He didn't u...
for her.

He'd never been a ...
man's woman. Ce... ... ... on the
receiving end of that game.

Still, Cara Merrill was the kind of woman he'd
wanted once upon a time. The kind he thought
he'd found until real life made mincemeat of
that hope.

His body was shot to hell, but his head still
worked. He knew damn well that this wasn't a
woman a man should become involved with
unless he was on for heavy talk about
commitment. A subject he wasn't willing to
think about, let alone discuss.

So why did she turn all his hard-won promises
to himself to shifting grains of sand? He'd
already made his decision on women. Except in
the most impersonal terms, they weren't to be a
part of his life. The price was too high...

Dear Reader,

What a fantastic month we have for you! First and foremost there's Linda Howard, back again with a new Mackenzie book. *Mackenzie's Pleasure* is a book hot enough to push the long, cold winter firmly behind you. Zane Mackenzie is this month's HEARTBREAKER and he's definitely one of a kind—the kind of man we'd all like to find!

Next, after the success of her trilogy about the McCall's, Judith Duncan's new novel is dynamite. Maggie Burrows can't keep her thoughts—or her hands!—off a man years younger than she is...

There's also the middle book in Pat Warren's REUNION trilogy, which can, of course, be read on its own. But if you've read Hannah's story, you'll be fascinated to see what happened to Michael. And don't forget that Kate's book is an April Special Edition.

Finally, meet a man determined to avoid women and commitment in Frances Williams' *Unbroken Vows*. You won't regret it!

Enjoy

The Editors

Unbroken Vows

FRANCES WILLIAMS

First published in Great Britain 1997
Silhouette Books, Eton House, 18-24 Paradise Road,
Richmond, Surrey TW9 1SR

© Frances Hardter 1996

ISBN 0 373 07724 6

18-9703

Printed and bound in Great Britain
by Mackays of Chatham PLC, Chatham

To my dear friends of many, many years,
Camilla Laking, Ginger Sexton, Eileena Murphy
and Sister Theresa Dalla.

Chapter 1

The man carving an impossibly direct path through the dark waters of the mountain lake obviously was not swimming for pleasure. He looked as if he were waging war against the water. A war he was determined to win. His arms knifed into the choppy surface with the relentless precision of a metronome. Left. Right. Left. Right.

Cara couldn't tell how long he'd been at it, but for the past ten minutes, simply watching him push to the end of the small lake, whip around and charge back again, left her feeling tired. She could guess at the pain such a degree of punishment must be inflicting on straining muscles of shoulders and back.

She dropped to one knee at the edge of the long wooden dock and dipped a hand into the gunmetal gray of the water. After only a few seconds of fanning her fingers through it, she shivered and yanked them out again.

The swimmer, she decided, had to be the man she was looking for. A genuine hero, Mr. Elliott had called him. Either that, she thought wryly, or the guy was just plain nuts. Only one or the other would explain why anyone would brave the bone-jarring cold of the late spring runoff draining from the hills walling in the small lake.

No one had answered her call up at the house, so she prayed the swimmer *was* David Chandler Reid. Learning about him had provided her first ray of hope in long, discouraging months.

The man pursued his exercise with such disciplined regularity that she hesitated to break into his concentration by calling to him.

She shook the water from her fingers and straightened. Skirting the pair of old scuffed sneakers and small pile of clothing topped by a towel carelessly tossed on the planks, she ambled over to one of the knee-high wooden support posts and sat down to wait until he returned to shore.

Her movements must have caught the swimmer's eye. The rhythmic swings of his head froze in her direction. The long, powerful strokes stilled. In a second or two they resumed with even greater fury, angling him away from the line of his laps and driving him toward her.

She pulled off her sunglasses, jabbed them into her hair and walked to the end of the dock, ready to greet the man whose help she sought.

A large hand slapped onto the planks at her feet bringing his rapid slice through the lake to an abrupt halt. His head pushed from the water in a hurl of white foam, followed by a pair of shoulders whose corded muscles certainly looked powerful enough to take the kind of punishment their owner had been inflicting on them.

"What are you doing here?" The scowling bark in the deep male voice backed her up a step.

A quick flail of his unfashionably long dark hair flung a halo of droplets into the air around him. He dashed back his hair and mopped a hand across his face to clear the water from his eyes. Eyes the same flat gray color of the lake, she noticed, and holding the same lethal chill.

"In case you didn't see the sign at the turnoff, it read, Private Property, Keep Off, This Means You."

The man's rudeness wiped from her mind the polite greeting she'd intended. She nodded briskly. "I saw it."

"Evidently you don't think that warning applies to you. It does. Go away."

After she'd looked forward to their meeting with such anticipation, the curt dismissal rankled. She bit back her immediate instinct to tell the man she now fervently hoped was *not* Reid that it wouldn't hurt him to be a little more polite.

But then, from his point of view her presence could be seen as trespassing, although she'd come with a purpose. And that purpose didn't include leaping into an argument with anyone. Especially not the person whose expertise she so desperately needed.

"My name is Cara Merrill. I came to see Commander Reid."

"I'm David Reid." She groaned inwardly. It had to be. "And I don't recall inviting you or anybody else here."

The reality of the man bobbing in the water below her sure didn't match the paragon of virtue Mr. Elliott had prepared her for. *Tough, brave, keenly intelligent,* those were only a few of the words Elliott had used in describing him. He'd said nothing about a complete lack of common courtesy.

She might not have come if she'd known her reception was to be so uncordial. She simply would have continued on with her own plans as best she could. And she'd turn and walk away right now if that darned hike up the long dirt road—sidestepping deep ruts and mud puddles her car could never negotiate—hadn't been so bothersome she hated to waste the effort.

"I assure you, Commander Reid—" She tried to keep any hint of the same tartness he'd used on her from leaking into her voice. "I do have a reason for coming. Roger Elliott suggested that I contact you. He told me where to find you."

"Elliott!" Reid let out a snort of disdain. "Forget it. Tell him I'm not interested in coming back. You've delivered your message. Now go away."

Not only was this guy about as civil as a cornered skunk, but he was also confusing. "I don't know what you mean. Mr. Elliott gave me no message for you. I'm here for reasons of my own."

"Which are?"

"Please, Commander, I can't talk to you like this." A hero David Reid might be, but a hero with an attitude. The fact that she was standing above him, as he tread water several inches below the level of her feet, should have afforded her some sense of control in their exchange. It didn't. "Would you mind coming out of the water so that we can talk in a more civilized manner?"

"I make no claims to being civilized, Ms. Merrill."

He'd get no argument from her on that. But the glint of self-deprecating humor brought a soft chuckle to her throat.

"Nevertheless, it's important that I speak to you, so I'd appreciate it if you'd climb up here on the dock."

"All right, lady. But be warned. I'm wearing nothing but water down here. You'd better turn around so that the sight of a naked man doesn't bring on an attack of the vapors."

"I've never had an attack of the vapors in my life. And you can't show me anything I haven't seen many times before."

"Well, even with your evidently wide experience at ogling naked men, I'd prefer that you turn around."

That a person so lacking in manners should demonstrate any personal sense of modesty whatever was surprising. But then, David Chandler Reid was turning out to be not at all what she'd expected.

Funny, though, how difficult it was to obediently force her gaze away from him.

Showing him her back, she strolled to the bottom of the long zigzag set of stone steps she'd walked down. Looking up, she fixed her attention on the elegantly designed house poised like a huge wing of silvery weathered cedar and glass on top of the hill.

She heard the loud splash and thump behind her as Reid heaved himself onto the dock. She wasn't quite as immune to the sight of a beautiful male body as she'd made herself out to be. The tantalizing view of the little of him that she'd already enjoyed tempted her to turn around and sneak a peek at the rest. She virtuously resisted the temptation.

"Didn't you find that water cold, Commander?" she called back to him, without turning around.

"Damn cold. That's the point." It was a point she didn't get. "And make that David. I'm no longer on active duty."

In a few minutes, the sound of his footsteps—strangely uneven and interspersed with a curious thudding—came closer.

"All right, Ms. Merrill, it's safe to turn around now."

The top-to-toe view of him startled her.

She'd noticed one end of the thick wooden staff fashioned from a tree branch sticking out from under the heap of shucked-off clothing, and hadn't thought anything of it. The rustic staff was a good six feet long. Reid topped it by several inches. But the pole was no mere walking stick for use in hiking through the woods surrounding the lake. Quite obviously, it served as a much-needed crutch. Leaning heavily on it for support, David Reid limped toward her.

Her physician's interest drew her gaze down the man's body. The faded black T-shirt emblazoned with a naval insignia molded a classically sculpted torso to the waist. One side of his damp jeans hugged a muscular thigh in a firm, unbroken line. The left leg, though, looked thinner and oddly stiffened.

Her surprise must have been written on her face.

"Evidently you didn't know I'm a cripple." He waved away any objection she might have to the word. "Forget the politically correct term. That's exactly what I am."

That he thought of himself as such went far to explain Reid's sharpness. Did that nasty temper of his mask a self-protective desire to keep people at a distance? Maybe. However, he might have been every bit as mean-tempered before the injury.

Roger Elliott hadn't struck her as a person of questionable judgment. Far from it. Yet knowing what the job entailed he'd sent her to Reid, who obviously was in less than top-notch physical condition. There had to be more to this man than what she saw. Still, she was beginning to have her doubts about Elliott's recommendation.

"Mr. Elliott evidently didn't think that your physical disability was worth mentioning."

"That astonishes me. He's usually no more forgiving of weakness in a man than I am. But let's drop the subject of my *disability*—" he spat out the word "—shall we? Get on with the point of why you're here."

"Very well. I'm here to ask you to help me find my fiancé."

Reid's dark eyebrows slashed upward.

"Well, Ms. Merrill, as opening lines go, that's sure a new one on me." An impatient pump of his walking staff ordered her to the steps. "Upstairs to the deck. I've got to sit down."

She stepped back politely to let him lead the way.

"No. You first."

He was sensitive, she suspected, about having her watch him maneuver the steep steps, just as he'd wanted to keep his damaged body hidden. She took the stones slowly, so she wouldn't get too far ahead of him. She heard him stumble behind her, but didn't look back. David Reid didn't seem the type to take kindly to any offers of help, no matter how well-intentioned. Especially not from a woman. Macho self-reliance was written all over him.

On the wide deck cantilevered over the hill, he lowered himself carefully into a cushioned, high-back wooden lawn chair.

His lips were clamped in a thin, tight line and his face was beaded with moisture. Not lingering evidence of his swim. Sweat. Since the day was no more than pleasantly warm, with a fairly stiff breeze, the perspiration was evidence of the effort it took him to climb the steps. Reid might have succumbed to a degree of bitterness about his injury, but unlike some of her patients, he sure wasn't one to pamper himself. If anything, he was probably pushing himself too hard.

Not so much as a small pot of geraniums softened the redwood planks running the entire length of the house. Nor, evidently, did the commander engage in a whole lot of entertaining. Only one other chair was set out on the deck. She hooked her shoulder bag over the back of the chair and settled into it.

A cat waddled by, brushing up against Reid's legs as it passed. The sight was so unexpected, she had to fight to suppress a giggle. A Doberman snarling by his side? Sure. But a blotchy white-and-brown angora so fat its belly dragged along the ground? She'd never have guessed.

"What's your cat's name, Commander?"

"I've no idea, and it's not my cat. I loathe the lazy beast." Maybe so, but he'd reached down to stroke its head before it flopped down beneath his chair. And its long fluffy coat was well-groomed. "The thing walked in a few months ago, probably abandoned on the main road. I made the mistake of feeding it." He shot a baleful glance down at the already snoozing animal. "Now I can't get rid of it."

She was about to decide that David Reid wasn't quite as uncivilized as he made himself out to be, when she noticed the half-empty bottle of liquor sitting on the low wooden table between them. The liquor was a fine, pricey old scotch. The glass beside it, heavy-leaded crystal whose faceted edges sparkled in the sun.

Navy pensions must be a lot more generous than she'd thought.

He poured a shot on top of the amber dregs of a previous drink, downed it in one gulp and poured another.

The drink in Reid's hand and the week's worth of grungy beard shadowing his face put him a long way from the spit and polish she'd expected from a much-decorated former naval officer. According to Elliott, Reid was an ex-SEAL, a member of the navy's elite Sea-Air-Land marine penetration and counter-intelligence unit. With his straggly black hair, streaked with gray at the temples, brushing his shoulders, he looked more like a denizen of some disreputable waterfront dive.

Catching her disapproving eyes on his drink, he shrugged.

"Kills the pain. Want one?"

"No, thank you."

She glanced at her watch. Barely noon, and it looked as if Reid already had gotten a head start on demolishing the bottle's contents. Apparently there were a number of things about him that Mr. Elliott hadn't bothered to mention. Obviously this was a man wrestling with problems of his own. The feeling grew that he wasn't the person she should ask to take on hers.

His drinking habits were none of her business: he wasn't a patient. But a professional concern for anyone's good health made her offer a caution.

"If I may say so, Commander, there are better ways to handle pain. If you'll give me a short medical history and a list of other medications you may be taking, I can write you a prescription right now for a very effective painkiller."

"You can—?" A profanity burst from his lips. He had the good grace to murmur a quick apology. "You're a doctor. Elliott sent me another damn doctor." He made it sound as if the profession made her first cousin to a horse thief.

"He did not. I'm a physician, yes. But Mr. Elliott told me to contact you for my benefit. Not for yours."

"Uh-huh." Reid held his glass up to the sun and squinted through the golden liquid. "If you think that, lady, you must not know Roger Bryce Elliott very well. Good ol' Roger does nothing except for reasons of his own."

"Frankly, Commander, I don't know what you're talking about. But if you'd seen Mr. Elliott with that little boy, as I did, you wouldn't say that. His grandson is a patient of mine. He came to the hospital to see the child every day, sometimes way past normal visiting hours. After meeting Mr. Elliott, I gave orders to let him see Jimmy anytime he chose.

"One quiet night we had a chance to talk. I don't usually talk about Tommy—Thomas Grant, my fiancé—but somehow or other, I found myself spilling out the story to Mr. Elliott." The man deserved a medal for how long he sat drawing out her sad story, even offering a pristine white handkerchief when she got a little weepy. "He's a good listener."

"Oh, yeah. He's a great listener, all right."

The tone of sarcasm couldn't quite disguise the disturbing new intensity in the steely gaze fastened on her.

Without breaking that fixed look, he sipped his drink.

"You said you want me to help you find your fiancé."

"Yes."

She glanced down at the diamond solitaire, which had fallen slightly askew on the third finger of her left hand, and twisted the ring back into place. It was always so painful to remember those last few months with Tommy. So painful to remember the biggest failure of her life.

"Rather a strange request, Doctor. How did your friend Tommy get lost?"

"About a year ago, he . . . disappeared."

"Disappeared. I take it there's no evidence that he's dead. Accident, murder, suicide?"

She hissed in a quick breath. "You don't mince words, do you?"

"Do you want me to?"

She had made up her mind finally to confront the facts head-on—especially the fact of her own guilt. She could hardly start by wilting under David Reid's tactless honesty.

She slowly shook her head. "No. I don't think Tommy's dead."

"So, how come you can't find him? Hard to believe that any man in his right mind would just up and walk away from a woman like you."

Cara snapped her gaze back to her interrogator. That last remark sounded suspiciously like some sort of compliment. The first time he'd given any indication whatever that he considered her anything more than a major nuisance and an unwelcome intruder.

"Where are you from, Dr. Merrill? Where was your Tommy when he disappeared?"

"I live in Baltimore. I'm a partner in a family practice there. Tommy was a resident at a New York hospital. He was last seen at his Manhattan apartment."

Rubbing her forehead against the beginnings of a headache, she gazed out over the lake and wished she didn't have to drag the whole excruciating mess through her mind again.

Reid gave an exasperated sigh. "Come on, Dr. Merrill. You didn't come all the way out to my little corner of the Blue Ridge to admire the scenery. Give. What's the story?"

The lungful of fresh mountain air she hauled in didn't ease the tightness in her chest.

"You put it correctly a minute ago. Tommy wasn't in his right mind when he disappeared. As I said, he's a doctor, too, with a brilliant career ahead of him if he hadn't—'' She leaned forward, clasping her hands together over her knees, trying to give Reid some understanding of a man who, from what she'd seen of the commander, was his psychological and emotional opposite.

"It was easy to love Tommy. He was such a sweet man. Gentle. Not coldly detached like some other physicians I've met." *Not like you,* she added silently. "I guess that was part of the problem. The pressure started to get to him. He began—"

She broke off and scraped her teeth across her bottom lip.

"He began taking drugs to help him cope. Oh, not much at first," she added hastily. Her hard-come-by promise to herself not to hide any longer behind pain and willful ignorance made her backtrack. "The truth is, I don't really know when he started, or how deeply he was into drugs before I noticed the change in him. When I did, I begged him to stop." At the memory of that agonizing confrontation with Tommy, she squeezed her eyes shut. "He assured me he could handle it. I'm afraid Tommy wasn't the first physician to abuse alcohol or drugs. He went on to cocaine. Then he made a serious mistake and almost lost a patient."

"I see. Bottom line, the guy's an addict."

She sprang to Tommy's defense. "You don't understand. The hours a resident has to put in are brutal. They take their toll on a person, both physically and mentally. Tommy's a sensitive individual...very sensitive. The exhausting work, the stress...it all had a devastating effect on him." She heard herself repeating the same rationalization for Tommy's actions that she'd made so often. Under Reid's unforgiving gaze those reasons sounded feeble.

"Yeah. Right. Sensitive." A quick flick of his hand brushed away her attempt at explanations. "Excuses, Dr. Merrill. Lame ones. You must have gone through much the same tough medical training, but you seem to have come through in pretty good shape. Great shape actually."

His gaze slowly raked up her body from her toes to the knot of straight blond hair swirled on top of her head, and back down again. His masculine scrutiny, though, seemed strangely impersonal, distant—and somehow threatening. As if he were interested in more than just checking out another female body. As if he were bent on ferreting out her private thoughts, her secret feelings.

This wasn't the first male once-over aimed her way. Usually she ignored them, or stared them down. This one sent warm blood tingling into her cheeks. She straightened in her chair and crossed her legs. Oh, for heaven's sake. Her fingers had actually flown to the top button on her white silk shirt to check that it was securely fastened.

Too much to hope that Reid hadn't noticed her ridiculously juvenile reaction. That hint of a mocking smile playing around his mouth told her he knew very well how much his scrutiny bothered her. He probably got a kick out of it. She was grateful when he dropped his gaze back to the liquor in his glass.

"Here's what you're facing, Doctor," he said flatly. "Evidently your Tommy has dropped into the drug subculture. He could be anywhere. He could be dead. You'll probably never find him. And if you do, believe me, you won't want him."

Lord! Reid gave no quarter. The man's only saving grace was that he seemed to be every bit as hard on himself. She sighed. The commander's personality grated, but a wimp would be of no use to her. And there was something to be said for honesty. Even the painful kind.

"Others have told me much the same thing, although they phrased it a little more delicately than you do. However, I intend to go on looking for him anyway." Absently she brushed her thumb over the diamond Tommy had given her. "I made a vow to myself to do everything I could to find him."

"There aren't a lot of women who'd go to this much trouble to find a man who deserted her." She flinched before she could catch it and hold back her reaction to Reid's biting words. "That's what he's done, you know. Tommy has chosen drugs over you—over his career, over every other meaningful thing in his life."

"It wasn't a free choice. It wasn't a fair fight." Wanting to show no sign of weakness in front of a man as hard as this one, she swallowed against the tightness that invariably rose in her throat when she spoke of Tommy. Controlling her emotions was always the toughest part of her job. "The drugs captured a man too gentle, too unaware of what was happening to him to be able to overcome his addiction by himself."

Unfortunately the small break in her voice hadn't escaped Reid.

"Look," he said. "I'm sorry, okay? I guess I've been away from polite society so long that I've forgotten how to converse in those more delicate terms you mentioned. I suppose I shouldn't have put it that way."

She lifted her chin and faced him squarely.

"Why not? It's the truth. It's also the truth that Tommy didn't get a whole lot of help in that fight from me."

Reid plowed a hand through his still-damp hair. "You don't need me to search for your fiancé, Dr. Merrill. Go hire a private detective."

"I already did. My man took a lot of time and a lot of money over the past year. He quit the case two months ago."

"He quit while you were still paying the bills?" She nodded. "Seems a little unusual. Why didn't he keep on with the job?"

"He said he'd run up against a brick wall and there was no point in going on. I pressed him for details. All I could get out of him was that there was a possibility that Tommy might have headed for South America."

"South America!" Reid's glass clunked down on the table. "That sure is a long way to go for a fix. South America's a very big place. Your man didn't narrow it down any?"

"No. He didn't tell me any more than that. There didn't seem to be any point in hiring another detective if Tommy isn't even in the country."

She leaned toward him. "I know I can't search the whole of South America, Commander. The most I can manage is one small part of it in a very limited amount of time. Mr. Elliott mentioned that you're familiar with several countries in that part of the world. I don't know it at all. My search for Tommy would be a lot easier with you as my guide."

"You don't mean you actually plan to travel all the way to South America to look for the guy?"

"I told you I intend to find my fiancé."

"You'd be going on a fool's mission, Dr. Merrill."

She managed, just barely, to hold on to her temper. "You misunderstand, Commander. I'm not asking for your approval, only for your help."

His eyebrows lifted in mild surprise, but her sharp retort didn't seem to annoy him any.

"I agree that my approval or disapproval isn't worth a damn thing."

"This will probably sound silly to you. But I feel that I took a big step toward that vow of 'for better or for worse' when I accepted Tommy's ring. I saw our engagement as a serious pledge. And if I'd stuck to that pledge at the time Tommy really needed me, I wouldn't be searching for him now."

A strange look flashed over Reid's face. Almost as if what she'd said had hurt him in some way, although she saw no reason why it should have. But she must have been wrong. The wince of pain was gone as quickly as it appeared.

A muscle flexed in his jaw. He slanted toward her and reached out to envelop her hands in his. An action that may have confounded him as much as it did her. He gave a quick break of his lips and a swift glance down at their joined hands.

She didn't mind the unexpected gesture, she discovered. Didn't mind it at all. The warm, strong clasp of his fingers sent a tingling wave of pleasure up her arms and through her body.

His movement brought his head into disturbing closeness with hers. One wouldn't have expected that a face carved of such severe angles would boast of black lashes so thick and long. It didn't seem fair, either, that a mouth set so implacably firm should be drawn so distractingly sexy.

"No, Dr. Merrill. I don't think you sound silly."

Where had the steel in his eyes gone? Cara wondered. The soft, smoky gray that now captured her gaze was fogging up her normal clinical detachment. Her heart gave a couple of crazy skips.

What in heaven's name was going on with her? She considered herself a reasonably intelligent woman, and had the diplomas to prove it. So why should this man's lingering look leave her feeling completely witless? Maybe she should have taken in more carbohydrates at breakfast.

"Listen to me, Cara." Reid's voice was quiet, earnest. "This really isn't something you should—"

He seemed to realize that he was still holding her hands, and yanked his away. He sat back in the chair. The rigid mask again dropped over his face.

Apparently his momentary lapse into civility was over.

"Listen to me, Dr. Merrill. You can't go prowling through the South American drug trade." He enunciated each word slowly and clearly. "It will chew you up and spit you out. No chemically dependent man goes there merely to get drugs for himself. He can do that right here. Chances are good that he became involved somehow in the production or delivery system."

"I don't believe that."

"Whether you believe it or not is irrelevant. If your idiot fiancé got himself tangled up in the drug trade, he hasn't a snowball's chance in hell of staying alive. Assuming he still is."

"Nevertheless, I'm going. I told Mr. Elliott that. I'm sure that's why he sent me to you. I don't even know where to start. I hoped you may be able to point me in the right direction." She wanted considerably more than that. "Actually I hoped you might agree to come with me. Naturally I'll pay for your time and all expenses."

"Hell, lady, it should be pretty clear to you that you've got the wrong man. Look at me! I walk like my grandfather." He slapped his injured thigh. She knew the self-inflicted blow must have hurt even before she noticed his hand lingering to rub the muscle. "I'm not in any shape to protect anyone. Certainly not among South American drug traffickers."

"I'm not looking for a protector, Commander. I can take care of myself. I need you for the brains Mr. Elliott says you have, not for your brawn."

"I've got brains enough not to do it," he snapped back. "And Elliott should have had more sense than to suggest me for the job."

Cara slumped in her chair, deflated.

"I see."

It was certainly Reid's right to turn down her request, but his understandable refusal gave her a surprisingly keen stab of disappointment.

For all the commander's off-putting ways and questionable personal habits, there was something admirably solid about him. The gray eyes held a penetrating intelligence and a dark intensity that suggested he'd be a good man to have around in a pinch. She wasn't naive. She knew darn well that tackling the job she'd set herself would be no picnic.

"Well, that's that then." Her letdown was her own fault for counting so heavily on the commander before she'd even met him.

She rose to her feet, picked up her handbag and looped its long gold chain over her shoulder.

"Mr. Elliott warned me that you'd probably refuse if I spoke to you over the telephone. It seems I had no better luck talking to you in person. Thanks for your time, Commander Reid. I suppose I can't blame you for not being anxious to make such a trip for a woman you don't even know."

"Put it down to cowardice on my part, if you want to."

His voice contained the bite of self-directed anger.

"Cowardice?" Cara shook her head. "Not hardly. Mr. Elliott said you were one of the most courageous men he'd ever met."

"I had courage once. It was burned out of me almost two years ago. I also used to think I was immortal. I learned that I'm not."

"That's no news to me. I'm a doctor. I learned a long time ago that no one is immortal. That's why we have to make each day count. And that's another reason why I have to find Tommy. To help him climb out of the mess he's in and make something of the rest of his life. I owe him that. He's too valuable a man to waste."

Reid levered himself out of his chair. She moved quickly to hand him his makeshift crutch. He slid his eyes away from her and grabbed it.

She fished in her handbag for the small silver case holding her business cards. She took one out and flipped it down on the table. "Just in case you change your mind." Not that she expected him to.

Reid ignored the card. Once again his face bore the closed-off look of rejection with which he'd first met her. True to form, he didn't offer his hand in farewell.

"Give up your crazy idea, Doctor. It's over between you and the very sensitive Tommy. You'd do better to write him off and get on with your own life."

Her cheeks flamed. She, like most people who'd known him, always called Tommy by the nickname that suited him. But every time Reid used it, it irked her. On his lips the perfectly good masculine name sounded dismissingly childish.

"Since you seem to have no problem dispensing blunt advice, Commander, I'll give you my professional opinion—free of charge—of what I've seen here today. You've undergone a serious physical trauma, which, I suspect, has led to a correlating deep emotional trauma. Different people have different ways of blunting that kind of pain. Evidently closing down your emotions, cutting yourself off from the world is yours. You've holed up to lick your wounds in the nice, safe cave you've built for yourself, complete with a warning sign at the front gate." Her gesture encompassed the house and its isolated surroundings.

"But you'd better be careful that you don't hide away for so long that you bury yourself in your cave for good. Frankly I think you may be well on your way to that already."

Not waiting to hear Reid's reaction—maybe not brave enough to face a predictably stinging counterattack—she hurried down from the deck. It took every ounce of professional discipline that she possessed not to look back at David Chandler Reid as she left him.

Chapter 2

David limped back and forth across the deck, pounding his makeshift crutch onto the planks as if it could stomp his irritation into submission. It was none of Cara Merrill's business how he chose to live his life. If he could no longer control his own body the way he once did, he certainly could control where he lived, who he saw.

What did she know of his life anyway? He was having a hard enough time trying to figure it out himself. He didn't even know who the hell he was anymore. The navy had given him a sense of purpose that had formed the bedrock of his life. What purpose did he serve now? Seeing how many laps he could force out before exhaustion drove him back to his empty house?

He hardened his jaw.

His house was empty because he wanted it that way. He was alone because he chose to be alone.

No one had ever spoken to him as she had yesterday. Everyone—with one excruciating exception—had been so damn sympathetic and kind, so damn pitying. At least the beautiful doctor sure as hell didn't pity him. He should feel grateful to her for that. What he felt instead was fury at himself for allowing her to get under his skin.

He hobbled down to hit the water.

The insomnia that kept his eyes glued open last night he was accustomed to. It was those damn pictures of Cara Merrill that kept flicking through his mind that bugged him. He could still see her as she looked standing on the dock, the breeze from the lake ironing the thin blouse and pants against her body, outlining those alluring breasts, that fabulous figure. The woman could bring a rock to life.

He quickly clamped off that train of thought. He wasn't man enough to risk putting the theory to the test.

She'd walked away from him yesterday without bothering to look back even once. That annoyed him. Especially since he only knew it because he'd kept his eyes on her until the trees hid her from view.

But then, why the hell should she have given him a parting glance? He'd turned her down flat. What's more, he didn't give a damn if he never again received any glances whatever from an attractive woman.

This one not only was damnably attractive, she was damnably determined. He still resented her for disrupting his self-imposed solitude, but demonstrations of tenacity, of sheer guts in anyone had always impressed him. He'd always liked formidable women. Why not? He'd once prided himself on being called formidable.

Not lately. Every faltering step he took drove the proof of his painful deficiency deeper into his soul. Only in the buoyant, forgiving water where his almost useless leg didn't matter could he come close to forgetting that weakness.

The woman sure didn't intimidate easily. He couldn't help but smile at the remembrance. In the water yesterday, he'd shot her the black look that had scared the hell out of hundreds of new SEAL recruits. Under it that female reporter who'd shown up here a few months ago turned tail and ran. Cara Merrill blinked. But she'd stood her ground.

She annoyed him, all right. But more than that, she piqued his interest. Curious. It had been a very long time since he'd reacted to anyone or anything with more than indifference.

He gave up on trying to work in his usual number of laps and headed for shore.

Up on the deck he slapped his wet towel over the railing.

She wouldn't quit. The decisive set of her lovely mouth when she left told him that. Damn. Nothing for it but to see her again, and take another shot at persuading her to give up this harebrained scheme. She could spend the rest of her life looking for that jerk and never find him.

He snatched up the small white business card from the table where it had lain overnight, and grumbled into the house.

He walked out of his room a half hour later, shaved and dressed in the custom-tailored dark gray slacks and the designer black silk sport shirt he'd bought back in the days when he cared what he looked like. He hoped he looked civilized enough to venture back into the real world for a few hours.

He hesitated for a moment before hoisting himself into the pickup. Until now, he'd used the vehicle only to run down to the general store. Someone always came to pick him up for trips into Richmond to see his doctor. On the long drive to Baltimore, working the clutch might be hard on his leg.

"The hell with it," he said out loud and pulled the door shut. If he'd gotten to the point where he couldn't even drive himself off this damn mountain, it was time he packed it in.

So much for heroics. By the time he reached the medical office, his leg was locked in one long agonizing cramp from the effort of stamping down on the clutch. He stumbled through the door doubled over and grasping his left thigh.

A stethoscope looped around her neck, Cara was speaking to the nurse at the reception desk. She took one look at him and her blue eyes flared wide. She was at his side in a heartbeat. He didn't object when she pulled one of his arms over her shoulder and slid her arm around his waist to tow him past the waiting patients into the examining room.

"Good Lord, Commander. What have you done to yourself? Sit down there." She pointed to the high examining table.

His teeth clenched against the torture in his leg, he dropped to the edge of the table.

She ran her hands down his leg, assessing the problems she could feel beneath the lightweight gabardine. "Severe muscle spasms of both thigh and calf." Without letting go of his leg, she hooked a foot around the low, wheeled examining stool and pulled it over. She sat down and carefully removed his black moccasin to gently flex the foot and begin to unknot corkscrewed muscles. Bracing his foot against the crook of her shoulder, she probed his calf.

"How did this happen?"

"I drove in—from the house—" he gasped out, his breathing ragged. "I ran into trouble with the—with the stick shift." He gripped the sides of the table with white-knuckled hands. "Stupid of me to drive myself—all this way. But from time to time—I try to pretend—that I'm still the man I used to be." He couldn't help the grunt of pain as her fingers found a particularly tender spot.

"Sorry."

She worked her way up to the bunched cords of his thigh. It felt like forever until the soothing warmth of her hands and their expert kneading of his twisted flesh eased the worst of the pain and quieted his screaming nerves. A big relief when he was able to take a more or less normal breath and release clenched stomach muscles.

"Just a small reminder, lady," he said, finally able to speak without choking out his words. "You're the one who wanted me to go galloping off to South America with you. Look at me. I can't even drive for a couple of hours without ending up in your emergency room."

"Over three hours, David," she countered quietly. "And I'll bet it's been a while since you've driven so far."

She stood up and kicked the stool out of the way. "Now that you can move without too much pain, scoot back on the table and lie down." She gave his chest a gentle push. "Let's get these pants off you." She flipped open the hook closure on his waistband and took hold of the zipper tab. He grabbed her wrist to pull her hand away.

"Oh, for... Come on, David. I've loosened up the muscles some, but massage will be much more effective if done directly on the affected limb."

That "affected limb" to her, was a repulsive mass of scarred flesh to him. Doctor or no doctor, there was no way in the world he was going to expose his ravaged body to her. "No need. It feels better already."

She shot him an exasperated look. "I *am* a doctor, Commander Reid."

Maybe so, but white coat or no, the lovely vision he saw in front of him was all woman. And he'd already undergone one searing lesson on how a woman reacted to the sight of him. He wasn't eager for a second. "But you're not *my* doctor."

"I sure don't envy whoever is your doctor. You probably drive him nuts."

"So he says."

"At least lie back so I can get at that leg a little more easily."

She pulled out the table extension and supported his damaged leg as he shoved himself carefully to the top of the table and gingerly lowered his back to the paper-protected leather.

"Interesting," she observed, continuing to rub her hands over the slowly relaxing muscles of his thigh. Her long tapering fingers looked as delicate as fine porcelain, but felt as if they were made of spun steel sheathed in velvet. "You insist on calling yourself a cripple—not a term I'd use, by the way—but you refuse to act like one. You won't even use a proper pair of crutches that would make getting around a lot easier for you."

"I did use them for a while, but I hated the looks of them."

It wasn't so much the looks of the crutches that he hated, but how he looked when dragging himself around on them. Especially after Anita got through with him.

He managed a halfway grin. "I've graduated to a cane. Don't I get any marks for that?" He pointed to the antique cane topped with a handgrip of smooth brass that he'd dropped to the floor.

"Okay. I guess you deserve a passing grade—for effort, if nothing else."

He'd drawn a smile from her. For some reason he felt quite proud of himself for that.

Her hands worked their way to the top of his leg, taming torment into a manageable ache. With the searing red flame in his leg subsiding, he gradually became aware once again of something outside himself.

And the closest thing to him was Cara. The only women who'd touched him in the past year and a half were medical personnel. And, of course, his grandmother. But Anne's touch had never brought him anything but comfort. Cara's hands on him should feel as neutral as their's had. They didn't. He was completely conscious of them as a woman's hands. As *her* hands.

Just looking at her did something funny to his chest. A few silky golden strands had escaped the knot on top of her head and fluttered against the softness of her cheek as she worked. Her full, pink lips were parted slightly and her breath came in fast little puffs from the physical effort of tending to him.

Lying flat on his back in front of her left him a long way from feeling comfortable. Instead he felt dangerously vulnerable. Vulnerable to what, he wasn't sure, since she was doing nothing but easing his pain.

Her knuckles brushed lightly against the lump of almost insensitive flesh at the juncture of his thighs. What had been almost insensitive flesh. Her accidental touch jolted a flash of heat through him. Startled surprise mushroomed into the beginnings of panic. But beneath the reflexive anxiety curled a desire to feel the animating touch again.

He pushed himself upright.

"You can stop now, Doctor." He felt like a fool for the harshness in his voice, but couldn't help it. "My leg feels fine."

"No more pain?"

"No."

She slipped a hand under his knee and gently worked the leg up and down a couple of times. "You don't have good range of motion in that knee. You've had surgery on it."

"Lots." It wasn't easy to shift his leg away from her when the pleasure of her touch felt so good, but he managed it.

"Very well, Commander." She shoved her hands into the pockets of her examining coat and stepped back from him. "You'd better stay off your feet for a while. Come into my office and rest in the recliner for the next hour."

He needed her help to edge himself off the table and onto his feet without sending his leg back into spasm. She stooped to recover his cane from the floor and handed it to him. He would have preferred not to accept the support of her delicately boned but surprisingly sturdy shoulder while staggering into the next room, but he wasn't sure enough of his leg to avoid it.

She was practically holding him in her arms as she helped him settle into the big black leather chair behind her desk.

Her breasts brushed electrifyingly against his chest. Her face was so close it would take only a slight tip of his head to touch his mouth to hers. And just as it had yesterday, looking into those blue eyes up close made him feel as if he'd knocked back one drink too many.

She quickly pulled back from him.

"There's coffee brewed," she said, lifting a hand to check the position of the silver comb anchoring her swept-up hair. "Help yourself."

Too bad he couldn't let her know that she was perfectly safe with him. Not pleasant to admit that he posed no sexual hazard whatever to any woman.

Still, he had to be careful around her. Yesterday, as she climbed the steps ahead of him, he'd been so busy admiring the enticing sway of her sweetly rounded little bottom that he'd damn near fallen flat on his face. Astonishing, because he'd thought himself completely immune to such enticements. Today he'd almost committed an even greater misstep. One he could hardly have predicted. And he'd make certain it would never be repeated.

The voices in the outer rooms finally died out, and in less than an hour she returned to him. She pulled the stethoscope from around her neck and dropped it on top of a bookcase near the door. With an exhausted sigh, she sank into the chair on the other side of the desk. Lines of fatigue bracketed the soft pink lips as her fingertips scribed tiny circles in the delicate skin at her temples.

"Tough day, Doctor?"

"Ordinary day—except for you. I just didn't get a whole lot of sleep last night."

He could relate to that. And he didn't have to add to her problems by badgering her about her fiancé. Regardless of his own opinion of Tommy the junkie, a woman so worried about the man to whom she considered herself bound didn't deserve to have her concern belittled.

"Thank you for helping me out in there." He angled his head toward the examining room next door. "God knows I needed it."

"Glad I could help. It's my job, you know."

"You do it well."

"According to Elliott, you did yours pretty well, too—although I'm not quite sure just what that job was. I guess that's why he figured you could do what I need you for."

It had been a long time since he'd felt that he was truly needed for anything. The idea that it might really be so was a seduction he resisted. He knew better.

"Assuming you ever find Dr. Grant, what do you intend to do about him?"

"I'll bring him back, of course. Maybe it's not too late for me to help him with his . . . his problem. I want to get him into the rehab program run for drug addicted and alcoholic physicians. Unlike most others, this facility can boast of a high success rate. Tommy needs to know I'm still there for him, that we can work this out together."

"You sound more like Tommy's mother than his lover. Is that what you'll settle for? Taking care of a man as if he were a child?"

She dropped her hands from her head and snapped her gaze to his.

"That's not the way I look at it. Is it so hard to see it as one person being concerned about another?"

David tossed her another fast ball, hoping he could hit on something that would dent her persistence. "Why weren't you there for him before?"

"I'm getting used to your penchant for blunt talk, Commander. That question didn't sting quite as much as it would have before you'd prepared me for it by our conversation yesterday. However, it deserves an honest answer. Tommy fell into a black pit because of me—because of what I didn't do, and should have."

"What does that mean?"

"It means that I let myself become so involved with finishing my residency and making the arrangements to open a joint medical practice with Tommy that I didn't pay enough attention to his problems. We went through med school together, but we were serving our residencies in different cities, so we weren't able to see a whole lot of each other. Both our schedules were chaotic. It wasn't unusual for us not to see each other or even find time to call each other for days. All we could do was squeeze in a few hours together now and then, either here or in New York. Tommy was out of touch for three weeks before I became alarmed enough to notify the police of his disappearance."

"Not exactly what you'd call a hot romance," David observed dryly. This Tommy must be an even bigger fool than he already thought him not to have hiked himself to this woman's bed every chance he could.

"I'm sure it wasn't what you're accustomed to." He almost laughed out loud at that. "But our relationship wasn't that unusual between busy medical professionals. That only made the time we were able to spend together more precious to us. We respected each other's work and we cared deeply about each other."

He could readily believe that. If not about Tommy, certainly about her. "You must really be in love with the guy to do all this for him."

She shot out of the chair and turned away from him. Her fingers curled around the back of her neck as if her headache had just spread to that region.

"I planned to marry him, didn't I?" Her voice was unusually sharp.

"Don't get all bent out of shape, Doctor. It was just a passing observation."

She turned to him, a look of contrition on her beautiful face. "I'm sorry. I've been on edge lately."

She slipped back down into the chair. "I've known Tommy for years. We grew up together. Went to grade school and high school together. Why do you seem to find my feelings for him difficult to accept?"

"Maybe I just don't understand it. Frankly I don't have a lot of experience with that level of commitment from a woman."

"Stand By Your Man." Foolish though it was in this case, she was sure taking the song to heart. He of all people ought to support her in that.

He wasn't ready, though, to buy her entire loyal angel-of-mercy bit. Anita laid on the same scene while he'd been in the hospital. Fluffing up his pillows, straightening the sheets, holding the straw in a glass of water to his lips when he hadn't the strength to lift his head. She dropped the act quickly enough that first night at home in their bedroom. The night she finally ran up against the sickening reality of him.

"Come right down to it, I don't think I really believe in love. Not the kind of romantic delusion that seems to have come over you."

"You consider love a delusion?"

"Let's drop it, shall we?"

This conversation was getting a little too personal. He jogged the subject back to the man in question by picking up the silver-framed photograph standing on the desk. While Cara was gone, he'd stared at the photo for several minutes trying to figure out what the guy had to so grab a woman that she wouldn't let go even after he'd kicked her in the teeth. The portrait had given him no clue.

"I take it this is your fiancé."

"Yes. That's Tommy." She leaned over and took the picture from him.

"As you can see, Tommy was—is—" she corrected hastily "—very good-looking. He could be very charming...when he wanted to be. He's always had a kind of boyishness about him." A gentle smile played around her lips. "You can see it even in this picture. I'm not the only woman who found that appealing."

"Boyishness, huh? For me a look of boyishness in a grown man shows nothing but his ignorance of the real world. And what you see as *boyishness,* I would read as helplessness. I did my best to knock that kind of boyishness out of any recruit that came into my training program."

"The SEAL program?"

"Yes. The training is tough. Most of the candidates washed out early. By the time they left me, the rest weren't boys anymore. They were men. And the only thing one could see in their eyes was sure confidence in their own abilities."

Her mouth thinned. "Sure confidence in their abilities to maim, to kill."

"If you want to put it that way. I wouldn't."

"That's how we differ," she said coolly. "I try to help people. You're in the business of hurting them. At least, you used to be."

"You're dead wrong, Doctor. I was in the business of keeping our people alive. I gave my men everything I knew to help them come out in one piece from situations people like you can't even conceive of. And, yes, if that means killing an enemy, then to kill. Better the enemy than one of our own."

At first he thought she was going to continue to argue with him and mentally started to line up his own verbal counterattack. He didn't mind an argument. Anger felt safer than some of the other feelings she provoked in him. But instead, she tilted her head and studied him for a long moment. The look of cool disapproval left her face.

"I understand what you're saying, Commander. We do have different ways of going about it, but at bottom we both try to take the best care we can of the people entrusted to us. I didn't take real good care of Tommy. I want to correct that."

She put the picture down on the desk and reached across to lay her fingers lightly over his. Just as it had yesterday, the direct skin-to-skin touch shot such a sharp stab of pleasure through him that it made him catch his breath.

"I'm sorry," she said. "I had no call to say what I did to you, just now or yesterday. I don't know what it is, but you seem to bring out the worst in me. Forgive me."

The grace of her capitulation left him nonplussed. "Don't worry about it, Doctor. I'm sure my worst is a whole lot worse than your worst."

Her bubble of laughter was the most delightful sound he'd heard in quite a while.

"You're a challenge for me, David Reid. You surely are. Now why did you show up in my office today? I guess we can rule out the possibility it was to get a medical checkup."

"The one thing in the world I don't need is another medical checkup. I came to have another try at convincing you that this mission you've set for yourself is a dangerous one. If you were going to South America just to check out the usual tourist sights primarily in one of the big cities, no problem. But if your search leads you into the drug trails out in some of the rural areas, you could run into real trouble."

"Like what?"

"Like bandits, competing bands of guerrillas, unsavory characters running around with guns they aren't afraid to use."

She arched a delicate brow. "You mean I might run into something like what goes on here every day in Baltimore, or for that matter in any other American city."

"No, Cara. You know the rules here. You know the places to stay away from. Here you can speak the language, read the signs, printed and otherwise. Do you speak Spanish?"

"Very little."

"So there you won't enjoy those advantages. You could very easily and very quickly stumble into something you can't handle."

"You've already convinced me of that, David. I don't have much faith in detectives anymore, but I intend to hire a guide in whatever country I decide on."

"The usual tourist guide isn't going to cut it. Not in the places you might have to go."

"How do you know so much about South America, David?"

"My parents had friends and business interests in several of the large capital cities. Ten years ago they died in a traffic accident in Rio. Sometimes they took me along on their trips. Later on, I did a lot of backpacking in the Andes and journeyed partway up the Amazon in a boat.

"So you really do know the area."

"Not all of it. Some of it."

"It's kind of you to be concerned, but you really don't need to worry about me. I'm pretty good at taking care of myself. Since my days in med school I've donated time at a free clinic in a very rough section of town. It seemed only prudent to take a course in self-defense."

He threw her a brisk salute. It was growing surprisingly easy, he admitted, to drag up a grin when with her.

"My mistake, Doctor. You could probably teach me a thing or two."

"I doubt that." She leaned forward eagerly. "So, does that mean you've changed your mind and you'll come with me?"

He shook his head. "I still don't think I'm the man you need."

"I'm sorry about that, but with or without you I'm going to look for Tommy. Can you at least give me some idea about where to start?"

He didn't even want to consider the first place that sprang to mind when she mentioned South America and drugs in the same breath.

"According to what you told me, Grant could be anywhere." He skidded his gaze away from her to a diploma hanging on the wall. "Lots of Americans go to Rio. Tommy could be one, especially if he likes to party. Buenos Aires would also be a good bet."

"I don't have the time to cover more than one city. I was thinking of Rio. I just wish I had a more solid indication of where he might be."

The way she so worriedly chewed on her lower lip pricked his conscience. The least he could do for her was to try to narrow down the lead she was bent on following. Maybe his instincts about where Tommy might be were wrong.

"Tell me more about your private investigator's last report."

"There really isn't anything more to tell." She absently fingered the smooth wooden edge of the desk. "Funny, though..."

"What?"

"That last phone call from him was kind of strange. Normally he's a talker. Usually I couldn't get him off the line. But that final call lasted no more than a minute or two. I thought he sounded—I don't know—a little nervous. Edgy. I had the impression he wanted to be done with me." She brushed away the idea with a little laugh. "Probably I was imagining things."

Maybe she was, David considered. Maybe she wasn't. "Is his office here in Baltimore?"

"Yes. Downtown."

He grabbed the cane and levered himself carefully to his feet. "Let's go have a talk with—what's his name?"

"Warren Baker."

"Let's go have a talk with Mr. Baker."

"You mean, right now?"

"Why not?"

"Well, I just..." She grinned. "Why not, indeed? I'm beginning to have a greater appreciation for your painfully direct attitude. But shouldn't we call first to see if he's there?"

"No point in alerting the enemy to our position."

" 'The enemy'. Good heavens, David. Is that how you look at people?"

"Let's just say I have a naturally suspicious nature. You drive."

According to the lettering on his office door, Warren Baker offered Investigative Services, Divorce, Missing Persons, Discreet, Affordable. The detective was in. And he was not happy to see them. Not happy at all.

"I told you, Dr. Merrill, I can't give you any further information on the whereabouts of your fiancé."

David strolled around to the detective's side of the desk. Even the limp didn't keep him from looking strongly intimidating, Cara noted. The way he used his cane made it seem more like a fashion accessory than a necessity. With its brass handle, he carefully shoved a stack of papers out of the way, parked himself on the desktop and smiled down at Baker.

The thin smile didn't seem to relax Baker any.

"How about repeating that information for me?" Reid said quietly, slowly twirling the cane between the palms of his hands. Cara couldn't figure out why the innocuous action should hold an undertone of menace. But, oddly, it did. "How do you know that Dr. Grant is in South America?"

"I don't *know* it." Baker eyed the cane warily. "Like I told the doc here, I just heard a rumor that Grant *may* have gone there."

"A rumor."

"Yeah."

"Where did you pick up this rumor?"

The detective squirmed in his chair. "In . . . in Miami."

"From whom?"

"Look, I don't have to—"

"From whom, Mr. Baker?"

Reid didn't so much as raise his voice, but Baker nervously licked his lips. "From a junkie who used to shoot heroin with the doc."

Cara gave a strangled groan.

"Go on, Mr. Baker."

"Said he talked about going to South America."

"South America."

"Yeah." Baker angled his head around David to face her. "Nobody can search the whole of South America, Doc. Give it up."

David didn't give her time to respond. "Wouldn't Grant have had a little trouble springing for the hefty airfare from Miami to any South American country?"

From the way Baker nervously swiveled his chair from side to side, it was clear he wasn't thrilled with David's questions.

"Said a friend was paying his way."

"What friend?"

"My source didn't have a name. Apparently it was a guy Grant met in some kind of street accident. That's all he knew."

"Good, Mr. Baker. We appreciate your cooperation."

This was a side of David she hadn't seen before. A lot different than simple rudeness, the unnerving mildness in his voice and the coldly approving smile he bestowed on the man veiled an implicit threat. She didn't much like the tactic, but it was certainly working a lot better than her own polite questioning on the telephone.

"Go on," he said. "Exactly where in South America was Grant going?"

"Look. I don't want to get involved in this, okay?"

"Involved in what?"

Baker pulled out a handkerchief and mopped his florid face.

"Involved in what?" David repeated with quiet but deadly persistence. He tossed the cane up a few inches and caught it again between his hands.

"The user," Baker mumbled, "said Grant mentioned something about Colombia."

Cara's heart sank. She knew as well as David did that Colombia meant drugs.

She glanced at David and did a double take. He'd gone strangely quiet and tense. His hands were vised tightly around his cane. The gaze that pinned Baker to his chair slitted to icy coldness.

"Colombia," David repeated.

"Maybe. He...he wasn't sure. Look, mister...uh... Commander..."

"Commander Reid."

"Yeah. Well. Both Grant and my informant are users. Who puts any faith in the ravings of an addict?"

"What has you so scared, Mr. Baker?"

"S-scared? Who's scared?"

"You are. Why?" David gave Baker's shoulder a gentle prod with the cane.

"Okay. Okay." Baker angled his head toward Cara. "Look, Doc. I like you. You're a nice lady. Drop this business. You don't want to get mixed up with whatever Grant has got himself into. It's bound to bring you nothing but trouble."

"Who threatened you?" Reid asked.

Baker flopped back in his chair. "I . . . I don't know who he was. I guess my snooping around rattled some cages. This guy caught me in an alley near my hotel in Miami. Told me to knock off asking questions about Grant."

"He leaned on you?"

"Not much. Didn't have to. Look, pal, I been in this business a long time. I don't scare easy. But this character was real big and real scary. His meaning was plain enough. Hey." He shrugged. "I dropped the case. So sue me."

"This man, your attacker." David pressed on. "What did he look like?"

"Hispanic. As I said. Real big. Bald. Ugly."

"Thank you, Mr. Baker. You've been very helpful. We're finished here, Dr. Merrill." David got up from the desk and took her arm to lead her to the door.

"If you're smart, Doc," Baker called after them, "you'll forget about Grant. The kinds of people he's mixed up with play for keeps."

In the elevator, David dropped his head against the back wall. "Colombia," he breathed in little more than a whisper. "Colombia."

She felt the same way, but it surprised her that David seemed to be taking their discovery so personally.

Out in the parking lot, she clicked open the locks with the remote and didn't bother to wait and help him into the car.

She'd already learned that he wanted no help except for what little he absolutely couldn't handle for himself.

He yanked open the passenger door, sat down and carefully lifted his bad leg inside.

"Baker wasn't just whistling Dixie about the dangerous kinds of people you'll find in Colombia," he said, his face grim. "But I don't expect you'll have sense enough to pay his warning any mind."

She snapped her head around to him, her eyes flashing.

"Excuse me?" she said, through gritted teeth. "I can do without you talking to me that way, Commander."

"Somebody sure needs to talk sense to you, lady. Looks like I'm it. I intend to keep on doing it. You've got yourself a partner."

Chapter 3

Cara had her mouth open, ready to continue her blast. Her irritation skidded into a hundred-and-eighty-degree turn. "You're what?"

"I'm going to ride shotgun with you on your crazy mission to Colombia. I understand your motivations well enough by now to know that what Baker said isn't going to stop you. You're sticking to idiot Tommy like a barnacle sticks to a boat. Or in this case, to a sinking ship. I sure can't let you go there alone."

Her eyebrows arrowed upward. "You can't *let* me go?"

"You heard me." Her satisfaction that Reid had agreed to accompany her was shot through with annoyance. "Look, Commander, you may be accustomed to giving orders, but it isn't up to you to *let* me do anything I want to do."

"Take it any way you want to. I'm going with you."

"Fine," she snapped. "Thank you."

"You're welcome."

Why did her nerves always end up wound as tight as harp strings around David Reid? The man had agreed to do her a very large favor and she was all but yelling at him.

"Hey, David." She gave him a sheepish glance. "Thank you. Glad to have you aboard."

"Sure."

"You can stay over at my place tonight."

His mouth dropped open. "Uh…" For some reason, the idea seemed to make him very nervous. "Uh… No. I don't think—"

"You can't drive all the way back to your mountain again today," she said, amazed that he'd contest a suggestion so reasonable. "Your leg would conk out on you before you were halfway there."

The alarm on his face provoked her soft laugh.

"I'm trying to save you some pain, Commander. Why are you looking at me as if I've stolen your wallet? Has word of my near-total helplessness in the kitchen leaked out? No problem. There are plenty of restaurants in my neighborhood. Or we can pick up takeout at a good health-food deli I know."

From the sound he made, she gathered that his appreciation of health food might not be as high as her own.

"I'd prefer to go to a hotel."

"We have a lot to talk about, David. Easier to do that at my condo than in a hotel dining room."

"Fine. We'll talk over dinner at your place. Then I'll find a hotel."

She shrugged. "Have it your way. If you change your mind, I have a perfectly good guest room. No complaints about it so far."

"What have you got in your fridge?"

"Fruit, a carton or two of yogurt in the refrigerator. Maybe some milk. Chicken and frozen vegetables in the freezer. I'm no great cook, but I can manage to sauté a couple of chicken breasts."

"Got any white wine?"

She'd forgotten his drinking habit. Might that become a problem on their trip? she wondered. "I have wine." He was asking about wine, but he probably wanted something stronger than chardonnay. "I also have a bottle of scotch. Not quite as good as what you're used to, but you're welcome to it."

"Chicken in white wine sauce tastes a lot better than chicken in scotch," he said dryly. "At least, I assume so. I've been known to down a whisky or two in my time, but I can't say I've ever poured it over chicken."

"Oh, I thought you meant . . ."

"I know what you thought. Don't worry, Doctor. My admittedly excessive fondness for the bottle is of fairly recent origin. I've never yet gone on a mission drunk. I'll cook."

"You'll cook? They teach you cooking in the SEALs?"

"No, they don't teach you cooking in the SEALs. I've had plenty of time to learn on my own lately. Throwing steaks on the barbecue is easy, but it gets a little boring."

"You shouldn't be eating a lot of steaks, anyway. Too much red meat isn't good for you."

"It's not enough that you criticize my life-style, you're going to take on my diet next?" She almost missed seeing the twitch of a smile accompanying the remark.

Her newly hired partner's abrasive self was growing on her. She was even starting to like him that way. The David Reids of this world, she decided, weren't meant to be polite and charming. They were more the doers, the risk-takers. Exactly the kind of man she needed right now.

She made the sharp turn into the parking area beneath the condominium tower where she lived. The resident key card she slid into the slot lifted the security bar.

Inside her apartment, David stood backed up against the door, surveying the large living room as if he expected something big and ugly to suddenly leap out at him and he intended to be ready for it. Caution, she decided, should be this fellow's middle name.

"Make yourself at home," she told him, gesturing toward the enormous sectional couch of textured white cotton that curved halfway around the room.

David's stilted stroll took him through the foyer into the main room of the apartment. Somehow his dark, vital presence made the all-white decor she'd thought so sophisticated appear flat and sterile.

"Nice place you've got here, Doctor. Elegant."

"I don't own it. No way I could afford it right now. I lucked into a sublet from a colleague who's spending a year studying infectious diseases in Africa. Everything in here is his, except for some of the books, the plants and those floral throw pillows on the sofa."

David didn't accept her invitation to sit down. Bypassing the couch, he walked toward the floor-to-ceiling wall of glass ten stories above the ground. She kicked off her heels and padded after him, her toes squashing into the thick snowy pile of the carpet.

Silently he gazed out on the wide arm of the Chesapeake Bay that formed Baltimore harbor. In the gathering dusk the lights of the restaurants and shops of Inner Harbor were beginning to wink on. A huge container ship rode the tide out to the open sea, the wide fan of its wake catching the angled rays of the lowering sun.

She joined him at the window. "The view is the best thing about this place. I've always loved being able to look at water."

He didn't respond. He sure wasn't one for small talk.

As he watched the rapid progress of a water taxi making for a shoreside restaurant, the hard lines of his face settled into more serenity than she'd seen on him so far. A strange melting feeling took over her chest. Not for the first time.

Now that she'd roped in this great growling intensity of a partner, might that have been such a great idea after all? David Reid provoked feelings in her she definitely was not interested in pursuing.

She hadn't been able to make sense of the flood of delight that came over her when she'd stroked her hands over him in her examining room. Nothing similar had ever happened to her before. She'd had to work hard to maintain her professionalism and not slide off into exciting awareness of the lovely feelings that touching him brought with it.

He rested his hand over one of the black metal bars holding a broad windowpane. Astonishing how difficult it was to keep her hand from connecting with the long, lean fingers lying so temptingly right there in front of her eyes.

"Thank you again for taking me on, David. I appreciate it even more since I know that coming with me isn't something you really want to do."

"I've bowed to the inevitability of you getting your way. And this is as good a time as any to prove to myself that you were wrong yesterday when you called me a quitter."

"I never said that, David."

"That's the way I took it. Besides, a request from Roger Elliott is tantamount to an order. I'm liable to have him on my back if I don't help you out."

"I see." She didn't really understand David's relationship to Elliott. But that request, of course, was his main motivation for agreeing to come with her.

An inexplicable twinge of regret nipped at her heart.

Staring at him wasn't polite, but she couldn't keep her gaze from his face. Her eyes strayed to his mouth and lingered on the firm, sensual lines of his lips. What would it be like to feel those lips on hers? she wondered. Good heavens! That thought was totally out of line. David Reid was practically a stranger.

A stranger whom she'd invited to share her apartment for the night. The pleasant warmth already lodging at the base of her stomach notched up a degree or two. No doubt about it. She should have given that invitation a lot more thought.

She cleared her throat. "Now that you're in on things, I'm much more hopeful about finding Tommy than I used to be." No harm in laying her hand next to his on the windowpane and lightly connecting with his little finger. She did it simply to lend a little emphasis to her expression of gratitude.

"If that's true, I haven't done you any favor."

He seemed completely unaware that he'd turned up his palm and that his fingers were making tiny investigating movements against hers.

"Yes, you have, David. You do a great job of trying to hide the fact that under that gruff exterior of yours, you're a good-hearted man, but I've uncovered your secret. What's more, I think that if I could scrape away a layer or two of that surly camouflage you wear, I'd discover that you're basically *nice.*"

He threw her a heavy-duty frown, as if being called nice was no compliment. But he kept her hand trapped in a gentle hold she had no desire to break.

His gray gaze speared down into her like an intimate touch. A flock of butterflies took flight in her stomach.

How was it possible to feel so comfortable with a man and at the same time feel so unnerved by him?

She was suddenly pulsingly aware of her femininity. In her profession, she always tried to push the fact that she was female into the background, especially with men who were uncomfortable dealing with a woman doctor. With David, it was impossible for her to ignore the fact of her womanhood.

His fingers gave a quick spasm around hers, then abruptly dropped away. That he'd released her should have left her feeling relieved. It only left her noticing the coolness of the room.

"Let's get at that chicken you mentioned," he said.

"Oh. Right. Chicken."

She led the way to the galley kitchen stocked with the finest in cookware, and took the chicken from the freezer.

He tore the wrapping off, shoved the meat into the microwave and touched the Defrost command. It took no more than three seconds for him to catalog the refrigerator's meager contents. He settled on a wilted clove of garlic and the single remaining onion. With an accusing glance at her he tossed the plastic bag of prepared salad fixings onto the counter.

"You don't need to buy this stuff. You can make a fresh salad from scratch in about five minutes."

"Sometimes I don't have those five minutes."

"You have time to fix fresh flowers," he observed quietly. "Pink roses on the coffee table." He pointed with the knife. "That little pot of violets on the counter."

She hadn't guessed that he'd even notice such small things.

"I like flowers."

"I understand. Priorities."

Sometime over the past few hours, his eyes had taken on a humor and warmth that gave the hard angles of his face a whole different cast.

"Think you can handle putting the salad together?" His mouth again crooked in that wry smile that broke out all too seldom. "Sure." She shrugged. "I've lots of experience in tearing open plastic bags."

It was a pleasure to watch him work. He moved with an economy of motion. Precise. Controlled. He'd have made a good surgeon, she thought, as he focused on the job of slicing the chicken and vegetables into neat, even pieces. And with the quiet authority of a surgeon confident of an immediate response, he demanded the cooking oil and sauté pan.

This was a kitchen planned to function around the needs of a single cook. As she eased by him to reach the pan in the bottom cupboard on the other side, her breasts and belly brushed against the solid, heated wall of his back.

He froze.

Thank heaven she was standing behind him so he couldn't see the flame rushing into her cheeks when she realized that she'd grazed his body on purpose. He mightn't have liked the delicious contact of their bodies, but there was no denying that she had.

As if nothing had just happened between them—and come right down to it, nothing had—she pulled out the pan and slid it onto a burner. With brisk efficiency she slapped the plastic bottle of oil into David's outstretched hand.

His alchemy at the stove produced a dish with a delicious aroma that made her mouth water. She carried the tray holding their filled plates into the dining area overlooking the living room and placed it on the glass-topped table.

As he walked around the kitchen's work island, he bumped his injured thigh against a corner and let out a small gasp of pain.

She hissed in a breath. The evidence of his hurt made her feel a little sick.

"Oh, David." She rushed toward him. "Are you all right?"

"It's nothing." He shrugged off the helping hand she offered. "Let's have dinner before it gets cold."

She filled his wineglass and sat down. "What's the official prognosis on your leg?" she asked bluntly.

His frown plainly indicated that he didn't cotton to much conversation on this subject. "After months of physical therapy, they told me the nerve and tissue damage was so great that I'd never fully regain feeling in that leg and I'd never walk without a cane."

Just about what she'd figured after working on him this afternoon. "You seem to be doing pretty well with it."

"Hobbling along with a cane is not my idea of doing pretty well."

"You don't hobble along."

"Close to it. But I guess I shouldn't complain. At first the doctors wanted to take my leg. It was necessary to save my life, they claimed. I refused to let them do it."

She wasn't surprised. The eyes of some of her most badly injured or most seriously ill patients bore looks of frightened helplessness. Not the square-jawed commander's eyes. In him, she sensed more of a baffled rage.

"It's not the pain, is it?" she asked with sudden insight. "It's not really the pain that drove you to that mountain or, despite what you said, to the bottle."

The slit-eyed look he shot her could cut steel. She didn't flinch.

"Seems to me I've a right to know a little more than what Mr. Elliott told me about the man I'm about to run off to South America with."

He pushed his plate away, set his elbows on the table and rested his chin on the hands clasped in front of him.

"For what it's worth, you're right. It was never the pain. I can handle the pain. I'm not complaining that my injury happened. I knew the risks and freely chose the life. But I know damn well that I'm not the man I was. I always wanted to make my life count for something—always wanted to contribute something that made a real difference. I succeeded in doing that. For a while."

"You can still do that, David," she said gently.

"Spare me the pep talk."

She debated with herself about voicing the rest of her thoughts. She hated the idea that he might go on living in iso-

lation and denial when he had so much going for him, if only
he'd give himself the chance. He mightn't like hearing what she
had to say, but she decided to risk his ire.

"You're to be commended for fighting so hard against your
physical impairment. But I hope you realize that no amount of
exercise will bring your body back to what it was before the
disaster that wrecked your leg. The kind of life you had before
that is over."

The astonishment on his face gave way to anger.

"You sure don't pull your punches, lady."

"Most of my patients want to hear the truth, and you don't
strike me as being a man who needs to have punches pulled. I
said what I did because the sooner you admit that hard fact, the
sooner you can get on with making something good of the rest
of your life. As for holding back in what I say, I haven't noticed much of that from you, either."

He looked ready to blow up at her. Instead he shook his head
and gave a sharp dry chuckle. He picked up his wineglass and
lifted it to her. "Touché. You've got guts, Cara Merrill. I like
that about you. Here's to no holding back for either one of us."

Not exactly a ringing endorsement of her on his part, but
she'd already decided that she liked him. As for not holding
back, he didn't know the half of it. She was doing her best to
hold back on the attraction he held for her. How smart would
it be to allow her emotions to get tangled up in a new relationship, when she was still battling her way out of the terrible re-
percussions of the last one?

"But you're wrong," he continued. "I'm very well aware
that the days of my being able to do what I want to do are over.
However, I'm not the reason we're here together. Your plan to
search for Tommy is. What does your family think about all
this?"

She recognized that he'd firmly shut the door on any more
talk of himself.

"They don't think any more of it than you do." Her family's lack of support for her commitment to Tommy remained
a source of deep regret. She couldn't fault them, though, for

being more concerned about her welfare than they were about his.

"Just a couple of days ago my sister, Kelsey, called and tried again to talk me into giving up on him. She claims I've always felt too blasted responsible for the rest of the world. To prove it, she reminded me of the time I spent weeks of summer vacation guarding a bird's nest on our back porch by shooing the neighborhood cats away."

Maybe Kelsey was right. But then, not even she knew the guilty truth about her engagement to Tommy. She'd never confessed that to anyone.

"A smart woman, your sister. You should listen to her."

"I should, huh?" Cara broke into a teasing grin. "I wonder if you'd have said that at the time she ran off with a prison escapee. A convicted murderer."

David choked on a mouthful of wine. Cara gave a satisfied smirk. It was fun to be able to shock him. He probably thought himself completely unshockable.

"Good Lord! What's with you Merrill women?"

"It wasn't as bad as it sounds. It turned out that Ben had been wrongly imprisoned. Kelsey helped him prove his innocence. They're married now. A few months ago they presented me with a darling little nephew."

She refilled his wineglass and her own.

"You have to understand, David. I owe Tommy. He did a lot for me. I've always been in awe of his intellectual gifts. He does have those gifts, even though he's made a complete mess of his personal life. He could read a text through and remember it almost word-for-word. I always had to work my brains out to make good grades. I might never have made it through premed without him. Because of his help I received the scholarship. My family and I never could have managed the tuition entirely on our own. I'm where I am today largely because of Tommy's help back then."

"You are where you are today because of your own hard work."

"That, too."

She stood up and started to gather the dishes. "You did most of the work on the dinner, David. Go sit in the living room. I'll clear the table and bring our coffee out there."

David picked up his cane and ambled over to take a seat on the sofa. She brought in the coffee tray and poured them each a cup. Settling back against the puffy down cushions, she folded her legs up under her and regarded him levelly.

"Back in Baker's office, you didn't seem too surprised to hear that Tommy had gone to Colombia."

"I considered it a possibility, especially with the drug and the Miami connections."

"Yet earlier you suggested that I go to Rio."

"Just trying to keep you out of trouble." He looked not the slightest bit contrite for deliberately misdirecting her. "I'm not surprised it didn't work."

"It doesn't bother you that I would have wasted weeks of my time in Brazil?"

He shrugged. "Rio's a great place. You might have enjoyed yourself there. Or is enjoying yourself against your religion?"

"I can enjoy myself as well as the next person," she snapped back. "Don't you think it was arrogant of you to take that decision on yourself?"

"Probably. I tend to be protective of women. No doubt that's considered a personal failing these days. Just one weakness among many in my case. Nevertheless, it's how I am. You might as well get used to the idea that I'll try to look after you in Colombia. Not that I'll be much good at doing that in the shape I'm in."

How could a woman stay angry at a man for wanting to protect her? Even though she didn't believe she needed looking after, she liked the feeling. She couldn't remember Tommy ever being protective of her. Usually it was she who was solicitous of him, listening to his complaints, taking care of whatever problems she could for him.

"Tell me about Colombia."

David set his cup down on the table. "Most people there are no different from people anywhere. They just want to be left alone to live their lives and bring up their children in peace. But the drug operations, leftist rebels, terrorists and scores of just plain bad guys have made it one of the most dangerous countries in the world, both for its citizens and visitors. The State Department has issued a travel warning for the country. You shouldn't take that lightly.''

"I don't. My brother works at State. How about Bogota itself? We won't run into any trouble right in the city, will we?''

"The main business and tourist districts are well patrolled by police and safe enough. But even in the city you'll have to watch yourself. There are muggers and scam artists everywhere. Come right down to it, Cara, the only really safe place for you will be in your locked hotel room."

"If you're trying to frighten me, David, you're succeeding."

"Good. Maybe that will keep you alert."

"What about visas, shots, inoculations?"

"All we'll need are our passports and a return ticket. No shots are necessary, except for trips into remote areas. I don't expect we'll be going there." His voice took on a brittle edge. "I strongly hope we won't be going there."

"So we can leave for Bogota fairly soon then."

"Anytime you want to."

"I made arrangements with my partners to have four weeks of free time so I could make a last concerted effort at tracking Tommy down. If I don't find him by the end of that time, I'll bow to everyone's opinion that I should quit looking for him. At least then I'll know that I've given it my best shot."

"I'm glad to hear that you don't intend to go around in sackcloth and ashes over the guy for the rest of your life."

She ignored the comment. "How about heading for Bogota next Monday?"

"Fine."

"I'll contact my travel agent tomorrow to order our airline tickets and hotel reservations. Naturally I'll pick up our expenses while we're down there."

"No. I'll take care of the tickets and expenses."

"But I already told you I planned to do that, David. It's only fair. You wouldn't be going at all if it weren't to help me out."

"Forget it. You picking up the tab would make me your employee, and I don't intend to take orders from you. Certainly not once we hit Bogota. This way, I'm in charge."

"But it's all so expensive." Cara worried her bottom lip. She already was in hock up to her eyeballs for college loans. Her income from her medical practice wouldn't pay off those bills for years.

"Don't worry about it. Money isn't a problem for me. Never has been. If I'd wanted to, I could have sat around Chandler Hall on my duff instead of joining the navy."

"So you've decided that you have to pick up the tab. You sure are into maintaining control of everything and everyone around you, Commander."

"You're no slouch in the control department yourself, lady. The first time I saw you, I ordered you off my land. But here I am preparing to jet off to South America with you."

She threw in the towel on the disagreement.

"Okay, you pay the bills for yourself. But I pay my own way. And we're equal partners. You're in charge of conducting our investigations in Colombia. I'm in charge of handling Tommy once we find him."

"Don't get your hopes up too high. Bear in mind that we're not even certain that Tommy is there. Bogota is a sprawling city of almost six million people. Even if he's there, your chances of tracking him down in the time you have aren't good. The only way you might find him is if he has contacts among the North American colony."

"I'll never know if I don't try."

Despite David's high-handed take-charge attitude, it was a huge relief to have found someone willing to share the burden of her search. And she suspected that injured leg or no, she couldn't have found a better partner than David Chandler Reid.

His home, Chandler Hall on Virginia's James River, meant he wasn't exaggerating about having the option of sitting back and enjoying a life of wealth and privilege without lifting a finger. He chose instead to enter a profession that would push him to his physical and mental limits, to risk his life in situations very few people could handle.

"One more thing, David," she said softly. "Graduating from Annapolis, making it to the SEALs and to the rank of commander isn't exactly just joining the navy."

She glanced at her watch. "I didn't realize it was so late. Doesn't make a whole lot of sense for me to drive you to some hotel, when there's a perfectly good guest room waiting for you right through that door."

"I guess I might as well stay."

Strange how much she wanted to go on sitting here quietly talking with him instead of leaving him to get the rest he needed after today's painful problem with his leg.

She didn't feel like examining why she should feel so glad that David Reid hadn't already walked out of her life for good. Not that he wouldn't someday, of course, but she'd be ready for it by then.

Not happy with the direction her thoughts were taking, she uncurled herself from the sofa.

"Let's see if I can find you something to wear."

The wave of disappointment that swept through him when Cara left, David thought, didn't make a whole lot of sense. He'd been in firefights that had tightened his stomach muscles less than had spending most of the day in close proximity to Cara Merrill.

It had been a long time since he'd enjoyed such a simple pleasure as dining with a woman, as having a real conversation with anyone. But those pleasures were enough to bring him a painful reminder of what real life had been like. And why he'd withdrawn from it to his mountain.

She returned holding a silk, paisley-print robe, and draped it over the back of the sofa.

He frowned down at the garment. "Tommy's?"

It made him furious that every time he noticed the ring on her left hand, every time she mentioned Tommy, a flame of anger licked through him. A man who didn't know what to do with a woman like Cara Merrill didn't deserve to be given a second chance. The possibility that Tommy might get exactly that brought an exasperated frown to his face.

"No. Tommy's never been in this apartment. My brother's. He brought the kids here to see the tall ships a couple of weekends ago, and left the robe behind. I haven't had a chance to return it yet. You'll find toiletries in the bathroom. If there's anything else you need, just let me know."

He planted the cane in front of him and used it to push to his feet. "Thanks. Good night, Cara."

She turned at the doorway to her room and loosed a smile on him that hit him like a blow right in the center of his chest.

"Good night, David. Sleep well. If your leg starts giving you trouble during the night, don't hesitate to call me."

Slowly she closed herself behind the door.

He scooped up the robe and made for the bedroom. He pulled off his shirt and pants and tossed them carelessly on the nearest free surface—a dresser—as usual. Then he went back and folded them neatly before laying them down again.

One quick look into the bathroom sent him scrambling for the robe. Why did they put in bathroom mirrors that were big enough for half a dozen people to use at the same time? All he needed to shave or comb his hair—when he bothered to do that—was the small mirror on his medicine chest.

After he'd finished in the bathroom, he parked himself glumly on the edge of the bed.

How in the name of everything holy did he get himself into this position? That threat of possible danger to her had pushed his mouth into volunteering the rest of him before his brain had a chance to kick in.

Evidently personal experience had made him too damn much of a sucker for loyalty in a woman.

He wasn't doing this because she asked it of him, he told himself. No, he was doing it out of sheer self-protection. If anything happened to her, he'd have to shoulder that guilt on top of everything else he was dealing with. And any more mental stress would surely send him screaming into the arms of the guys in the white coats.

Damn Elliott. The man had to have a sadistic streak in him. The same suspicions that crossed his own mind about Grant's whereabouts must have occurred to the intelligence officer. He'd gone ahead anyway and pointed Cara in David Reid's direction. Not that this was a mission that required a whole man to do it. He'd be little more than a glorified tour guide. Action that shouldn't prove too much for a cripple.

His mouth twisted in a self-directed grimace of disgust.

Never mind Elliott, an undiscovered streak of masochism must lurk inside himself, too. What kind of fool would head right back into the place that wrecked his life?

He hoped he'd be up to handling any danger they might run up against in Colombia. There'd been a time when he'd been convinced he could handle anything. Convinced, that is, until he came up against the frightening fact of his own physical weakness.

What he wasn't at all sure he could handle was the different kind of danger that tugged at him from only a few feet away.

Returning to Colombia would be tough enough. Based on the kind of reactions the beautiful doctor already raised in him, he had the sinking feeling that returning there with her would be like walking on fire.

He didn't like these new and chaotic emotions she inspired in him. He'd arranged his life neatly and orderly, exactly the way he wanted it.

What he didn't want was to feel the softness she called to life within him. Didn't want to feel the urgent need to touch her that had bedeviled him all evening. For sure, he didn't want to feel that warm swelling between his legs. Not with this woman. And what irony that was. Be careful what you pray for, you might get it.

But how could he be expected to overcome these dangerous feelings that tempted him down pathways he didn't want to go, when he was lying in a bed separated from hers only by thin sheets of wallboard?

He doused the lamp on the bedside table and slid between the sheets. A faint sound from her room reached his ears. In the darkness his eyes turned toward the wall between them. He fought off the visions that kept assaulting him. Tantalizing visions of her wandering around in there dressed only in some skimpy night thing.

Call her, she'd told him. Call her? He wouldn't call the woman if his whole body seized up into one giant charley horse.

Chapter 4

Cara peered out through the small window next to her seat and watched the broad blue length of the Caribbean unrolling thirty thousand feet below.

This wasn't how she'd envisioned carrying out her search for Tommy. She'd expected to track him down through the mean streets of Baltimore or New York, not have to fly to another part of the world to find him.

David dropped his head on the seat back and closed his eyes.

One of his hands rested on his left leg. The long, lean fingers curving around his thigh moved back and forth. He drew his mouth tight and shifted slightly, obviously in some pain.

She felt a startling desire to comfort him. But if ever a man appeared completely self-contained and self-sufficient, it was David Reid. The fact that he might be locked in an emotional cage of his own making shouldn't concern her as much as it did. She wasn't responsible for him. She was responsible only for Tommy, who was locked in a tighter cage. One from which he probably could never escape without her help.

She laid her hand beside David's on his thigh. She should have foreseen the shock of pleasure that streaked through her when her palm met the tingling warmth of his body.

His eyes immediately flew open and his gray gaze cut quickly to her. For a moment she thought she read an unexpected defensiveness in his eyes. Defensiveness about anything other than his disability didn't seem a part of his makeup. He always seemed primed for attack.

"I'm sorry," she said. "I didn't mean to wake you."

"I wasn't asleep." The huskiness in his voice suggested otherwise.

A subtle change had come over him during the days they were making preparations for the trip. There was a banked energy about him now, like a slow-burning fire glowing beneath graying ashes.

She couldn't believe how unshakable was the attraction he held for her. That testosterone-driven stoicism of his, that irritating lack of sensitivity represented so much of what she'd never cared for in a man. Somehow on David, those weaknesses came across as personal courage and plain truth-telling.

He'd made a surprisingly good impression on her family. She was a little annoyed to find out that her brother had checked him out without first letting her know. But Stephen's report on Commander David Chandler Reid had calmed her family down about her trip to South America. It couldn't have been David's charm that so easily won them over, but they all seemed comfortable about taking him on trust.

They weren't alone in that reaction. She hadn't known David long, but she'd never been able to trust Tommy in the way she'd already learned to trust her partner.

Trusted him in most things, she thought glumly. Not in their seesawing personal relationship that she refused to call romantic, but felt a long way from platonic.

A line of thought she didn't want to pursue.

"What did you do with the cat, David?"

"Huh?"

"The cat. You're not at the house to feed it."

"I took care of that problem."

Alarm shot through her. "David! You didn't—?"

"The woman who runs the general store down in the village is looking after it while I'm gone. I'll probably have that nuisance animal on my hands for the rest of its miserable life."

Cara smiled. He'd have the animal on his hands because he couldn't bear to get rid of it. The hard-as-nails commander harbored a soft spot a mile wide.

The beautiful dark-haired flight attendant who'd been eyeing David since he first came on board, strolled over to him again. She noted Cara's hand lying on his thigh and slid her an openly envious glance. Cara went right on with her gentle kneading. She didn't care if the woman thought her action was a sexual one instead of a simple soothing of a man's painful muscle.

"May I get you anything, Commander Reid? Coffee? Something from the bar?" Cara couldn't blame the attendant for her interest in the man. His now always clean-shaven face and a decent haircut had enhanced the rugged good looks that had been evident even beneath his former grunge.

"Coffee, please. Cara?"

She nodded.

David had hardly glanced at the attendant. Cara wondered if he'd even noticed her interest. For some unfathomable reason, it pleased her that he didn't.

"I have to admit," David said, "that I never really believed you'd get this far. I hoped you'd come to your senses and bail out at the last minute."

"Why does everyone think I'm crazy for wanting to find Tommy and help him?" she asked with some irritation. "If something terrible happened to me, I'd want someone to care. What if he'd been involved in a car accident that left him in a wheelchair? Should I have abandoned him then?"

David pressed his lips together and didn't answer.

"If he'd been injured in some way, or if he'd come down with some life-threatening disease, I wouldn't have deserted him. So why should I write him off now?"

"You didn't desert him," David said pointedly. "He deserted you, remember?"

"Thank you for reminding me."

The acid tone of her voice didn't deter him.

"Besides, drug addiction is hardly the same as an accident, and I don't buy the theory that it's a disease. A man makes a choice to use drugs. He has no choice when he's hit by a car, or when he's shot up trying to rescue a couple of DEA agents held hostage in a jungle drug lab."

Cara jerked her cup to a halt halfway to her lips. David had finally volunteered a mention of the incident that left him with a ruined leg.

"Is that what happened to you, David?"

He gave a deliberately offhand shrug and found a sudden interest in the contents of his coffee cup. The man seemed embarrassed that he'd ventured even that much.

"We were talking about you and Tommy-the-Sensitive."

That David so quickly clammed up about himself didn't surprise her. She already knew that he wasn't a man to let it all hang out. Over the past few days, he'd turned away most of her inquiries about himself. But for his sake she was sorry he hadn't been able to go a little further about the incident that left him so badly wounded.

"Wouldn't you stick by someone close to you if they were injured?" she asked.

"Maybe I would. But not everyone is as adept as you are at the self-sacrificing little woman bit." She'd already decided that he tried to push her buttons on purpose, just for the fun of seeing her get riled. This time she didn't rise to the bait. "My wife for one."

"You're married?"

That important little nugget of information exploded like a firecracker in her mind. The subject of his marriage had never come up. He'd spoken fondly of the grandmother at Chandler Hall who insisted that he call her once a week to let her know that he hadn't fallen off the mountain. Nothing about a wife. He wore no ring. She had simply assumed he was single. Why it should matter so much one way or the other, she had no idea, but she held her breath for the few seconds it took him to answer.

"I was. I'm not anymore. The final divorce papers came through last winter. Except for a few minutes in court, I haven't even seen Anita since the day I came home from the hospital nineteen months ago."

Was there something in the coffee that was loosening his tongue? Cara wondered. He hadn't taken any alcohol but that glass of champagne with lunch. In fact, she hadn't seen him with anything but the occasional glass of wine since that morning on his deck.

"When my wife saw what was left of me she did some serious backpedaling about our relationship."

Cara's heart contracted painfully. How could the one person a man should be able to count on run out on him at a time of such aching vulnerability? But she was in no position to throw stones. Hadn't she herself done something similar to Tommy?

She touched David's hand.

"It's not uncommon for serious disease or injury to take its toll on personal relationships." Her professionally correct attempt at consolation fell so far short of what she wanted to say. "I'm very sorry that it happened to you."

"Take its toll on a relationship? I'd say so. Anita took one look at me after I came out of the hospital and ran into the bathroom to vomit. When she came out, she bolted to the man she already had waiting in the wings."

David had thrown out the words with clipped coolness, but a nerve worked in his jaw. And his hands were clenched in his lap.

His wife's brutal rejection coming on the wings of his injury must have destroyed him. Just listening to his recounting of it made her flinch. Tears burned behind her eyelids. She turned away to make sure he wouldn't see. He'd probably read her tears of sympathy as a sign of pity, and would hate it.

Muttering a soft curse, David raked a hand through his hair.

"I don't know what made me tell you that. It's not something I usually inflict on people."

"You haven't inflicted anything on me. I'm honored that you shared that confidence with me. You've listened patiently enough to my problems. I'm afraid we've both learned a lot more than either of us ever wanted to know about the pain of loss, the pain of rejection.''

He didn't say, as he might have, that his pain was worse, that he'd done nothing to earn his rejection, as she had.

Why had she ever thought David Reid cold and withdrawn? It was a wonder he was able to function at all after what he'd been through.

''We have more than that in common, David. I berated you for withdrawing into your own closed little world, but just now I realized that in a way I did the same thing. I closed up when I found out what Tommy was doing. It's true that my workload at the time was crushing. But to some extent I used that as an excuse not to deal with a situation I felt was beyond me. I was scared. I didn't know how to handle it. I thought if I threatened to leave him, Tommy would come to his senses and quit the drugs. He didn't.''

Her voice dropped. ''The hurt was awful. I still feel like the survivor of a loved one's suicide. I should have found some way to save him. Instead I failed him badly.''

She was looking down at her hand and twisting her engagement ring on her finger. It startled her when she felt the welcome warmth of David's hand on her cheek. He gently turned her face to his.

''You didn't fail. Tommy did.''

She tried to ignore how his touch turned her insides to warm jelly, and hoped that he couldn't feel her tremble.

''I did fail. By the time I lost track of him, he was using heroin. That so frightened and confused me that I gave up on him much too soon. Maybe if I'd pulled out of my residency and moved to New York to be with him, it might have made a difference.''

David drew his fingers away. She resisted the urge to grab his hand and put it back on her face where it felt so good.

''Most likely it would have made no difference whatever. For a smart lady you suffer from a major blind spot. You can't live another person's life for them. It simply can't be done. Each of us is responsible for ourselves. It's not only patronizing to think otherwise, it's useless."

"It's not that I'm trying to lead Tommy's life for him," she protested. "It's just that I feel I owe him this. He never said in so many words that he was breaking our engagement. Neither did I. After your experience with your wife, I'd expect you to appreciate that simple loyalty to another person counts for something."

"It counts for a great deal. SEALs have the bedrock of team loyalty to count on. We bet our lives on that loyalty. It saved my life in South America. A buddy came back and got me out of there at risk to his own life. If he hadn't shown me that kind of loyalty, I wouldn't be sitting here now."

He turned his face away. "You might as well know, too, that for a long time I didn't thank him for that. In fact, at one point, I even thought about—" He gave a short, quick shake of his head. "Never mind."

She went cold. If those chilling words meant what she thought they meant, David's retiring to his mountain retreat had been a positive choice rather than a negative one. He'd been dealing with his physical and psychological problems as best he could, yet she'd castigated him for it. His bout of ill temper back at the mountain house was now a lot more understandable.

The implications of what he'd said a moment earlier finally struck her.

"South America? You almost lost your life in South America? Oh, Lord, David. Not in Colombia? Tell me that didn't happen in Colombia."

His nonresponse spoke louder than words.

"It did." She flopped back in her seat in dismay and closed her eyes. "Of course, it did. I should have realized that from the way you looked when Baker mentioned Colombia." Willing her eyes not to mist up, she turned to him. "And now I've forced you to return to a place you probably never wanted to see again. Oh, David. I wish you'd told me."

"You knowing it wouldn't have made any difference. Coming with you was my choice."

.

"But I—"

"Drop it. It was about time that I made a conscious choice about something other than myself. As for your unusual loyalty to Tommy, Cara, frankly I don't believe it stems from true, undying love. I think you're really doing all this for yourself more than him. At bottom this search is a way to salve your conscience for what you see as letting the guy down in the first place. I'm surprised that a woman as intelligent as you are can't see that."

Cara drew in a quick breath.

She couldn't deny it. Guilt rode her like a fiend. "I do feel guilty for having failed him. And it's true that I find that guilt very hard to live with."

David Reid was more astute than he knew. He'd seen through a secret she'd never told anyone. Never had the courage to admit even to herself for a long time. She'd so concentrated on what Tommy had done to her, how he'd hurt her, that it had taken her a while to recognize how unfair she'd been to him.

David shrugged. "I still don't see why you should feel so damn guilty. And how come you've got the job of finding him all by yourself? Doesn't the guy have any family?"

"His parents are divorced. When I met him he was living with his mother and her new husband, and he didn't get along too well with his stepfather. They were pretty cold when they learned about the drugs."

"I suppose if it means that much to you, then maybe you're doing the right thing after all. For your sake, I hope that all this will help you dump that useless load of remorse you're carrying around."

She wondered if there was any personal caring whatever behind his words. But why should there be? He wasn't doing all this for her. As he'd said, he was helping her simply because Mr. Elliott had asked him to. That reminder always brought a strange tightness to her chest.

"I think I'll close my eyes for a few minutes," she said, as the flight attendant took their cups away. She didn't feel much like talking anymore anyway. She pushed her pillow between the seat and the window and rested her head on it.

David looked over at Cara dozing against the pillow, and shook his head in wonder. She was for real, this lovely, graceful woman. These few engaging days with her had convinced him of that.

What he wouldn't have given to have received just a fraction of the loyalty she offered to a man to whom she was merely engaged. He'd received none at all from a wife of three years. A wife who had elaborately taken him for better or worse in the august presence of Richmond high society.

He'd never met anyone who presented such an intriguing mix of cool professionalism and emotional sensitivity as did Cara Merrill. They'd given him a medal or two for heroism under fire, but he hadn't one-tenth the bravery she had when it came to laying herself open to her feelings, and acting on them.

Maybe because he'd been out of practice in handling a close association with a woman for such a long time, some of that emotional openness of hers was starting to rub off on him. He couldn't believe he'd actually told her about that last horrible scene with Anita. The still-hurtful confession just seemed to burst out of its own accord. He'd never breathed a word of it to anyone else. Hell, a wife's total rejection wasn't something a man was eager to admit.

The shock of Anita's blistering reaction had shoved him headfirst into hard reality. Lying in the hospital, he'd managed to convince himself that he'd ultimately come through his ordeal little changed from the man he'd been. The wounds would heal, he told himself, maybe leaving an intriguing scar or two. Perhaps that very self-delusion helped keep him alive. The gut-wrenching moment he realized it wasn't going to happen was the moment he began his slide into despair. A despair capped by his wife's desertion.

The scene remained as searingly vivid in his mind as if it had happened yesterday. They'd decided—actually Anita had decided—so as to allow him to rest properly during the night, that he should sleep for a time in the guest room. When he hobbled into their bedroom on his crutches, he'd been seeking the comfort of her arms rather than sex.

The look on her face when she'd turned and seen him was branded deep into his memory. Complete disgust twisted her pretty features. She slapped a hand to her mouth and rushed to the bathroom.

While he stood there stunned, listening to the mortifying sounds from the bathroom, his reflection in the mirrored closet doors showed him exactly what his wife had seen. No wonder the sight of him had sickened her. A hollow-eyed man he could hardly recognize stared back at him. A man hanging between metal crutches like some loathsome living scarecrow. A frightening number of jagged red scars, stitched through with ragged lines of black thread, slashed down almost the entire left side of his painfully naked body.

After that, it had taken a very long time for him to screw up the courage to see any woman other than his grandmother and the nursing professionals.

Why the hell he hadn't brought out his big guns to send Cara packing right there on the dock almost a week ago, he still didn't understand. All he had to do was climb out of the water and stand in front of her. The ugly sight of him would have done it.

Or maybe not. She was a doctor. Maybe she would have calmly inspected his scars and offered the same coolly clinical comments the others did. No big improvement over her taking to her heels.

Restless, she shifted in her seat beside him and turned to drop her head against his shoulder. He looked down at the gentle rise and fall of the soft mounds of her breasts, and smiled. Never slept on planes, huh? She was out like a light, completely oblivious to the fact that she'd snaked her hand under his arm.

The perfume of her hair teased him. The nearness of her sent a soft prickle of want over him, just as it had been doing every time he saw her. A want that both gladdened and tormented him. A want he wasn't ready to test. Not with this particular woman. Not after that humiliating experience in the darkened hotel room with the woman who'd been coming on to him for years, always unsuccessfully until that night.

Even thinking about what happened to him then—or rather what didn't happen—made him cringe. From that day to this, he'd allowed no woman to touch him except in the most distanced of terms. Except for Cara. No way in the world could even the lightest of her touches be called distanced. When she'd fondled his thigh earlier, he was afraid he might actually whimper in pleasure.

And as unlikely as it seemed, he couldn't deny that many of the thoughts about her sparking through his mind the past few days were definitely of the carnal variety.

She made a little mewling sound of distress in her sleep. Probably some unhappy dream about her fiancé. He stroked his hand gently down the side of her head and she stopped. Her commitment to the worthless Grant left her so vulnerable. He didn't know what they'd find in Colombia, but it wasn't likely to be anything good.

He pushed away the rush of sympathy for her that came over him. He didn't want to feel anything for her. He'd never been a man to move in on another man's woman. Certainly not after being on the receiving end of that game.

Still, Cara Merrill was the kind of woman he'd wanted once upon a time. The kind he thought he'd found until real life made mincemeat of that hope.

His body was shot to hell, but his head still worked. He knew damn well that this wasn't a woman a man should become involved with unless he was on for heavy talk about commitment. A subject he wasn't willing to think about, let alone discuss.

Why did she set all his hard-won promises to himself to shifting like grains of sand? He'd already made his decision on women. Except in the most impersonal terms, they weren't to be a part of his life. The price was too high.

He could do it, he told himself one more time. He'd already done it for almost two years.

Chapter 5

The Spanish conquistadors came to the area of Bogota in search of El Dorado, the legendary City of Gold. They found that those mythical treasures didn't exist. Present day Colombia found its fortune mainly in coffee, emeralds and flowers. Its most infamous export—cocaine—brought the country to the attention of most Americans and to the world.

David had already informed her that Colombia wasn't the tropical jungle country she'd expected. Parts of it still held miles of steamy uncharted rain forest, but Bogota was built on a high plateau ringed by a ridge of the Andes. At eight thousand feet, the temperature usually ranged in the comfortable sixties. Within minutes of walking out the door of El Dorado Airport, she had to work harder to drag enough of the thin mountain air into her lungs.

He could never have prepared her for her first shocking sight of horrifying third-world poverty in the sprawling, squalid slum thrown up near the airport. On the edge of the *barrio* loomed a mountain of trash. People, many of them children, scuttled over the heap like a horde of miners digging for gold.

"They're scavenging for recyclable material to sell," David told her.

Beyond the soul-searing territory of the desperately poor rose the domain of the comfortable: a large cluster of modern apartments and office towers.

Jammed in among the traffic chaos of cars, trucks, long streams of *busetas,* and other traffic, their taxi was going nowhere fast.

A small arm jutted through the open window. The ragged child the arm belonged to was so young he—or maybe she— could barely peer in over the edge of the door. The little one's face was filthy, black hair matted into clumps.

The driver's shouted curse didn't faze the tiny beggar. David reached across Cara and pressed a two thousand peso note, less than two dollars American, into the little hand. She quickly did the same. The small creature scampered off to the car behind them.

Cara twisted in her seat to watch the tyke. "He's just a baby, David. We've got to do something for him."

"We've already done the only thing we can do. The money we gave the kid means that he'll eat today. Believe me, Cara, we'll have plenty of opportunity to do the same thing every day we're here. There are hundreds, thousands of these street kids in the cities. Begging and scavenging is the only way they can survive."

The little boy disappeared into the traffic.

"It hurts to see it, David."

He covered her hand with his.

"It hurts. But it doesn't take long in a place like this to realize that you can't save the world single-handed."

That didn't stop her from wishing she could wave a magic wand and give the little one—all the little ones—a decent life.

Impatient drivers unleashed a deafening crescendo of car horns. David cranked his window closed, and so did she. The wrathful outburst apparently blew away whatever obstruction had been holding them up. Their cab crawled ahead.

"Tomorrow I'll show you the old colonial Bogota," David said. "You'll like it."

"I don't want to waste time sight-seeing. I'm not here as a tourist. I want to get on Tommy's trail as soon as possible. We'll start this evening."

"We will not. You've got to give yourself time to adjust to the altitude. Take it easy for the first day or so, or you could find yourself laid up with *soroche,* altitude sickness. And as far as the rest of the world is concerned, you *are* here simply as a tourist. So am I. We don't want to get the police or anyone else interested in us. We're just a couple of harmless *turistas* in town to view their spectacular collection of pre-Columbian artifacts and pick up some emerald jewelry. While we're here, we thought we'd try to look up a friend we heard might be in Bogota."

David's background in the military might be leading him to be overcautious, but she wasn't up for debating the point. He seemed to win most of their arguments. Even when she was convinced she had logic on her side, it usually felt as if he were the one who was right about their difference of opinion.

He'd booked rooms for them in a large luxury hotel belonging to a well-known American chain. She was too keyed up to follow his suggestion that she take it easy for the rest of the day. She didn't like to admit that she might be feeling antsy because she hadn't seen David for a couple of hours and came close to missing him. They'd spent so much time together these past few days, it didn't feel quite right to be separated from him.

She felt a little guilty about ringing his suite. He picked up the receiver on the first ring, though, so he couldn't have been resting, even though he'd ordered her to do that.

"I want to get started," she told him. "Surely it won't do any harm to go out for a stroll around the area while we decide how we're going to go about our search."

"I didn't expect to have much luck keeping you quiet in your room for any length of time. I'll meet you down in the lobby."

She had mixed feelings about the gun-toting security guards ambling around the pleasant tree-lined avenue holding restaurants and upscale shops. That the intimidating guards were necessary at all only made her wonder what she was being protected against.

They skipped an elegant French restaurant for a café that served a traditional Colombian specialty, a bowl of thick, creamy chicken soup with vegetables.

"After what happened with Baker," Cara said, "I suppose there's no point in hiring another detective here."

"No. I don't think we should chance it."

"Tommy may have gotten a job in some kind of medical capacity at a hospital or a clinic," she suggested. "He might even be practicing as a doctor somewhere, although he has no right to do that. I think our first step should be to contact the local medical associations and hospitals for any word of him."

David agreed. "As a physician yourself, Cara, you should be the one to do that. They'll probably open up to you quicker than they would me. You'd better see them in person, rather than talk to them by phone, so that you can show Grant's photograph around."

"Among medical professionals, I should find some who speak English."

"Yes. But keep your questions low-key. Don't push. That incident with Baker and the thug in Miami still worries me. We don't know yet why or with whom Tommy might be here. Until we do, we don't want to rattle the same cages that got your detective into trouble. In Colombia, no one with any sense asks too many questions about anyone with any connection whatever to the drug scene. Which may include Tommy."

"And may not," she added quickly.

"He's in the cocaine capital of the world, and he's with a guy who travels with protection. You figure it out."

She didn't want to figure it out. "I'll start in on the hospitals first thing in the morning."

"Be careful who you talk to on the streets. The city is crawling with dangerous scam artists. While you tackle the medical community, I'll check out the hotels where a visiting American is likely to stay. I already spoke to the manager of our own hotel. It's the largest in the city. I thought Tommy might have stayed here."

"I take it you had no luck?"

"No. Their computer files showed that the only guest named Grant who'd stayed there lately was a woman."

A well-dressed Bogotano who'd been sitting in the rear of the small restaurant got up to leave. As he walked past their table, he slowed and gave Cara an appreciative smile. *"Buenas noches, señorita."* Even though Cara ignored the man, he seemed inclined to linger.

"Adiós, señor," David said flatly.

The man looked at the cane leaning by David's chair and at the stiffly bent leg, and insultingly ignored him.

David's eyes narrowed into slits. *"Adiós,"* he growled.

She'd already seen the effect of David's withering look on Baker. Apparently deciding there might be more to this *gringo* than he was willing to deal with, the man *adiósed.*

She rather liked the idea that it irked David that a man would come on to her.

On the walk back to the hotel, her jacket wasn't enough to cut the chill wind sweeping down from the enormous Andean chain. Folding her arms tightly over her chest didn't do much to keep her warm.

"You're cold," David said. "Come here."

She dutifully stepped closer. He carefully fastened every button on her jacket, and flipped up its collar. The tantalizing brush of his fingers against her nape skipped a shiver of delight through her. She thought she'd learned just about all there was to know about the human body. But no medical text had warned that a man's touch—this man's touch—could send her blood rushing hotly through her veins.

"Better?"

She could only nod. What she really wanted was to be closer to him.

He rounded an arm over her shoulders and drew her protectively into the windbreak of his body.

He'd been doing that increasingly often lately: reading her mind. That intangible connection he seemed to be forging between them was unsettling. Yet it continuously tempted her into wanting more of it.

It felt wonderful to be pulled up close to the heated wall of his chest, wonderful to breathe in his clean, already comfortingly familiar scent.

They reached the hotel much too quickly. She could have happily stayed within the enlivening circle of David's arm all night, no matter how low the temperature dropped.

·He clicked on the light and saw her safely inside her room.

With a tenderness that ran straight to her heart, he stroked his knuckles slowly down her cheek.

"I hope you find what you're looking for here."

It was a second or two before she could call up breath enough to speak. "Thank you, David."

"Right now, it's into bed with you. That's an order."

An order she realized she wouldn't hesitate to comply with if it included him. "Yes, Commander."

He smoothed the backs of his fingers under the curve of her chin. Her pulse raced into overdrive. The soft, warm whisk of his lips on her forehead sent a sparkling mantle of electrifying sensations cascading over her.

His breath caressed her cheek. A quiver started up inside her chest. The pads of his fingers, rough from splitting logs or whatever other outdoorsy things he did up there on his mountain, dripped an energizing heat into the little hollow at the base of her throat.

She'd never felt anything so pleasurable.

All her senses were springing to inflaming life. She should open the door for him and tell him good-night, but a deep ache to know his mouth—a yearning that had been growing for days—held her back from ending their closeness.

His lips parted slightly. His head bowed a little closer.

Oh, yes. She desperately needed to feel his arms tight around her, desperately wanted to feel his mouth on hers. She tipped her head back, offering her lips.

Her eyes drifted shut.

A shock of cool air rushed between them. The door clicked shut.

Her eyes flashed open. She'd done everything but carry a sign saying she wanted David to kiss her, and he'd just walked away.

Leaving her aching for him.

Trembling between twin urges to hurl a string of curses at him and to run after him begging for the embrace he'd denied her, she slumped against the door.

Cara tossed her crumpled list of hospitals and clinics, every one crossed out, on the small table in front of the window in her room.

"Nothing." She dropped disconsolately into a chair.

Three days of covering the obvious places where a man with medical training might be working had brought her several offers of personal tours of the facilities, two invitations to dinner and one request that was considerably less polite. Other than that, she'd gotten exactly nowhere.

David had fared no better.

"No one at any of the hotels or restaurants I visited remembered seeing the guy in the photos at all," he reported. "I'm beginning to wonder if that private investigator of yours hasn't sent us off on a wild-goose chase. As Baker pointed out, you can't rely on the ravings of an addict to be the truth. If Grant is in Bogota at all, he's keeping a very low profile."

Running the edge of a thumb back and forth along the hard line of his jaw, he considered the problem. "Could be he's out of sight because he's haunting the underground drug scene."

Cara bit her lip.

"Sorry, Cara, but it's a possibility. We're not exactly searching for a candidate for sainthood here. If Grant is using drugs in Bogota, he'd better be doing it quietly. No matter that cocaine fuels much of the economy, the local authorities come down hard on open drug using."

David heaved a sigh of frustration. "I wanted to avoid bringing myself to the notice of the police, but I guess I'd better go down to headquarters tomorrow and see if they've got our boy in jail. You have to be prepared, though. If Tommy's in prison, we probably won't be able to get him out."

"I understand, David. I'll just have to deal with that situation if I come to it."

The year-long depression over Tommy that David's vital presence had warded off, began to creep back. He might be right about her having brought them all this way for nothing. She raised her hands to the back of her neck to rub out tightness caused as much from the tension of finding no trace of her friend as from exhaustion.

David came over to stand behind her. He nudged away her fingers to replace them with his own. Her whole body immediately tensed. Her instinct was to get up and run away from the stimulating touch. But moving away would look as if she were afraid of it. And that idea was just plain silly.

David had already made it clear that he wasn't on for any romantic scenes by totally ignoring her all too blatant request to be kissed the other night. A good thing, because she really was no more interested in him than he was in her.

Telling herself that often enough might eventually make it true.

The warm strength of his fingers subdued the ache at the base of her neck, but incited a different kind of tautness in the rest of her.

"Aside from checking with the cops," she said, with as much coolness as she could muster, "what will our next step be?"

David's thumbs stopped drawing soothing circles at the top of her shoulders. He didn't answer immediately. She dropped her head back to look up at him.

"What do we do next, David?"

"I'd better handle that part alone. We've already covered the trendy bars and nightclubs without success. This evening I intend to start checking out some of the less fashionable *rumbeaderos* in areas where you won't feel very comfortable."

"You mean the red-light district."

He nodded. "Colombia is a very conservative country, nevertheless there are *putas,* prostitutes, everywhere."

She was about to argue that Tommy wouldn't frequent those places, but she was no longer sure of anything about the man with whom she'd once been ready to spend her life.

"The streets I have in mind are where much of that activity is concentrated. You won't want to see it, and the area isn't safe. While I'm out, you can spend a nice relaxing evening here in the hotel. They're putting on an exhibition of Latin American dance this evening. I'm sure you'll enjoy it."

His fingers picked up where they'd left off. It was all she could do not to collapse into a fluid heap under his gentle stroking. If he thought the action would lull her into agreement, he had another think coming.

"No way. I'm not going to just sit here by myself while you are out doing what is, after all, my work. Do you think I've never seen a prostitute? I've treated several of both sexes at the free clinic. This is my search and I'm coming with you."

He gave up his massage and stalked around in front of her.

"Believe me, Cara, you won't like it."

"Probably not, but I'm not a child. I can handle it."

David glowered at her for a moment and then shrugged. "As you wish. But don't say I didn't warn you."

He still had a tendency to order her around as if she were one of his recruits. Maybe he was finally learning that tactic wouldn't work with her.

"All right then," he said. "The nightlife around here doesn't get started until late. We can have a leisurely dinner at the hotel and then head on out."

On a Friday evening, it seemed as if the whole city was in the streets partying.

The area in which the taxi deposited them was considerably less well manicured than the streets around their hotel. Radios and TVs blasted a cacophony of noise from every open door and window for blocks. Groups of men clutching bottles of beer loitered against the graffiti-splattered walls of low, seedy buildings. Yet another beggar came up and asked for money. David had a few pesos ready for him.

A slight young man jingling under the weight of several heavy gold chains sidled up to David. The man's pants matched the spiky punk shock of fluorescent yellow hair marching down the center of the black head. With a predatory grin, the *mestizo* of mixed Spanish-Indian blood murmured something to David. Cara had a feeling it was just as well she didn't quite hear what the man said.

David shook his head, but held out a photo of Grant and evidently asked if the man had seen him. The man spat out a *no* and hurried on to collar another potential customer for his girls.

They had no choice about entering the first *rumbeadero* they came to. The group of laughing party-goers in back of them swept them right into the enormous hall pulsing to strobe lights and earsplitting music.

A bevy of giggling young women descended on David and pulled him into a seat at a long table where the night's festivities were well under way. Before she could follow, a couple of young men sat her down in the chair between them.

On every available inch of the floor in the smoky room, men and women, all swaying bodies and revolving hips, flaunted themselves in a flagrantly joyous celebration of sex. Intimately and suggestively they slid their bodies up and down those of their partners in blatant imitation of lovemaking.

The men sitting on either side of her shouted twin invitations to dance. She smiled and shook her head at each of them.

David leaned across the table to be heard above the din.

"Go ahead and dance if you'd like to, Cara. I can do the questioning here."

The pounding beat of the *salsa,* the sight of so many sweaty bodies writhing in the sizzling dance made her wish she could do the same with David. His were the only arms she wanted to feel around her. His the only body she longed to feel pressed up close to hers.

Her gaze flew to the cane hooked over the back of his chair.

She and David could never hold each other close and sway together romantically on a dance floor. His injuries prevented it. The man seemed so completely capable, she'd almost forgotten his wrecked leg.

A sharp sense of the depth of his physical and emotional loss swept over her. Her throat tightened.

He bought a round of drinks for the crowd at the table and passed around the photographs that elicited only a mass shaking of heads. They followed the same scenario in several more *rumbeaderos,* showing Tommy's pictures to waiters and customers, with equal lack of success.

After a few hours, both the noise and the repugnant solicitation of David by the *putas* who apparently found the woman with him completely invisible finally did her in. That the search for Tommy had led her to such an area left her feeling tired and dejected.

David, on the other hand, seemed to have the stamina of the pink bunny endlessly drumming in the commercial. Despite his damaged leg, he brimmed with more personal energy than anyone else she knew.

He must have noticed her flagging steps, because he led her to a table at an outdoor café. "I'll pick up coffee for us both," he said, and headed inside.

Even the limp didn't prevent him from holding his back warrior-straight as he walked. Simply watching him move brought her a surprising pleasure.

Not that she wanted it to.

Through the grime-streaked glass of the café window, she saw a tiny old Indian woman shuffle into line behind him at the counter. He bowed slightly and stepped back to let the elderly lady go ahead of him.

The courtly action tugged at Cara's heart. That was the real David Reid. Hidden beneath the toughness that was no mere pose was a kind and considerate man. Look how far he continued to put himself out for a woman who held no claim on him whatever.

She cut her gaze away. She was with him, she reminded herself, for the sole purpose of finding Tommy.

Nevertheless, the man so arousingly crowding her every daytime thought and nighttime dream was David Chandler Reid. When she was with him, all she knew were the heated, exciting feelings he continuously called up in her. She couldn't go on pretending that those feelings stemmed only from sympathy, from gratitude, from admiration. Try as she might to deny it, what she felt for David was pure, unadulterated desire. A craving she'd never felt even for the man whose ring she wore.

David returned with two mugs and set one in front of her.

"Do you mean to cover very many more places tonight?" she asked.

"No. I'll just do a couple more blocks. Then we can call it a night."

"If you don't mind, David, I'd like to just sit here and wait for you."

To his credit, he refrained from actually speaking the phrase, *I told you so.* "I'll send you back to the hotel in a cab."

"No. That isn't necessary. I'll be fine here. You go ahead by yourself."

He flicked his gaze around the crowded tables. "All right. The next blocks are the worst yet. I'd hate to take you there. You should be safe enough with all these people around. I won't be too long, maybe forty-five minutes or an hour."

He pushed back his chair and got up to leave. She reached for his hand. His strong fingers immediately enveloped hers. That alone was enough to make her feel better.

"Thank you, David, for doing so much for me."

"I haven't done a whole lot so far."

He'd done more than he knew. And not all of it had anything to do with the search for Tommy. Maybe it wasn't right, certainly it wasn't very intelligent of her, but the fact that they hadn't yet found her fiancé didn't dismay her as much as it should. The longer it took to find Tommy, the longer she could stay with David. A little frightening to admit how important he'd become to her in only a week.

She knew full well that her partner didn't share the feeling. He was concerned only with what he called their mission, and held no personal interest in her.

Quick pain squeezed her heart.

David caught the sudden slump of Cara's shoulders. He didn't like to see her looking dejected. "Don't give up hope, Cara. Maybe all this questioning will eventually pay off."

"You're right. Maybe word will get to someone who knows Tommy and he'll get in touch with me."

Sure he would, David thought. Just like he'd gotten in touch with her since his disappearance. That their questions would lead to anything solid, he very much doubted. He'd suggested it simply to cheer her up a little. Everything he'd learned about Grant implied that the man was working hard not to be found. Hearing that someone was looking for him might just drive him further underground. Not that he had any problem with that. Cara would be better off if she never found the brainless boyfriend.

He was getting mightily fed up with everything about Dr. Thomas Grant, especially with Cara's single-minded focus on the man.

"Let's hope this next round of questioning comes up with something," he said. "While I'm gone, you're to stay right here. Don't go wandering off on your own in this neighborhood."

"I won't budge." She crossed her heart and shooed him away. "Go on. I'm a big girl, David. You don't have to worry about me."

David forced himself to let go of the feminine fingers electrifying his skin and sliding a ribbon of heat down to wrap around his groin. How it would be with any other woman, he couldn't say. Wasn't even interested in finding out. But for sure this one could light the beginnings of a fire in him without half trying.

That intriguing talent of hers left him both glad and wary at the same time.

So far he'd gotten exactly nowhere in trying to divorce himself from the strong feelings she continually raised in him. He didn't get it. He'd never been an emotional man. How could this particular woman so quickly and so effortlessly keep filling him with incomprehensible aching needs whenever she came near?

He was never able to stop thinking about her. Not when he was with her, ostensibly absorbed in something else entirely. Not when they were apart and that uncomfortable itch to get back to her took over.

So much about her had become precious to him. The way a few delicate blond strands fell down over the sensitive curve of her neck. The way the azure of her eyes darkened to indigo when he took her in his arms. The way her lips quivered the other night when she thought he was about to kiss her.

He was quite proud of himself for being able to limp off down the street without looking back at her.

Cara had just ordered a refill on the coffee when a woman selling handmade *ruanas* stopped by her table to show her wares. Maybe the natives were used to Bogota's evening chill, but she wasn't. A beautiful woolen wrap with blue and gold stripes caught her eye. She paid the woman, and draped the *ruana* over her shoulders.

For almost an hour her cool lack of response kept unwanted visitors at bay, until a paunchy American, who obviously had downed one drink too many, swayed over to her and began to make suggestive remarks. Her quick tongue-lashing didn't discourage him. He groped for her breast. She slapped his hand away.

Two young Colombian men sitting at the next table came to her rescue. They grabbed the obnoxious *gringo* by the arms and shoved him into the street. Hurling back a string of curses at the two, the American stumbled off.

Cara knew enough Spanish to thank the men for their help. The tiny monkey belonging to one of them had sat on their table angrily yelping and chattering during the commotion. Now that things had settled down, the cute little animal scampered over and leapt onto its master's shoulder.

Her rescuers' English wasn't too good, but they were polite and charming as they assured themselves that she was all right. They asked to buy her a drink. She pointed to her full cup of coffee and smiled her refusal.

She hadn't exactly invited them to join her at her table, but after what they'd done for her, she could hardly refuse their company. Besides, having this pleasant pair sitting with her might ward off any others with the same ideas as the drunk. With a lot of laughter and descriptive waving of hands, the three of them managed a conversation of sorts.

The monkey skittered into her lap and started playing with the fringe on her *ruana*. Working around the pet, she fished her photo of Tommy out of her handbag and showed it to the two men, who were jokingly struck with disappointment to find she had such a good-looking boyfriend. With comically doleful expressions, they shook their heads.

A series of yawns came upon her from out of the blue. She had no luck suppressing them. Hopefully, David would be back soon. She glanced at her watch to check the time. The physician's timepiece held a large face and easily read numerals. Even squinting, she couldn't quite make them out.

She tried to blink away the strange blurring that had come over her eyes. It didn't work. The men with her now looked a little fuzzy around the edges, too. And the dizziness that had taken hold of her was getting worse. One of her newfound friends held her cup of coffee to her lips. Hoping the strong brew would help clear her head, she took a sip.

Vaguely she realized that the monkey man had pulled his chair uncomfortably close and was fumbling for her hand. The hand bearing Tommy's ring. Alarm speared through the cotton batting in her mind. She tried to push the man away. Her hand flopped ineffectually against him. She tried to get up from her chair. Her body wouldn't obey.

She heard shouts. A long, brown stick cracked down on the table in front of her. She tried to make sense of the apparition that came out of nowhere. Through the fog in front of her eyes, she saw the monkey man running away.

A man's arms slid under her own from behind and started to lift her from her chair. What she intended as a scream came out as a squeak. The man pulled her up and held her close to him. A scent, familiar and comforting, pierced the haze in her mind.

David. David was with her. She could barely make out his grim face frowning down at her. She turned and sagged against him. His arm clamped around her waist.

David struggled to get a good one-armed grip on Cara, while bracing himself with the cane. Trying to hold her up was like trying to stand a rag doll on its feet. She looked up at him with unfocused eyes. The only word he could make out from her mumbling was his name.

This was all his fault. He knew the dangers lurking in the streets of Bogota. He should have overruled her objections and

left her back at the hotel. If he hadn't returned when he did . . .
He hated to think about what might have happened to her.
With some women, thieves wanted more than just their jewelry and money. A woman as beautiful as Cara would surely
have been one of them.

He glanced down at her coffee cup. Almost full. And she was
drowsy, not unconscious. He prayed she hadn't swallowed too
much of the *burundanga.*

He slipped over her head the strap of the handbag he'd
grabbed back from the man with the monkey. Cara swayed
dangerously against his arm and almost broke his hold. He
cursed his bad leg. If only he could pick her up and carry her
out to the waiting cab.

It wasn't easy maneuvering her into the taxi. As he heaved
himself onto the seat next to her, he happened to glance
through the rear window. The pimp with the straw-colored
streak in his hair, who earlier had tried to line him up as a customer, was standing in the shadows of the café wall, watching
them.

That observation flew from his mind, quashed by a new,
strongly agitating one.

The hot velvet of Cara's lips grazed his ear. He swallowed.
Hard. She had no idea how tough it had been to tear himself
away from her their first night here when she'd offered him her
lips. And perhaps more. No idea how difficult it was to hold his
flaring reactions under tight rein every arousing moment he
spent with her.

With a little giggle, she pulled back the collar of his shirt and
nibbled downward along his suddenly sensitive skin. He blew
out a long, shaky breath.

"Ah . . . Cara . . . don't do that, honey . . . please don't do—
uh—"

She slipped her fingers between the buttons of his shirt and
pressed them directly against his chest.

His gasp had the driver peering wide-eyed into the rearview
mirror. If she kept this up, the distracted man was liable to run
them right off the road.

She did keep it up. It was a miracle his mind was still functioning by the time they reached the hotel. Another miracle that they made it in one piece.

The driver accepted the tip, but his appreciative grin indicated he'd already received one.

It wasn't hard to guess what the people in the lobby were thinking as he half dragged, half carried Cara, who was softly chuckling at some private joke, to the elevators.

At the door to her room he propped her against the wall and held her there with his body while he rummaged frantically for her key in the purse dangling from her neck. Tantalizing female softness teased him from shoulder to knees. Desperately he willed himself to ignore it.

She looked up at him, her forehead creased in puzzlement, and made a questioning sound.

"Forget it, Doctor. You're in no shape to figure things out."

He pushed the door shut behind them with his cane and hauled her over to the bed. Unceremoniously he let her drop. She bounced on the mattress and bubbled a trill of laughter.

He pulled off her shoes. She splayed her arms above her head and smiled giddily up at him as if she didn't have a care in the world.

Unfortunately he had enough for both of them.

Chapter 6

Cara lay precariously half on, half off the bed. He couldn't leave her this way, in danger of slipping to the floor. Setting his hands at her waist he tried to shove her farther onto the bed. A dead weight, she scarcely moved.

Awkwardly he scrambled onto the bed and straddled her, with one knee bent at her hip and his bad leg drawn up alongside her. He yanked his arrested gaze away from the sweet sight of her lying so incitingly beneath him and succeeded in pulling her more firmly onto the bed. Her legs dangled over the edge only from the knees down. Enough to keep her from falling off during the night.

Before he could back off the bed, she threw her arms around his neck. They flopped off. She tried again, and succeeded in draping them loosely around him.

He couldn't make out all her mumbling, but one word leapt out at him with mind-focusing clarity. "Kiss..."

He tried to brace himself above her on his hands. She wasn't having any. Her hard tug on his neck flattened him on top of her. Searing fire leapt into the already smoldering part of him pressed into the soft warmth at the top of her thighs.

How was any man expected to resist this? A flood of sensations, dammed up for what felt like a lifetime, raged through him. The sheer wonder of feeling her sweet, yielding body brought a choking ache to his chest.

God help him, he was ready to take her.

He *could* take her.

The realization of the miracle of his arousal flooded through him. Already he was as rigid as he'd ever been. As he'd never been for almost two years. What a way to learn that every throbbing part of him, except his leg, was now fully, painfully, operational.

The *burundanga* wasn't making her do anything she didn't already want to do. The quickness and heat of her previous responses to him made him certain of that. The apparently small dose of scopoline had simply removed her inhibitions. The knowledge did nothing to lessen his predicament.

"P-please, D-David...I want...I want..." In case he hadn't heard her whispered pleading, she repeated it. Several agonizing times. Pure torture to keep himself from giving in to her entreaty.

She braced her feet against the edge of the mattress and lifted her pelvis hard against him. His instinctive convulsive thrust against her came so quickly he couldn't prevent it.

"Yes," she gasped. "Oh, David...yes."

She fumbled with his jacket, trying to push it off his shoulders. Her short, fast breaths puffed hotly against his neck. He groaned. He couldn't take much more of this.

"No, Cara. Quit it."

Feeling foolish at being forced to demonstrate the indignation of a maiden aunt, he pulled the protective blazer back into place. While he was busy with that, Cara took the opportunity to jerk his shirt from his pants. Her hands and forearms slid under the shirt and ranged over the burning skin of his sides and back.

The sweet assault taunted him almost beyond endurance. Never had a woman's touch, a woman's softness robbed him so quickly of so much of his mind.

She found his hand and planted it over her breast, even softer
and warmer than he'd imagined it to be. Without his express
orders, his thumb brushed over its already beaded tip. She
moaned in pleasure. Her eyes were dilated. An effect of the
scopoline. She trembled with need.

So did he. His protective instincts warred with his raging desire for her. It had been achingly long since he'd been with a
woman. Would it be so wrong to give her what they both ardently desired?

It would, the part of his mind still functioning insisted. Bastard he might be. Some had called him so. But he wasn't bastard enough to take advantage of a woman who wasn't in full
possession of her senses.

He couldn't pretend that no more than the honor of an officer and a gentleman held him back from doing what he so
wanted to do. He'd coped with a lot, but he knew he could
never handle the contempt she'd surely show him if she learned
that he'd taken her while she was helpless.

Soft kisses rained over his face and every inch of bare skin on
his neck and upper chest her lips could reach.

Hell's fire, he wasn't made of stone. On a moan of defeat, he
turned his head and captured her mouth.

Immediately she opened to him. Wild horses couldn't have
prevented him from plunging his tongue into the intimate wet
secret of her mouth. The honeyed taste of her broke a flood of
want, white-hot and urgent, through him.

Cursing himself for taking any advantage whatever of a
woman at a time when she was so piercingly vulnerable she
wasn't able to defend herself against her own physical needs, he
pulled his mouth away from hers.

Her hand slipped beneath his belt and trailed an arrow of
flame down his stomach. Every fiber of his being lusted for
more of the fiery caress.

If she reached his throbbing arousal, he knew damn well that
his command of himself would be over.

In one of the most difficult actions of his life, he took hold
of her hand and withdrew its inflaming contact. He shifted his
weight and rolled to the bed beside her.

Frantic, she grasped his jacket and curved back into him. It was impossible to hold his mouth from hers when it felt so much at home there. She drew a knee up over his thigh and pressed herself against him.

How could he possibly abandon her in this condition?

Heartless to refuse to bring her the release she needed. His own need wasn't important. Hers was.

He gathered her close and slid his hand down between them to cup the soft joining of her thighs. Only the sheer nylon of her panty hose barriered her hot damp center from his direct touch. She gasped and moved against his hand.

He gritted his teeth and forced himself to ride on top of the pleasure threatening to claim every last shred of his control. Fortunately for his sanity, it didn't take long until she gave a sighing shudder and went still.

Drenched in sweat he sank back and hauled in a deep breath.

When he finally recovered enough strength to do it, he carefully worked his arm out from under her head, and struggled to a sitting position. Given a little more room in which to move, she heaved a contented sigh and curled up into a ball like a kitten. She looked as if she'd sleep for a week.

He hunched himself off the bed and pondered whether or not to undress her and slip her nightgown over her head. No way, he decided. If she awoke and launched herself at him again, he'd be a goner. Safer just to flip the bedspread over her.

At the door, he looked back at the most heart-tugging scene he'd enjoyed in ages.

He deserved another medal, he thought grimly, for having the strength to drag himself out of her room and back to his own.

Cara tiptoed across the lobby as carefully as if she were walking on eggs. She'd never been intoxicated in her life—as far as she knew—but right now she had a strong understanding of how a hangover must feel.

Sprawled in a chair beneath a potted palm, David waited for her. He didn't look all that good himself, she noted. They must have had one heck of a night, although she couldn't remember any of it. He saw her and rose.

"It's almost noon, David. You should have called earlier to awaken me."

"I figured you needed your sleep."

"Sleeping in didn't help. For some reason I woke up with a dull headache and a bit of an upset stomach." She laid her hand cautiously on top of her head, to make sure it was still there. "Funny, I can't seem to remember a whole lot about last night. I don't usually have too much to drink. Did I go overboard while we were out?"

David cleared his throat. "Not when I was with you."

"I don't even remember us coming back to the hotel." She started to shake her head in puzzlement and was forcefully reminded that moving her head even a fraction wasn't a real good thing to do right now.

"You did seem to be a little . . . um, out of it when we got here."

"I must have been really tired. I just tumbled on top of the bed and fell asleep without getting undressed."

A vague recollection of an incredibly erotic dream involving David shimmered into her mind. Thank God he didn't know what her subconscious kept coming up with when she was asleep.

"Not surprising you're exhausted," he said. "You're a strong woman, but you've been going nonstop since we got here. And from what you've told me, for months if not years before this. You've graduated from med school, completed your residency, started your practice and had to deal with the emotional shock of having the man you love fall into drug use and disappear. It's a wonder you've kept going this long."

She rubbed her forehead. "You could be right. I woke up feeling totally wrung out."

David gave another little cough. She wondered if he might be coming down with a cold.

"We could both use a break," he said. "We're supposed to be tourists. Today we'll take in the colonial mansions and churches of La Candelaria. You'll enjoy seeing the beautiful old cathedral on the Plaza de Bolivar. And the fresh air might help you feel better.''

His prescription worked, David was glad to see. Their stroll in the comfortable coolness of the afternoon brightened Cara's mood. Her cheeks regained their color and she quickly became interested in the cathedral.

As she took the time to inspect the intricately carved altar heavily ornamented with gold, he walked back to sit down and rest his leg. As he turned into the pew, his glance snagged on the movements of a young man lingering at the back of the church. A *mestizo*. With a shock of yellow hair.

He snapped back a second look just before the man disappeared into a side chapel. Had the *mestizo* ducked out of sight to avoid his attention?

David shrugged. Ridiculous to think so. Just his ingrained sense of caution working overtime. The man posed no threat.

Nevertheless, when they left the cathedral habit prodded him to look back. As expected, he saw no sign of the *mestizo*.

Cara strolled a little ahead of him into the small garden next to the church.

The shining crown of her hair blazed gold in a shaft of bright sunlight that broke through another of Bogota's usual gray days. She balanced herself on parted legs and swayed slightly on the balls of her feet as she gazed at the small grotto holding a rose-ringed statue of the Virgin of Guadalupe.

He was sure Cara didn't realize that the gauzy cotton of her skirt threw up little defense to the sun's penetrating rays, giving him an entrancing view of long, elegantly shaped legs. He knew he was courting danger when he allowed his slow gaze to follow their narrowing V up to its intimate merging.

He swallowed a groan. If only he could make his mind as blank as hers about what happened between them on her bed. What right did she have to bounce along in blissful ignorance, he grumbled silently, when tormenting memories of last night were driving him crazy?

He hoped the fervent prayer he sent up that she wouldn't touch him too much would be heard and answered in this holy place. Heavenly intervention might be the only way he could resist taking her in his arms.

She gracefully lowered herself to the small wooden bench near the grotto. He folded himself down beside her, being careful to leave a good six inches between her bare arm and his. She turned her head and smiled at him. The beauty of her eyes bathed his brain in a blue fog that turned off all logic and urged him to close the frustrating gap between them.

A terrible yearning came over him to someday see her look at him clear-eyed and fully aware that he was kissing her. To have her know—as during last night's intimacy she didn't know—that the man embracing her was David Reid. Not anyone else. Not Tommy.

Tommy. He dragged up the aggravating name. Stupid, worthless Tommy. That was why he was here with Cara, instead of back in Virginia swimming interminable, punishing laps in the frigid mountain lake.

And he'd better stop forgetting that. Or worse, trying to convince himself that dumb old Tommy really didn't matter, when Grant's disappearance was the only reason he'd ever met Cara Merrill in the first place.

"I have some good news for you," he said. "I didn't tell you earlier, because I wanted you to have a few hours free of worrying about Tommy and his problems. Last night I found someone who recognized the photograph I showed her. The girl told me that a couple of months ago she'd met a man who looked a lot like Dr. Grant. She remembered him because she thought him so good-looking."

Cara's hand darted to his arm. He tensed.

"Who, David? What girl? Not one of the *putas,* I hope."

"No. A—a waitress I spoke to in a cantina." That the girl made a living by giving paying customers—Grant among them—a sexual massage was a hurtful fact Cara didn't need to know.

"That's good news."

To his surprise, she didn't leap up and shout for joy at this first nibble of intelligence about Tommy since they'd arrived. She wasn't even smiling.

He hiked up an eyebrow. "Somehow I thought you'd be more excited when you heard it."

"I am. I guess that after all this time it's hard to get excited about something experience tells me might not pan out. But I am glad we've been able to establish that Tommy has been seen in Bogota. I was starting to lose hope of finding any trace of him."

Every time she spoke, he could hear again the enticing sound of her fevered pleading for him to make love to her.

"There's always the chance that the woman told me only what she thought I wanted to hear," he said. "However, I'm ready to accept that it confirms Baker's information. Nothing more. She only saw Tommy that one time and had no idea where he was staying. She never even knew his name."

Cara sighed. "So we'll just have to keep on looking."

"At least now we know we're looking in the right city. This complex is a tourist attraction. We're as likely to run into Tommy here as anywhere."

"I doubt it, David. Museums and churches aren't exactly his thing."

She retrieved her hand from his arm, allowing him to pole himself to his feet with his cane.

Cara wasn't sure how she felt about the possibility of finally coming face-to-face with Tommy. Aside from trying to convince him to come back with her and go into treatment, what on earth would she say to him? The thought of plunging back into any kind of relationship whatever with him was troubling.

She and David didn't speak as they rambled the secluded courtyard hemmed in by a looming row of trees. As she strolled by his side, his hand brushed against hers—by accident, she was sure. Instead of moving away, his fingers danced around hers. Their two hands linked together.

Just a friendly gesture, she told herself. Whatever it was doing for David—probably not much—being connected to him even in a way that might seem insignificant to anyone else, gave her a feeling of intense satisfaction.

David came to an abrupt halt. Since their hands were joined, she did, too. His hand tightened around hers.

She was constantly aware of him, even when they were apart, but now his vital nearness swallowed up her senses. His chest rose and fell on a deep inhalation. She could hear the whisper of his breathing. A great pot of pink blossoms nearby threw an exotic perfume into the still, thin air, the fragrance underlaid with the light tang of David's unique scent.

Her mouth went dry.

His cane clattered to the ground.

With a muttered curse, he snaked out an arm and pulled her to him.

The heat of his body radiated over her breasts and thighs. She couldn't have escaped the sensual bliss of his hold on her even if she wanted to. She didn't want to.

"Tommy's a fool to have let you go," David growled.

The intensity of his words sent a nebulous yearning shuddering through her. He wore no jacket, only a royal blue shirt that clung so closely to his skin she could make out the faint outline of his tiny male nipples. Before her mind could prevent the thoughtless and provoking action, her fingers flew to one of the intriguing nubs.

He hissed in a rapid breath. His heart suddenly jumped beneath her hand. Her own heart lurched into a quick stuttering drumbeat that pounded in her ears. A soft, swelling spasm rippled through her womanhood. Emotions layered through her. Confusion. Guilt. Anxiety.

Above them all, utter, eager delight.

A remarkably distinct remembrance of last night's dream flashed into her mind: David—the whole hard length of him— stretched out on top of her. Not only could she see him looking down at her, but she also felt as if she knew exactly how her softness fitted into the weight of his hard body. She flushed at the alarming pleasure recalling the dream brought her.

He broke the tight link of their hands and drew a finger over the arch of her eyebrow. Her legs threatened to buckle under her.

"You're so beautiful," he murmured. "I should have told you that long before this." The low, harsh rasp of his voice sent a delicious shiver down her back.

He stroked down her cheek and along the ridge of her jaw. Every nerve in her body was suddenly attuned to the inciting warmth and stimulating pressure of the male fingers ranging slowly over her skin.

She couldn't still the quivering of her mouth.

David's hand skimmed lingeringly down the front of her throat and spread wide across her collarbone exposed in the dipping neckline of her dress. A languorous, enveloping heat suffused her muscles and deepened her breathing. In the afternoon's coolness, a bead of perspiration trickled down between her breasts.

The gray of his eyes turned a deep silver, sharp and wanting. His face looked carved from stone. He gave a low, strangled groan and bent his head. His lips met hers.

She could work up not the slightest scrap of resistance.

Her eagerness tempted him to draw the tip of his tongue over the outline of her lips. Even that sensitive, explorative touch made oatmeal of her mind. Thick, hot, sugary oatmeal.

This is not smart, her brain babbled faintly from some deep recess in her head. *You'll be sorry.* But it was unthinkable to try to halt the warm shower of pleasure drenching her. A warmth that softened and parted her lips beneath his.

The firm, moist fullness of his mouth closed hotly over hers. His tongue demanded entrance. She gave it to him. The enticing taste of him seemed dizzyingly familiar.

Desire rolled through her in hot sluggish waves commanding that she fit herself closer into the solid wall of his body. His hand drifted down to mold her breast within a crescent of warmth. A heat and a gentle pressure that seemed to belong there.

She hardly noticed when her fingers tangled themselves into his hair to hold his mouth deliciously fastened to hers. But she felt every inflaming inch when he stroked down over her back and curved his hand over her bottom to lock her to his hard, hot center.

She reeled under a barrage of tantalizing sensations.

Sensations that teased familiarly at her mind.

She skimmed her hand over the muscles of his back, mapping warm, hard shapes her palms seemed to recognize. A sudden conviction came over her that she knew precisely where David's skin bore a thick, raised scar. Wondering why she was having such crazy reactions to their embrace, she slowly inched her hand over his shirt to his side and down to his waist.

Her fingers fell on the smooth hard ridge of the scar angling into the waistband of his slacks.

Weird. How could she possibly have known that scar was there? How could she have known precisely how it would feel?

Another arousing picture of her lying on her bed with David flared into her mind. A picture of her flattening her hand against the bare skin of his stomach and stroking downward to his—

This didn't make sense. Not possible that they'd made love. Fourteen bottles of champagne couldn't have eradicated that exciting incident from her mind. The shape of his fingers would have left their searing imprint on her breast. The feel of his mouth would have been burned onto hers—exactly as her lips felt now. How could she possibly have forgotten anything so wonderful?

Much too wonderful to halt right now and try to figure out answers to the questions tumbling through her mind.

He could spend the rest of his life, David thought hazily, doing nothing but holding this woman in his arms. Doing nothing more than holding his lips bonded to the lush, giving mouth burning beneath his.

The captivating taste of her made him drunk, and wanting, craving, more.

He came to with a start. What the hell had he been thinking of?

He shouldn't be doing this. He couldn't be doing this. He had no right even to hold her. No right to practically wallow in the stunning pleasure she gave him.

She'd made him a man again. He owed her big-time for that. But falling in love with *anyone* wasn't an option. Allowing himself to fall in love with any woman would be downright irrational. With his ugly, ravaged body he shouldn't even dream of making love to her for real. Cara Merrill wasn't for him. A woman as marvelous as she deserved a whole man. She surely deserved a lot better than Tommy the user.

And much more than a cripple like himself.

He dragged his mouth from hers.

Even without his humbling impairment, only a fool would let himself become involved with a woman so fiercely loyal to another man she was willing to do whatever it took to find him.

That enraging thought gave him the strength to drop his arms and step away from her.

"Let's find a restaurant and take a break." The gruffness of self-directed anger colored his voice.

Cara blinked up at him, looking dazed at the suddenness of his turnoff. He couldn't blame her. She must think him the fool he already knew himself to be.

She was still trembling and looking painfully baffled when he bent to scoop up his cane. Leaning heavily on it he turned to head them back toward the plaza.

Her breath in shreds, Cara needed a few seconds to gather her thoughts. One minute David was kissing her as if his life depended on it. The next he was walking away from her.

Just as well he'd called a halt to their lovemaking she decided, as more of her mind settled back into place. It didn't make sense that his arms, his kiss should feel so blazingly right when she knew darn well he was with her only because he saw Roger Elliott's request to help her as an order.

His kisses so addled her senses, she couldn't think straight, but why did these foolish, all-too-realistic pictures of them in bed together keep popping up?

"Wait, David." Her call halted him, but he didn't turn to face her. "Why can't I recall last night more clearly? This isn't normal. Tell me the truth. Did I drink too much and make a fool of myself?"

She detected a curious wariness in the glance he shot back over his shoulder.

"You weren't drunk. That's the truth."

"I can remember us leaving the hotel together, what happened after that?"

"We went to a few *rumbeaderos* to ask about Tommy."

"*Rumbeaderos.*" She closed her eyes and tried to dredge up memory. "Yes. I seem to recall a place with lots of noise. People dancing. What else? When did you speak to the woman who saw Tommy? Was I with you?"

He turned and waited for her to catch up with him.

"No. I left you waiting for me at an outdoor café."

"I don't understand, David. Why can I remember only bits and pieces of last night?" How did a woman tell a man that she couldn't remember if he made love to her?

He sighed. "All right. Here's what happened. You were the victim of the local version of a Mickey Finn. While you were alone at the café, someone gave you a dose of what they call *burundanga*. Scopoline."

Her mouth dropped open. "Scopoline? That's not a street drug."

"No. It was supposed to knock you out."

"It can certainly do that, especially if given intravenously. It's a derivative of scopolamine, twilight sleep, an anesthetic sometimes used during childbirth." She shuddered. "An overdose can kill."

"Thank God you didn't get much of it. You never completely lost consciousness, but you were out of it. *Burundanga* is the weapon of choice among the thieves here, who use it to rob their victims of resistance while they relieve them of their valuables. They can easily make the substance from trees found all over this country. It's a major problem both for foreign tourists and native Colombians."

She rubbed her forehead. "Was there something about a monkey?"

David nodded. "There were two men with you when I returned to the café. They probably used the pet monkey to distract you while they slipped the powder into your coffee."

"Scopoline. That explains why I can't remember much about last night. Scopoline can cause loss of memory that can last from a few hours to several days."

Hot astonishment suddenly hit her. What she'd thought was merely an erotic dream was real. Specific, face-warming memories were flooding back. She'd thrown herself at David like a wanton. Begged him to make love to her. Touched him intimately. Or tried to. He'd touched her, too. Very intimately. Her breath caught at the remembrance of that searing touch.

No way she could deny that she'd loved it all.

Not everything came back, though. She still couldn't remember the final outcome of their lovemaking. How far did she push him last night?

"David. I need to know. Did we...?" She lifted her chin and met his gaze. Making love with David Reid was nothing to regret, although practically attacking him the way she did was embarrassing, even if she couldn't be held entirely responsible for her actions. "Were we intimate last night?"

"No. There's nothing to worry about. I tucked you into bed and left."

He'd tucked her into bed and left? Senseless disappointment rushed over her. She should thank him for having had the strength to keep his head when hers had floated off in a scopoline haze. But gratitude wasn't the emotion taking hold of her.

She'd begged David to make love to her. He hadn't wanted her. That was the bottom line. He didn't want her. Sure he'd kissed her in a thoughtless male way when given the opportunity. But the embrace that meant so much to her, to him was close to meaningless.

The scopoline had given her a headache. Knowing how little she meant to David made it worse.

David had no trouble reading the dismay written all over Cara's lovely face. From the look of her, she now remembered too much of what happened on her bed. As he'd feared, she was none too pleased to know that her helplessness hadn't kept him from plundering her mouth, caressing her with the intimacy a woman like her would grant only to a lover.

"What happened wasn't your fault, Cara. As I said, you were a helpless victim of Bogotano thieves. If you need to blame someone, blame me for not taking better care of you."

"Taking care of me is not your job, David."

In her books maybe it wasn't. In his, it certainly was. He cared nothing about Tommy and his problems. He saw his mission mainly as protecting Cara Merrill from her own misplaced loyalty to the man.

As they walked back across the wide plaza he didn't venture to take her hand again. She'd only pull it away.

On one side of the square, street vendors hawking postcards and souvenirs jostled for position among potential customers. Since Cara showed no interest in them, he intended to avoid them all. Before they could escape, a woman jangling a handful of colorful Indian bead necklaces fixed herself persistently in their path.

Cara indifferently examined the jewelry. He didn't bother.

Out of the corner of his eye he caught a small flash of yellow. He quickly ran his gaze over the area. It wasn't hard to spot the punk blond streak at the back of a group of black-haired Japanese tourists gathered around their lecturing tour guide.

Twice in under an hour, David noted. Last night in the cab made a fourth time he'd seen the man who'd approached him on the street earlier. And it sure looked like the *mestizo* was trying to keep from being seen.

Why should a pimp be tailing them? Or him? There were plenty of other foreign men around. Surely he wasn't such a prize catch that a Bogotano procurer would dog his heels in hopes of snagging him as a customer.

He didn't believe in this level of coincidence. He needed to have a talk with their stalker. He could find out soon enough whether there was anything to the peculiar blond's repeated appearances in their vicinity.

"Cara, I—"

Before he could tell her to wait while he sprinted as best he could over to the man, his quarry scurried away into one of the waiting line of *busetas*. He abandoned the idea of trying for a chase. He might have made it to the vehicle moving slowly in heavy traffic. But after last night's incident, he was loath to let Cara out of his sight even for a few minutes.

"What, David?"

"Uh . . . nothing. Let's get out of here."

Cara had enough to deal with already. No point in bothering her further over a so far minor episode. But if Yellow Hair showed up anywhere near them again, he wouldn't get away without providing acceptable answers to several pointed questions.

Chapter 7

She was grateful to David for keeping the conversation light and businesslike at the luxurious restaurant where they dined that evening.

He was so darn good at keeping his thoughts and feelings to himself. His face gave absolutely nothing away about his reactions to their kiss or to their previous intimacies. Maybe he simply didn't have any. For all his distanced demeanor they might never have come close to having sex—she couldn't really call it making love. She didn't even want to think about the shattering power of those arousing memories, let alone talk about them.

She'd worked hard all evening to avoid any lengthy eye contact with him. She was afraid her eyes might disclose how strongly she had to fight to keep herself from reaching for him.

David's inflaming embrace had brought something new to life within her. Emotions she wasn't ready to handle. Feelings she hadn't even known she harbored. She was used to dealing with problems in a logical manner. With the uncontrollable problem of David Reid and his effect on her, she didn't even know where to start.

She'd faced more than her fair share of problems with Tommy, but never had their relationship posed this particular kind of dilemma.

A wild thought took sudden root in her mind. An idea so uncomfortable it set her to gnawing on her lower lip. Might she have slipped into a more personal relationship with Tommy precisely because, up to the moment it exploded on her, that relationship was so controllable, so predictable?

In a way, Tommy, even with his faults, was safe. Although he always asked a lot of her in other ways, always leaned on her so heavily for support, he never demanded much on a sexual level. David, on the other hand, without uttering a word, with only a look, could set her sexual responses racing, her deepest emotions churning.

When she'd had her hands full with med school, perhaps a quiet, unthreatening relationship with a man was what she needed. From here on, that would never be enough. Not after experiencing the magic of David Reid's embrace.

"Cara? Cara?"

David's voice jolted her back from the wild blue yonder of trying to make sense of her reactions to him.

"Yes?"

"Are you ready to leave?"

Cane in hand, he was standing by the table waiting for her. She nodded and picked up her handbag.

The evening was pleasantly cool. An easy stroll back to the hotel seemed in order. The business district around them had closed up for the day. Only a few people were on the streets.

The breeze tugged a strand of her hair from its anchoring comb. Tucking it back, her absent glance landed on a man lingering in front of the display window of a small shop half a block back. There was something familiar about him. His hair, she suddenly realized. The slight illumination from the shop window picked out the pale streak in the *mestizo*'s hair.

"David?" Cara touched his arm to get his attention. "I think the man who approached you outside a *rumbeadero* last night is back there behind us. Do you think we should ask him again if he has any information about Tommy?"

David ignored her comment.

His indifference irritated her. He could at least have taken a moment to glance back. But he never pulled his gaze from the lighted windows of an office tower soaring above the others a couple of streets away.

"I know," he said quietly. "He picked us up as we left the restaurant."

Picked us up? A strange way of putting it.

She looked back again. The street was empty. "Oh. He's gone now."

David still wasn't interested. They came to the corner of a dark side street. Even though the hotel lay a few blocks straight ahead, David suddenly pivoted on his good leg and disappeared around the corner. Before she could even voice her astonishment, he reached out and pulled her around the corner with him and set her close to the white stone wall of an office building.

She opened her mouth to ask what the heck was going on. He jerked his finger to his lips warning her to be quiet.

He flattened himself against the wall a foot or so from the corner, and kept his eyes glued on the end of the building. Obviously he was waiting for someone to show up.

She couldn't figure out why he was acting so strangely. The only person in sight behind them had been the blond-streaked man. Surely a short, slight individual didn't warrant this kind of wary reaction from a combat-hardened military man.

The rapid *click-clack* of metal-heeled boots hitting the pavement came closer. The man with the streaked hair—definitely the same man they'd seen last night—rounded the corner at a fast clip.

David shot out a hand and yanked the man off his feet. He let out a yelp. In the blink of an eye the cane angled across his throat pinned him roughly against the wall.

"David!" Cara gasped, shocked that he'd manhandle a person so much smaller than he. "What are you doing to that poor man?"

The *mestizo*'s flailing arms and legs had no effect on his captor's iron grip. David bit out a few words in Spanish. The

Colombian gave up the useless struggle. His whole body was shaking. He was wide-eyed with fright. Cara didn't blame him.

Being cornered by the lethal-looking opponent towering over him, would be enough to scare the devil out of anybody.

"Okay." David bit out the word. "In your line of work, you probably speak English. The show's over. I don't take kindly to being tailed. Don't provoke me any further. Find the fellow's billfold, Cara," David ordered without taking his icy stare off his victim.

She nodded and began to search the man's pockets. Not a pleasant task. Inside his jacket she found a cheap black leather wallet.

"See if you can find some identification," David told her.

She took out a driver's license and held it up in the dim light for David to scan, then dropped it back into the wallet.

"All right, Manuel Pereira." David took the billfold from her and slapped it into the man's hand. "Let's have it. Why have you been following us all day?"

The pimp had been following them all day? She sure hadn't noticed. David needn't play his cards so irritatingly close to the chest. He could have let her in on that.

The hapless man hadn't responded to David's question. He clamped a hand on his prisoner's upper arm, jerked him off his feet and gave him a hard shake.

"Okay, okay," the man yelled. "No hurt Manuel. I talk. You show me photograph. You look for man in picture, *sí?*"

"Yes. What's that got to do with you? Have you seen Thomas Grant?"

The man's black eyes narrowed. "You *norteamericano* drug cops?"

"Drug cops? No. We're not any kind of cops."

A hint of craftiness snaked into the man's look of anxiety.

"I follow to find out who you are, why you look so hard for man in picture."

"Why is that of any interest to you?"

"Information you want worth money."

Their shadower still looked worried, Cara noted. Evidently, though, he wasn't frightened enough to fend off his greed entirely, even in a situation that couldn't be too comfortable for him.

David's growing impatience showed in the nerve jumping in his jaw, but he fished for the wallet in his back pants pocket and took out a handful of bills. The *mestizo*'s hand darted out and closed around the money.

"Information 'bout *you* worth more somebody else." The man shoved the money into his pocket and slid David a sly glance. "Lot more."

If I were you, mister, Cara thought, *I wouldn't press my luck too far.* David didn't seem inclined to put up with too much nonsense from this predatory creature.

"Oh? Like who?"

The *mestizo* hesitated. But apparently a quick study of David's face brought their stalker to the same conclusion she'd reached a moment before about her partner's probably limited supply of forbearance.

"Okay. I tell you. You nice guy. You no cop." The man's toothy grin contained all the sincerity of a hyena. "Hey, man. I just try make honest living."

"Right. Real honest."

"Information worth more to my connections work for *mafioso,* drug lords ship *perica,* cocaine, to your country."

Cara's eyes flashed wide. Drug *lords?* Drug users, sure. Tommy unfortunately was one. But how did drug lords figure into this? She had the sinking feeling that she didn't really want to hear the answer.

"What do cocaine traffickers have to do with our search for Dr. Grant?" David demanded.

"Very dangerous talk about these guys. Must have more pay."

David took hold of the man again and looked as if he were ready to convince him to cooperate in a manner a whole lot less pleasant than paying for it.

"I'll be the judge of how much your information is worth. Now talk."

Apprehension flew back into the man's expression.

"The *gringo* Grant," he spewed out rapidly, "he come Bogota maybe two months ago."

"That's not worth a single peso. We already knew it."

"You know he come with son of Dan Kane?"

David's face took on a look of amazement, followed by a frown that suggested he'd just smelled something putrid.

"Nice company your Tommy keeps," he said to Cara.

"You know who is Dan Kane?"

"I know."

"Then you know is not good talk about him. He *mafioso*. Powerful man. No like people talk about son, Robert. No like people chase after son's friend."

Even though Cara didn't know who they were talking about, she didn't like the sound of it.

"All right, Manuel," David snarled. "Seems to me your problem right now is figuring out who can pay you more. Us, or your contacts among the traffickers."

Fishing out a hefty wad of American dollars, David waved it temptingly in front of the man's eyes.

"I'd like to point out that we're the ones with cash in hand, whereas your friends may or may not find your information about us worth the price. It's not like we haven't been spreading the word around that we're looking for Grant."

"Hey, man, no worry. I like deal with *norteamericanos*. Not dangerous like *perica* guys." The wide mouth split into a hopeful grin. "Sometimes can be more generous."

"You'd better remember that. And don't assume that we're less dangerous than your drug friends. Trust me, you don't want to find out what I can do to someone who seriously annoys me. Now where can we find Robert Kane?"

Pereira let out a high-pitched giggle of derision. "You no find Robert. He gone home. You try go Kane's place with no invitation, his men kill first, ask question later."

The man's eyes stayed glued on the roll of money in David's hand.

"But maybe way you can see Robert soon, find *gringo* friend."

Pereira's crafty smile suggested that he was about to one-up his captor. In the uncertain glance David threw her, Cara could sense a slight shift in the power structure involving the Bogotano and the American.

"All right." David nodded. "We're listening."

"Robert come Bogota often. He like buy clothes. Buy jewelry. Play clubs. Like go where pretty girls friendly. He come see me. My girls good." The man preened. "Got good reputation. Clean. No cheat clients."

"I'm sure you're a saint," David said dryly. "Do you—"

"Manuel." Cara broke in. She couldn't hold back the question. "Does Robert's friend, Dr. Grant, does he come to see you, too? Is he one of your, uh, clients?"

She steeled herself for the answer.

David's attention sliced to her. Both men looked as if they'd forgotten she was there.

The *mestizo* shook his head. "I see friend of Robert two, three times in clubs. No my client."

Thank God for small mercies, Cara thought.

David took over the questioning again. "Do you expect Robert Kane to return to Bogota soon?"

The man shrugged. "Maybe. He don't like stay with father too much. Like it here. Like go Miami, too. He say mucho fun in Miami. Maybe sometime I go America. Where you live in America? Maybe I come visit you."

"Don't count on it." David again held the roll of cash up to the man's eyes. "And if you want any more of this, don't make any travel plans until after you let us know that Robert or Grant is back in town."

He released their newly hired informant. The man grabbed the money.

"I tell you 'bout Robert. No worry."

"You're the one who'd better worry if you don't," David grated. "Keep your mouth shut about us and we'll make it worth your while to keep us informed. Just don't forget who's paying you." David gave the man his name and the name of the hotel where he could be reached. "Now get out of here."

With a last relieved but feral grin, Pereira bolted up the street.

Cara's head was still spinning from the astonishing incident. To her the whole thing felt like a scene from a bad movie. David, on the other hand, was taking the bizarre episode with remarkable composure. He quite calmly limped to the edge of the sidewalk and scanned the street for a taxi. His piercing whistle and an imperious wave of his cane skidded a passing cab over to them.

"What on earth was all that about?" she asked as he held the automobile door open for her.

"It's a long story. I'll give you the details back at the hotel."

Cara poured two tall, frosted glasses of sangria from the large crystal pitcher and dropped a half-moon of sliced orange into each. Using the silver tongs set out on the tray, she fished a few extra cubes from the ice bucket and clinked them into their drinks.

"Tell me about this Robert Kane," she prompted, handing David his glass.

He settled back on the sofa. "Robert, quite the playboy from Manuel's account, is the son of a notorious American drug kingpin now living here in Colombia. I don't know anything about the son. Didn't even know he existed. I do know enough about Dan Kane to understand that he's scum the world would be better off without. Back in the late sixties he was a businessman involved with the construction of military bases in Vietnam. Even then he was a bottom-feeder. Made a fortune on the black market mainly by stealing Uncle Sam blind and importing drugs to supply the users among our troops stationed over there."

"That's horrible."

"It is. And it gets worse. After the war, Kane's colorful résumé bought him entry with one of the cartels here. I'm sure his bosses found Kane very valuable to them. Still find him so, or he'd no longer be one of their top lieutenants. He has an insider's knowledge of the U.S. and he'd built up an important network of transportation contacts stretching back to the States.

I'm sure he made it his business to find out which ones wouldn't pay too close attention to what they were shipping by plane, boat or truck. Despite what Manuel says, Robert's trips to the States can't be simple pleasure junkets. No doubt his father uses him to keep his hand in among those contacts.''

Cara sighed and shook her head. ''I hate to think that there are Americans at every level willing to cooperate with drug traffickers, but there must be.''

''Yes. However, there aren't many who've set up shop right in Colombia. Apparently Kane has gone native. Spends most of his time here. Although precisely where his headquarters are located no one seems to know. These people don't hang out signs on their front doors. He's probably somewhere in the mountains.''

· The way David paused and frowned made her think his mention of those mountains brought him unpleasant memories.

''Even if we did know where he makes his home base, aside from the strong possibility of running into competing guerrilla groups, bandits and the cartel's mercenaries, just getting around up there among them poses a big problem. Outside the cities, there aren't many good roads, mostly just dirt tracks, many of them cocaine trails. The only Americans who show up there are backpacker types. We'd stand out in the area like a sore thumb. Manuel wasn't exaggerating when he said Kane's private army would shoot first and ask questions later. All the mercenaries in the pay of the drug lords would.''

David took another long swallow of the fruited wine. ''No, Cara. There's not much else we can do now but wait to hear that young Kane is back in town and hope that he brings Tommy with him.''

Cara put down her glass and rubbed her forehead worriedly. ''I hope that's soon. I don't want to give up on Tommy, but I also have a responsibility to the physician who's covering for me and to my patients.''

''We'll be lucky if your limited time is the only problem we face. I just hope the bribe I gave Manuel was big enough to ensure his silence about us. It worries me, though, that our investigations may already have alerted people we don't want to meet. Manuel was right. It's not healthy to ask any questions whatever about members of what they call the *mafioso*, or about any aspect of their business. I'd just as soon not have drug traffickers find out for sure that we're trailing one of their own.''

"Please don't call Tommy that," Cara snapped. "Just because he knows this man Kane doesn't mean he's *one of their own.* He could be just a friend."

David's mouth tightened. He didn't argue.

"It's hard to believe," she continued, "that anyone would threaten us just because I want to talk to Tommy. I don't want to attack these criminals. I would if I could. But I know I can't."

"Believe it. Warren Baker did."

What with all that had been going on lately, she'd forgotten that her detective had been scared enough to drop her case. And that had been back in the States. They were a lot closer to the vicious drug traffickers here in Bogota. Despite David's warning back in Baltimore, she'd never really felt any sense of personal danger during her search for Tommy. For the first time, a spurt of fear leapt into her veins.

"What have I gotten myself into, David?" She twisted her hands together tightly in her lap. "More important, what danger have I placed you in? If anything should happen to you because of me, I don't know what I'd—"

"Don't worry about me. I can take care of myself. But as I told you that first day, I'm not at all sure I can take care of you. You'd be a lot safer at home."

He turned to her on the sofa. The gentle hands he wrapped over her shoulders shivered an instant thrill through her body.

"Haven't you heard enough to make you want to give up this business and go back to Baltimore? By anyone's standards, you've already paid your dues to Tommy. And more."

She shook her head. "I don't want to quit before accomplishing what I set out to do. I don't handle failure real well. I'm not accustomed to it—except for Tommy, that is."

"It's not a personal failure if you give a mission your best shot, but it doesn't completely succeed because you're outgunned by superior forces."

"I'm not stupid, David. I know that if Tommy really is with this man Kane, he could be into things that would turn my stomach. But the fact that he's been seen, well dressed and apparently rational might mean that he could be getting some kind of handle on his addiction. I owe it to what we once meant to each other not to convict him of being personally involved with the actual production and delivery of drugs until I have solid proof that it's true."

"I hope Grant has enough sense to appreciate that kind of loyalty, assuming he ever finds out about it."

He raked his fingers angrily through his hair.

"How in the name of all that's holy did a woman as generous, as smart as you ever fall in love with a guy like that in the first place?" His voice rang with fury.

"I'm not in love with him," she blurted out. "I never was in love with him."

Her outburst left David looking blank.

"I want to help Tommy mainly out of the guilt I feel about him. You already know that. But there's more to that guilt than I've told you."

Cara took a deep breath. David set such great store by what he called her loyalty to Tommy. She wasn't sure of his reaction to the confession she was about to make.

"In a way I might have abandoned Tommy before he abandoned me. As I said, I love him, but . . . I loved him only as a longtime friend. I was never truly in love with him. When he asked me to marry him, I said yes. It seemed the right decision at the time."

David looked completely focused on what she was saying, but he didn't throw any questions into the pause she needed to take.

"My whole life revolved around the study of medicine. I wanted more. I wanted to be married. I wanted to share the kind of strong relationship between a man and a woman that my parents, my sister and brother, enjoy. I was ready to start a family of my own. Showering my niece and nephews with love and affection wasn't enough. I longed for children of my own. Of course, that dream is down the tubes now.''

"Let me get this straight." The flatness in David's voice gave her little clue to his reaction. "You're doing all this for Tommy because you're *not* in love with the guy?''

"I've never put my motivation exactly in those terms, but I guess it's something like that. It's true that I had so much on my plate when Tommy started to fall apart that I had little energy left to take on his problems, too. But I can't get over the feeling that if I'd been truly in love with him, I might have done more. I would have knocked myself out for him.''

"You're doing that now.''

"Maybe. But I didn't do it back when it would have counted. Whatever my reasons at the time, I did make a commitment to Tommy Grant. If I don't do this for him now, I know I'll regret it the rest of my life.''

David heaved a great sigh and fell back on the sofa. Staring at the ceiling, he threw up his hands and let them flop down on his thighs.

"All right. That's it, then. We'll stay and hope that Manuel gets word to us before too long.''

That was it? David wasn't disgusted with her for not being as honest about Tommy, as loyal to him, as he'd thought she was?

"Right now," he said, "there's not much more I can do for you.''

"You've already done much more than I could have expected. More by far than you need have done.''

"Don't hand me any medals, Cara. This trip has done more for me than the little I've done for you. It's good to feel that I'm doing something meaningful, contributing something important to someone. I didn't realize it at the time, but maybe my need for that was another reason I volunteered to come on the mission.''

She covered his hand with hers. Finally she allowed herself to look deeply into the gray eyes that always generated such a visceral effect on her.

"I want you to know something, David. You've been a friend to me in a way Tommy never was. I've known *him* for years. I haven't known you very long at all, but already I know that I can count on you. I have every confidence that you can keep us both safe."

"I hope that confidence is justified. Somewhere along the line we might find ourselves up against some very tough customers."

"Perhaps. But I doubt if a Navy SEAL will be any pushover."

"An ex-Navy SEAL." David corrected her. "And only half a SEAL at that. I'm not exactly in top condition."

"Come on, David," she scoffed. "You're not exactly helpless, either."

"No. But I'm so disabled I couldn't cut it any longer with the Navy." He snapped his gaze away, as if he wished he hadn't added that remark.

"Is that how you see yourself?" she asked, astonished. "As weak? Helpless?" Hard to believe that could be the negative self-image of a man who exuded such an air of personal power.

"In some things, no. In what I've managed to do since I met you, no. In terms of what I used to be able to take on, absolutely."

"Then maybe you need to get on with the things you *can* do."

A corner of his mouth hooked upward.

"You sure don't do a whole lot of sympathizing with a man, do you, Cara? But I already knew that."

"I save my sympathy for people who really need it," she said flatly. "You don't."

She smiled.

"It's good to be able to talk to you so easily like this, David. With Tommy I always had to be careful about how I put things. Sometimes I found myself having to talk down a little to him to avoid the appearance of criticizing him. Strange, considering that he's smarter than I am."

"Book smarts, maybe. Life smarts? Forget it."

She could talk to David about most things, Cara allowed. But did she dare bring up what happened between them this afternoon? Maybe last night didn't really count, since neither of them had planned it, but they were both in complete possession of their senses when they kissed this afternoon. He must know as well as she did that the kiss had jogged their relationship onto an entirely different level.

She'd stuck her head in the sand about what was going on with Tommy those last terrible months. She refused to do the same about her feelings for David.

"About what happened this afternoon at the church—"

David catapulted from the sofa so quickly, he had to struggle to maintain his balance.

"That was a mistake on my part," he said, limping to the darkened window. "I'm sorry. It should never have happened." The back he held turned to her was rigid. His words delivered in a clipped, cool tone. "Don't worry. What happened this afternoon won't happen again."

His words cut her to the bone. He was sorry? He wished that the kiss that seared her soul had never happened?

Shaken, she tipped her glass to her lips so quickly the ice tumbled against the tip of her nose and a little cold wine trickled down her chin. She dashed it away with her fingertips.

At least the man was up-front with his feelings. He let her know where she stood with him. Absolutely insane to give any thought whatever to embarking on a relationship with a man who'd done everything but carry a sign saying he wasn't interested in serious commitments.

If only she could remember that.

"I guess if you can forget it—" she said, with as much dignified reserve as she could manage. "I can, too."

She pushed herself slowly to her feet and walked over to hand him his cane.

"Good night, David."

He bit off a short hard curse and spun around to vise his hands just above her elbows.

"Cara—" His eyes were angry dark slits. A nerve throbbed wildly in his clenched jaw. He looked as if he were about to jerk her off her feet and shake her the way he did Pereira.

"If I ever meet Grant, I'm going to knock him senseless for what he's doing to you."

She could feel the crushing strength in him, feel his trembling anger. Anger supposedly aimed at Tommy, but which felt as if it were flaring white-hot at her.

As suddenly as he'd grabbed her, he let her go. Without another word, he snatched his cane from her and stalked from the room, his limp more painfully pronounced than ever.

Even if he'd stayed, she wouldn't have told him that what Tommy was doing to her was nothing compared to what David Chandler Reid was doing to her.

Chapter 8

"You'll enjoy it," David insisted. "People for miles around come to see the religious procession this town lays on."

"Frankly, David, I'm not much in the mood for a drive out in the country to watch a parade of any kind."

"After hearing what Pereira had to say last night, I don't want us roaming around the city any more than we have to. Either we spend the day out in the countryside, where I hope we'll be safer, or we wait around in the hotel for Pereira to get back to us. That could be days. It could be never."

Cara sighed. "You've made your point, Commander. We'll take in the religious parade."

The town was located a two-hour drive from the city, on the shore of a narrow river winding through a mountain valley. David manned the oars of their small, rented boat. A powerboat raced noisily past them, showering them in its wake. They stared at each other, startled at the sudden sprinkling. Both of them broke out laughing at the same time.

After what David said yesterday, how could it still feel as if some invisible bond kept her linked to him even when they weren't together? Linked, that is, from her point of view. But she didn't understand how a link could go only one way.

Half a dozen boats belonging to visitors in town for the religious procession were strung prow to stern alongside the town center. Not only were the people from surrounding villages streaming in to take part in the ritual, but they were toting their wares to sell to the temporary influx of customers. A bevy of tiny shops and food stalls opened expressly for the occasion wafted delicious odors by Cara's nose.

The weather was cooperating. Bright sun smiled on boats, trucks and donkey carts weighted down with baskets of exotic fruits and vegetables. From a small stand on the bank, the local version of the neighborhood ice cream man busily doled out ice cream to eager young customers lined up on the path.

In a scene that could serve as a movie set, forest jungle swept down to the riverbank. Through the trees she glimpsed a meandering line of dingy whitewashed mud-brick houses. The small dwellings looked like something left over from another time, but the TV antennae sprouting from their roofs anchored them firmly in the present of CNN and endless repeats of Lucy driving Desi crazy. In Spanish.

Cara trailed her fingers in the water, hoping there were no piranhas or alligators around who might view her hand as an invitation to lunch. They passed under the arched branches of a palm tree dipping low overhead. She reached up to swat lazily at its dangling fronds.

David drew their boat alongside a larger one almost buried under a wild rainbow of flowers. A little girl about five years old with bright black eyes waved and called out to them. Apparently bent on selling her mother's wares, the child, her long black hair bouncing down her back, skipped surefooted from her boat into theirs. David greeted her in Spanish, and soon the two were laughing together and chatting back and forth as if they were long-lost friends.

Man and child swiveled their heads toward Cara at the same time. She found herself the object of disconcerting scrutiny by two pairs of eyes. David's expression mirrored the solemnity on the little girl's face as she studied her customer, but amusement flickered in his eyes.

"I asked Maria, here," he said, "for her expert opinion on which flowers would best suit the pretty lady with me. As you can see she's giving the matter some serious thought."

The youngster switched her attention from Cara to her mother's boat and contemplated the brilliant pile of flowers. With an emphatic nod the child finally pronounced her judgment.

"*Sí,*" David agreed, returning the nod.

The girl trilled the order over to her mother. The woman immediately broke into a wide grin, evidently at the prospect of a lucrative business transaction. She gathered up an enormous cluster of deep yellow orchids and stacked them into her daughter's outstretched arms.

Chattering at Cara in Spanish, the child carefully laid the blossoms in Cara's lap. Cara looked to David for a translation.

"Maria says the beautiful golden orchids are a special gift of the Virgin to a beautiful golden lady."

Cara took the little girl's tiny brown hand and smiled her thanks. "Please tell her for me, David, that I think the flowers are lovely."

The child scampered up to him and looped a long circlet of crimson blossoms around his neck. She clapped her little hands together and stood back to admire the effect. Apparently satisfied, she bowed to each of them in turn and danced back into her own boat. With a flurry of head bobs, waves and best wishes for their good fortune, mother and daughter waved goodbye.

"By the time that little salesgirl gets through," Cara laughed, "there won't be a petal left in their boat." She lifted the sweet-smelling sheaf of flowers to her nose. "Thank you, David. These really are beautiful. I've never enjoyed the luxury of receiving a whole bouquet of orchids before."

Settling back on the none-too-clean cushions the boat rental man had tossed in for her comfort, she twisted off one of the yellow blooms and threaded it into her hair.

She wondered if David had even noticed that she'd taken off the ring. No point in encouraging any more thieves. Besides, for a long time the ring had served mainly as a symbol of her vow to find Tommy. Like the POW-MIA bracelets some people wore.

David rowed them farther upriver, leaving behind some of the bustle at the town center. He faced her in the other end of the boat. She had little choice but to look at him hunkered down on the ridiculously small seat of the low-sided rowboat.

His bad leg was stretched out in front of him, the other jackknifed up to his chin.

He was enduring the uncomfortable position solely for her benefit. He'd showered her with flowers in a generous effort to please her. And he'd been touchingly gentle with the little girl.

No matter that she was trying to maintain an emotional distance from him, a strong swell of affection for him flooded her heart. It was okay to like the man, she told herself. Stupid to let liking grow into anything more.

"You're constantly surprising me, David. I wouldn't have expected you to have such a natural way with kids, but you certainly hit it off with little Maria. I think you'd make a very good father."

"I used to think so myself. I do like kids." The lingering smile the little girl had left him with vanished. "But I had no more luck with my plans for a family than you did. Anita and I talked about it . . ." He stared off into space for a moment. "She never did get around to deciding the time was right." He shrugged. "Just as well, in view of what happened. Divorce is hard enough on adults. From what I've seen, it's murder on children."

He pulled the oars inside the boat and lifted the floral necklace from around his neck.

"Here. This will look a lot better on you than it does on me."

Lunging forward with a heavy awkwardness that made the little boat sway, he leaned over the mound of flowers in her lap to drape the delicate scarlet circlet over her head.

Instead of drawing away, he lingered. His eyes locked on her mouth. His lips parted slightly, as if he planned to speak. But he said nothing.

He wanted to kiss her. She exulted in the longing she could read in the darkening gray in his eyes. The deep furrow between his brows, though, betrayed his mental debate about doing that.

Her pride came in a distant second to her aching desire to feel his lips on hers again. As if he could read her mind, David erased the distance between his mouth and hers.

She forgot the flowers. Forgot the river. Forgot everything but the sweet thrill of David's kiss, the perfect way his arms fit around her.

Again and again their parted lips fused, their tongues darted to each other. His ranged over the soft, moist cup of her mouth as if he meant to assure himself that he hadn't left one tiny bit untasted during his last inflaming visit there. She'd been kissed before. None but David's kiss had ever fired up that wild undertone of need within her.

A hard jolt of the boat jerked them apart.

David whipped a barely focused gaze around in an effort to get his bearings. His neglect of the oars had bumped their vessel into a spit of land jutting into the river.

David gave a weak imitation of a laugh. "I'd better keep my mind on my work instead of slacking off like that."

He tried to look completely composed as he regained his seat and rowed them away from shore. But she hadn't missed the dazed look in his eyes that matched the way her own head was spinning.

Maybe she wasn't as experienced in lovemaking as he, but to her, that kiss hadn't felt at all one-sided. She was sure that he'd been as caught up as she in the pleasure of it. She'd felt his rising passion in the hunger of his mouth, in the tightening of his hold on her.

"Why do you keep on pretending that our kisses don't mean anything, David? That there's nothing special going on between us?" She couldn't believe she'd actually spoken those words out loud, but she'd started this, so she might as well finish it. "You sure don't act as if I were only a...a client of some kind."

"Oh, for—" He raked back his hair. "Look. You're into the talking everything out thing. That's not me, okay?"

From the irritated way he threw back his answer without looking at her, she figured she'd touched a nerve. Exactly which nerve, she intended to find out. This confrontation frightened her a little. Exactly why she pushed it. She'd let fear—not her usual response to a problem—overcome direct action with Tommy. Never again.

"It was you on the plane when you opened up to me about your wife. You said you seldom do that with anyone. You don't seem to have a lot of trouble talking to me."

She stretched out her hand. He was too far away to reach.

"Talk to me now, David. Rowing this boat doesn't take nearly the amount of attention you're giving it."

"All right," he said, still peering as intently over his shoulder as if he were piloting the *Queen Mary* into berth. "Sure I care about you. I don't want to see you get hurt. And you've set yourself up for that with this pointless search of yours."

Her brows hooked upward in open skepticism. "I see. Your feelings for me are completely altruistic."

"No. They're a lot more than that." He turned and balanced the oars on the sides of the boat. "Just remember that you asked for this."

He tilted his head to one side and looked at her through slitted eyes. She wondered if provoking him this way had been such a good idea after all.

"Yeah. I like kissing you," he said flatly. "In fact I'd like to do a whole lot more than that to you. After the tease you gave me the other night, I want to take you to bed so bad I can taste it. Shall we stop in right now at that small hotel we saw in town? What do you say?"

The shock of his blunt proposition, David noted with grim satisfaction, produced its desired effect. Cara's face flushed pink. Her open blue gaze jerked away.

Maybe it was the coward's way out, but since he wasn't able to keep his hands off her, he hoped he'd fixed it so she'd keep a safe emotional distance from him.

It didn't help that she'd told him she wasn't in love with Tommy, and that the ring had disappeared from her finger. If anything, the fact that she didn't belong to another man only made things more difficult for him.

She had him against the ropes. He was afraid he'd soon go down to defeat in his battle with himself not to make love to the woman who played such havoc with his mind and body.

The problem was she felt good in his arms. So damn good it scared him. But his arms were the last place in the world she belonged. He was no good for her. You'd think she'd be able to see that for herself every time she watched him hobble along next to her.

She broke the simmering silence between them.

"What do I say?" she repeated levelly. Her mouth tight, she lifted her chin. "I say it's time for you to take me back to our hotel in the city, where I'll go to my room alone."

The flurry of traffic on the river and the dirt road running along its banks had slackened off considerably. He'd been so focused on Cara, he hadn't noticed. Theirs was just about the only boat still moving. The others floated empty by the shore.

A loud blast of tinny music erupted from the town center. The religious ritual was scheduled for noon. David glanced at his watch. It was just about that now.

He started to row back toward the area where he'd parked their rental car. Cara sat in hurtful silence that made him feel like a heel. That he'd said what he did to her only for her own good didn't help him feel any better.

While still four or five hundred yards from the rental dock, he spotted the man on the road.

Behind the heavyset man in the short-sleeved white shirt and dark pants, stragglers on their way to the procession hurried along the road. The man who'd caught his eye, though, was going nowhere. Standing by the side of the road, he stared in their direction. Hard to tell for sure from this distance, but he seemed to be intently observing their approach.

Big. Bald. Scary-looking Hispanic. The investigator's description of his attacker lit up in David's mind. A perfect description of the watcher on the road.

He let up on his hard pull on the oars and scanned the area ahead. A second man stood eyeing them from the small pier where they'd rented their boat.

And where they had to return it.

He felt a creeping of the skin at the back of his neck. Over the years he'd learned to trust the sixth sense that lodged there. Right now, that internal warning system was prickling like all get-out.

Cara. He didn't know what the men had in mind for either of them, but these didn't look like the types of guys who'd think twice about attacking a woman. His mind raced through the precious few scenarios that might get her away from the hazardous confrontation evidently looming ahead.

She was in good physical shape. Given a head start, she stood some chance of outrunning the men. With any luck she'd make it as far as the nearest crowd that might provide her some measure of protection. How much, he couldn't predict. Anti-Americanism was prevalent in the country. The crowd might not have much of a problem with watching native Colombians beat up a couple of *gringo* tourists.

Reaching the crowd, though, was the only chance she had. To give her that chance, he'd have to hold off the two goons as long as he could. He prayed to God there were no others lurking somewhere out of sight.

"Cara," he said briskly, holding the boat in place with the oars. "Two men I don't like the looks of are waiting for us over by the dock. I'm going to pull up to this side of that clump of trees on the riverbank up ahead. That should give us a bit of cover. When I do, I want you to waste no time in getting out of the boat and making for the crowd."

He dug into his pocket for the ignition key to their rental car and tossed it to her.

"Try to make it to the car. If you manage to do that, take off. Don't wait for me. I'll be okay. Just get out of here. That's an order," he snapped. "Follow it."

Cara didn't waste time asking for lengthy explanations. The incident with Manuel had given her warning enough that they could run into a dangerous situation. From the alert tenseness in David's body and voice, she gathered they now faced exactly that.

She grabbed her purse, shoved the car key into it and looped the shoulder strap diagonally across her body.

They'd almost reached the spot David mentioned. He stabbed an oar into the shallow river bottom and swerved the boat toward land. The little craft butted into the bank.

"Move!" he commanded.

She moved. Flowers scattered into the river as she leapt from the boat.

David followed. His cane caught in the thick underbrush. He stumbled.

She stopped, ready to run back and help him. He imperiously waved her on.

"No. Keep going."

He pulled his cane out and struggled after her as best he could through knee-high vegetation. The lei around her neck bobbed distractingly. She tugged hard at the flowers. The cord holding them broke. With a spasm of regret, she tossed David's lovely gift away.

They made it only to a clutch of small buildings on the edge of town before the two men began to close in on either side of them.

"Let's both try for the crowd, David. Your leg. You can't fight those two."

"The hell with my leg. They're not going to give me the option. Get going."

He set his back protectively against the wall and flipped his cane around to use the heavy brass handgrip as a pointed weapon.

"Damn it, Cara," he shouted. "Run. I'll hold them off."

Run and leave him to battle two assailants alone? No way. She might still be able to race away fast enough to escape the heavyweight pair. David couldn't possibly elude them.

She opened her mouth and forced out an ear-shattering scream for help. If anyone heard over the racket from the procession, they didn't shout back in return.

The larger of their two attackers positioned himself to take on David. With an evil grin, the Colombian slashed at him with a long, vicious-looking machete.

A quick whip of David's cane whacked the blade away.

She had no more time or energy to keep on screaming.

The second man advanced on her. She fell into the defense position she'd been taught: alertly balanced on both feet, hands and arms angled up in front of her ready to tighten and strike. Her assailant, who outweighed her by more than a hundred pounds, laughed derisively at her stance.

He lunged at her.

Her well-aimed karate kick to the side of his knee stumbled him to the ground. He wasn't laughing anymore. He looked up at her, openmouthed that she'd managed to put him down. Without compunction she launched another kick, this time to his ribs.

She connected.

The force of the hit traveled all the way up her leg. Unfortunately it seemed to have little lasting effect on her adversary's heavy body. He moved quickly enough to grab hold of her ankle and yank. Sharp pain speared up her leg. She landed on her stomach in the dirt. The hard thump drove the breath from her lungs.

Furiously concentrating on recalling moves she'd performed only in class under no real stress, she couldn't spare a glance to see how David was faring. The best thing she could do for him was to take care of herself as best she could.

She flailed at her assailant's head with her free leg and twisted onto her back. He let go of her ankle and got to one knee, his arms outstretched, ready to hurl himself upon her. If he succeeded, he'd bury her under his bulk. One blow of his massive fist to her head and the uneven contest would be over.

He gathered his heavy legs under him, ready to spring.

She drew up both knees to her chest. With all her strength she kicked his face.

He reared back, blood spurting from his nose.

His grunt of pain and the sickening feel of her feet thudding into his face brought her a rush of nausea. She'd devoted her life to the easing of pain, and had practiced self-defense moves only on well-padded pretend opponents. Deliberately hurting anyone, even a real attacker out to do her serious harm, wasn't easy.

Her ankle throbbed. She pushed the ache from her mind. Thinking only of David, she scrambled to her feet.

His opponent was moving in on him again. The man had recovered the knife. David's legs were useless as defense, but his upper body strength made a formidable weapon of the cane he gripped with both hands and flailed around him like a sword.

He was holding his own right now, but he couldn't do that forever. Neither could she. Her attacker was already struggling to his feet. A man that size could take a lot of punishment. More, she was afraid, than she'd be able to dish out. Already she was gasping for breath. And her antagonist had learned that overcoming her would require a more brutal attack. One she was sure he was ready to employ.

"I told you to get the hell out of here," David yelled. His cane cracked against his attacker's bare, knife-wielding arm. This time the Colombian managed to hold on to the blade.

"Forget it," she hollered back.

She jerked her heavy bag over her shoulder. Holding it by its long strap she whirled it out to thump into her man's head. The action gave her another couple of seconds to ready herself for another onslaught.

David's ugly opponent tried again to grab for the cane inflicting so much damage on him. David kept him so busy trying to protect his head from its blows that he wasn't able to catch hold of the weapon. Sooner or later, though, he'd manage to do that and things would get a lot tougher for David. And for herself.

The sharp clatter of drums and the wail of flutes grew louder. She stole a quick look down the narrow alley between the buildings. A group of hymn-singing young girls dressed in white streamed past the lane's exit at the next block.

"David. Down here. We can—"

A massive arm locked around her throat. She couldn't breathe. Couldn't twist her head away. A shower of bright red sparks danced in front of her eyes.

David's cane landed with a hard thud across her assailant's back and broke his hold. Two quick blows to the back of his legs flopped the man back on the ground next to his partner, who was doubled over holding his bloodied head.

"Down the alley," David ordered, hooking his free arm around her shoulder. Between the support of her body and the cane, he was able to manage a fairly rapid, if ungainly, lope down the lane.

She glanced back. The two men were already picking themselves up off the ground. It hurt to put her weight on her injured ankle, but worse hurt was gaining on them from behind.

Gasping with exertion, she and David broke into the religious procession. Just ahead, a group of men loudly chanting prayers held the ends of thick silken ropes attached to a huge banner brightly painted with a sacred image. The gold-fringed flag effectively hid them from anyone in back of it. But the men bearing the religious symbol were marching at such a slow pace, Cara was afraid their stalkers could soon catch up to them.

A man dressed in white, an official badge pinned to his shirt, gestured them to the sidelines. It was clear they couldn't push rapidly through the milling crowd to reach the car that offered escape.

"Those two goons face the same problems we do in getting through this crowd," David said. "Our only chance is to keep from being seen long enough to make it to where the car is parked." Ignoring the orders of another parade marshall, David steered them as quickly as possible along the edge of each group of chanting marchers into the cover of several banners.

Trying to locate their tormentors, David pulled his arm from her shoulder and turned to peer around a banner.

"They're back there, all right."

Up until now, she hadn't had time to take stock of the fight's effects on the two of them. No wonder they'd garnered official frowns. Everyone else was cleanly dressed in Sunday best.

AN IMPORTANT MESSAGE
FROM
THE EDITORS OF SILHOUETTE

Dear Reader,

Because you've chosen to read one of our romance novels, we'd like to say "thank you"! And, as a **special** way to thank you, we've selected <u>four more</u> of the <u>books</u> you love so much, **and** a lovely necklace to send you absolutely <u>FREE</u>!

Please enjoy them with our compliments...

Jane Nicholls ___ Editor, Silhouette

P.S. And because we value our customers we've attached something extra inside...

EDITOR'S
FREE
GIFT
SEAL
THANK YOU

PEEL OFF SEAL AND PLACE INSIDE

HOW TO VALIDATE
YOUR
EDITOR'S FREE GIFT
"THANK YOU"

1. Peel off gift seal from front cover. Place it in space provided at right. This automatically entitles you to receive four free books and a lovely silvertone heart necklace.

2. Send back this card and you'll get four specially selected Silhouette Sensation® novels which are yours to keep <u>absolutely free</u>.

3. There's no catch. You're under no obligation to buy anything. We charge nothing for your first shipment. And you don't have to make any minimum number of purchases - not even one!

4. The fact is thousands of readers enjoy receiving books by mail from the Reader Service™. They like the convenience of home delivery and they like getting the best new novels at least a month before they're available in the shops. And, of course, postage and packing is completely FREE!

5. We hope that after receiving your free books you'll want to remain a subscriber. But the choice is yours - to continue or cancel, anytime at all! So why not take us up on our invitation, with no risk of any kind. You'll be glad you did!

6. Don't forget to detach your FREE BOOKMARK. And remember... just for validating your Editor's Free Gift Offer, we'll send you FIVE MORE gifts, *ABSOLUTELY FREE!*

You'll look like a million dollars when you wear this lovely necklace! Its silvertone chain is a generous 18" long, and the exquisite heart pendant completes this attractive gift.

Only the two Americans looked dirty and bedraggled. David's shirt was torn, as was her dress.

Her horrified gaze riveted on the stream of blood flowing from the back of his arm.

"David! You're bleeding. Why didn't you tell me you were hurt?"

"No point in it. Nothing we can do about it now anyway. Keep moving."

The relative cover the parade gave them was running out. Not far ahead, a high, gold-and-white canopy rippled over an altar erected on a flower-bedecked stage. Their car was parked on a side street down to the left. She craned her neck, but couldn't make out their vehicle among the others.

David pulled her up short and led her off to the side to mingle with the spectators.

"More trouble. Looks as if our friends have left a lookout behind. There's another big guy standing a few feet away from the car. I don't think he came to town simply to join in the hymn singing."

"So what do we do now?"

"We've got to get to the car. I don't know when the next bus leaves for the city and we're not in any position to wait around. Frankly, Cara, I wouldn't bet on the crowd being much help in a dispute that pits us against their fellow Colombians. They may not want to get involved."

"The fellow at the car, d'you think we can take him?"

David looked startled at the matter-of-fact way she asked the question. He broke into a grin.

"Hey. There are two of us, only one of him." The grin didn't last long. "The others didn't have guns. Let's hope this guy doesn't, either."

The procession flowed by as David stood and pondered a battle plan. His gaze lit on a young boy lugging a plastic bucket of water up a path leading from the river. David limped over to the boy and spoke to him rapidly in Spanish. Pesos and bucket changed hands.

David handed her the filled bucket.

"Try to keep from being seen until you let the guy have the water in the face as hard as you can. That should surprise him enough to give me time to get behind him and clobber him." He hefted his cane admiringly. "This thing is coming in a lot handier than I ever expected."

It might work, Cara considered, if they actually had time to do it. Her quick glance back over the crowd showed her one of their attackers elbowing his way through a band of men following a white surpliced acolyte bearing a golden crucifix atop a tall pole.

She maneuvered herself into a small group of passing women chanting their rosaries. When her part of the procession turned and flowed toward the altar, she broke from the group and sped to the cover of a small truck.

She peeked over the hood and went cold. The man standing guard at their car was looking in her direction. The only good thing about his perusal of the area of her hiding place was that he didn't see David working his way to the other side of the street.

She had no other choice. She stepped away from the truck.

God must have been listening to her prayers. At the same moment she readied her watery weapon, her target jerked his gaze off to the side, apparently caught by something or someone in the crowd. She glanced behind her. The shouts and wild gesticulations of their pursuers, instead of calling their partner's attention to her, only served to distract him.

Mentally thanking them for the favor, she dashed across the street and hurled the water full in the backup's face.

Stunned, the man coughed and sputtered and wiped his arm across his eyes.

David wasn't at all gentle when he conked the lookout over the head with the cane.

"Give me the car key," he ordered, limping quickly to their rental car.

"I can drive."

"No." He grabbed the key from her outstretched hand. "Get in."

They slammed into the car.

Their two assailants broke free of the crowd. All three were running in their direction. The enraged man she'd soaked was almost on them. He grabbed at the door handle on her side.

David wrenched the wheel, swerving the car out of the line of parked vehicles. The third attacker lost his hold on the door and fell into the road.

The way ahead was blocked with people. David had no space in which to turn the car around. He threw it into Reverse.

The vehicle sped backward, leaving the thugs shouting curses at them in the dust. Half a dozen people had to leap out of the way, but David miraculously managed not to hit any of them.

He knew what he was doing when he demanded the car key. She could never have driven like a madman and still kept the vehicle under control the way he did.

With barely an inch to spare between their back bumper and an extremely solid-looking tree, David spun the car around and took off. Her last glimpse of their pursuers showed them pushing back through the crowd, evidently trying to make their way to their own vehicle.

"Think they'll catch up to us?" she asked, finally being granted a second to snap her seat belt into place.

David stole a glance in the rearview mirror. "I don't see them. I think we'll be okay."

A few minutes later he allowed the automobile to slow to a civilized speed. He glanced over at Cara and gave a sharp, ironic laugh.

"How can you laugh after what we just went through?" she demanded.

"I'm laughing at myself. At one point I actually thought you might need a big, strong protector like me to look after you. My mistake. You handled yourself well back there."

"I told you I'd taken some self-defense courses."

She knew darn well, though, that she'd reached the limit of her expertise. In another few seconds she'd have been out cold flat on the ground and David would have been on his own, battling two opponents at once.

"You sure did. But you have lots to learn about following orders."

"I follow all kinds of medical orders. I'm just not real good at taking yours."

She pulled a scarf from the handbag that had made it through the scuffle. "Now fasten your seat belt and let me take care of that arm."

Fortunately the wound was in David's accessible right arm. They wouldn't have to stop in order for her to tend to the deep cut. She expertly wrapped the rectangle of white silk around his upper arm to stanch the bleeding. "You'll need to have that taken care of at a hospital when we get back."

David's mouth crooked. "Handy to have my own personal physician along when I get knifed."

His face turned grim. "But I react badly to being attacked. Even worse to having the woman I'm with exposed to that kind of thing. If I ever get my hands on that bastard Pereira—"

He gripped the steering wheel with white-knuckled fury.

Chapter 9

From his chair next to the sofa, David folded his arms in front of him and looked down at Cara. He gave her a morose frown.

"That's the problem with con artists like Manuel," he growled. "They're not honest enough to stay bought."

She'd refused the doctor's suggestion that she spend the rest of the day in bed. She lay stretched out, her head and shoulders resting on pillows David had carefully arranged on the sofa in her room.

Fortunately X rays had shown no broken bones in her bandaged ankle, only a minor sprain and bruises.

Anesthetizing adrenaline had long since worn off. Her whole body ached from her run-in with the thug. David, settled on a chair next to her, the stitches in his arm covered by a bandage more professional than a scarf, had to be in even more discomfort. He'd taken a worse pummeling than she. The only sign of pain he allowed, though, was a certain extra carefulness in moving.

Taking her cue from him, she hadn't raised any objection when medical and police officials chalked up the incident to just another regrettable tourist mugging.

"You think Manuel set those thugs on us?" she asked.

"He'd be my first choice."

"Trying to kill us is pretty drastic, isn't it?"

"They weren't trying to kill us. If wasting us was their aim, they'd have come armed with more than muscle and a knife. No. They were trying to do what one of them did with your detective back home—put the fear of God into us so we'd quit looking for Tommy."

Cara shuddered. "Well, frankly, they came pretty close to accomplishing that with me."

David rubbed pensively at the back of his neck.

"I don't know. Something about that whole episode doesn't add up. I'd have thought that a man of Dan Kane's resources would have sent goons with a little more finesse to take care of us. Personally I'd have given them orders to jump us quietly sometime when we were alone, instead of within a stone's throw of a sizable audience. And you'd think that a beating designed to send us packing wouldn't stop short of leaving us ready for pickup by an ambulance."

"For heaven's sake, David, it almost did."

He was complaining because she suffered only from a painfully wrenched ankle, and he was stabbed merely in the arm instead of an artery?

"Not really. Not all three of those guys were that good, and the fellow at the car was an outright idiot. No offense, Cara, but the hood you bested wasn't a professional who could have put you away in three seconds."

"Oh, really? Well, to me he seemed expert enough at beating people up. And your attacker sure looked like he meant business with that terrible knife."

"Okay. That one was a pro. I'm sure he was the man in Miami who scared Baker into dropping your case. That must have happened when Robert was there and somehow or other got together with Grant."

"Well," she groused, irritated at having to defend the expertise of the low-life pair who'd jumped them. "You might see something wrong with those horrible men not leaving us completely mangled in the street. I'm not complaining about it."

David hastily pushed himself from his chair. Cara shifted her hips to give him room to sit beside her. He leaned over her and rested one hand on the back of the couch, his mouth a thin tight slash.

"Believe me, I'm not sorry about it, either. Thank God you weren't badly hurt." He drew a finger lightly alongside the two-inch scratch inflicted on her cheek during the struggle. "I should have been able to prevent this."

David was most dangerous when he was gentle, Cara reminded herself. That was when she tended to forget why he was with her. Forget that he'd already told her the only thing he wanted from her. She wasn't proud of the fact that back in the boat her first instinct was to agree to his cold proposition. But she'd be no man's one-night stand. Not even David's.

A nerve throbbed at the top of his jaw.

"I should have been able to stop that lout from laying his filthy hands on you at all."

"I don't see how. Have you forgotten that at the time you were pretty busy yourself?"

"I won't forget anything about that incident."

The icy fury flashing in his eyes softened into a look of tenderness. "You saved my hide by keeping that second goon off me until we had a chance to get away. Thanks."

"I'd say we helped each other."

For a long time now David's face hadn't seemed nearly as hard and distant as it had when she first met him. Contemplating that face shouldn't continue to bring her such a deep degree of contentment. But it did.

"You handled yourself so well today, Cara, I should make you an honorary SEAL."

"Thank you, Commander. I'm honored."

Though she'd thanked him with a smile as light as his, she wasn't kidding. She was deeply pleased to receive David's open admiration. "But I know I can't come within shouting distance of being in your league in dealing with bad guys. You were astonishing this afternoon, David. I can easily understand why Mr. Elliott called you a hero."

David's eyes widened. "He what?"

"He made you sound like a cross between a Rambo with a bit of self-control, and Indiana Jones. Plus a little Captain America thrown in for good measure. That's why I was so disappointed when you refused to help me."

"That Elliott likes me at all is news to me. He kept sending me out on the worst missions that came along."

"Believe me, Mr. Elliott said words to that effect, and more." Cara tossed him a teasing smile. "Would you like me to quote him exactly?"

"Please don't."

It was fun to watch David's red-faced embarrassment. She never suspected that he possessed any at all. He looked so much like an abashed little boy that she had to reach up and brush back a stray lock of black hair.

"So what's the deal on Mr. Elliott, anyway? I take it he's a CIA spook, or something?"

"Or something. And I believe he'd prefer the term intelligence officer to the word spook."

"But you were navy."

"Elliott is occasionally authorized to use specially trained members of the military on particularly important and sensitive missions."

"Like going after some captured DEA officers?"

"That's all I'm going to say on the subject."

Since she was still gently twisting the ends of his hair around her fingertips, it seemed only natural to slide her hand down to his cheek.

As if he'd caught himself gazing too long at her, David skidded his eyes away. She dropped her hand.

The lull in the conversation lengthened as he contemplated the blue plush carpet at his feet and rubbed a hand absently over his injured thigh.

The silence between them lengthened. She was willing to bet he was again getting ready to say something to her that she wouldn't enjoy hearing.

"All right, David, let's have it. What has you frowning so furiously?"

He didn't try to pretend he didn't know what she meant.

"There's a significant possibility you haven't considered yet."

"What's that?"

"The possibility that Tommy may not thank you for this search. Hasn't it occurred to you that he may not be interested in returning to the States?"

"No, it hasn't."

"It has to me."

"Why wouldn't he want to go home and take back his real life, when he hears that I'm ready to help him do that?"

"What if he thinks his real life is here?"

"What do you mean?"

"It wouldn't surprise me if Grant has found precisely the niche he wants with his pal Robert and intends to keep it. Dan Kane is very wealthy. His son can buy himself—and any friend of his—anything he wants. Except, I suspect, freedom from his father's grip."

David caught her hand.

"Try to think about this whole thing objectively, Cara, instead of with that ridiculous blind loyalty of yours not only to a man who doesn't deserve it, but to a man who doesn't really exist."

"I'm not blind to Tommy's faults," she insisted. "Maybe I was at one point. All right, I know I was. Not anymore."

Certainly not since she'd met the man who embodied all the strength of character she admired in the other important men in her life, such as her father and her brother.

"Good. Because the real Tommy may feel that he lucked into a very good deal. Think about it. Someone else paying the bills for a life of luxury, access to all the high-grade cocaine and heroin he wants. And all of it with no hassle."

Cara angrily hunched her hips away from their pleasurable contact with David.

"You're saying that Tommy may have set those thugs on us to get me to quit trying to find him."

"I don't think he'd have the authority to do that on his own hook, but he could have approached Robert or Dan Kane about us."

She set her mouth and gave her head a fierce shake of denial.

"I don't believe it. I refuse to believe it. In all the years I've known Tommy Grant, I've never seen the slightest hint of violence in him. In fact, I believe that it was his lack of personal toughness that led him into drugs in the first place."

"I'm sure you know that drug abuse can change a person's whole personality."

"No matter what he's gotten himself into, I'm convinced Tommy would never do anything to hurt me."

"Just like you knew he'd choose you over the cocaine when you offered him the choice."

"That's a low blow, David. You know I meant that he'd never hurt me physically. We're talking about a man who hardly ever so much as raised his voice to me. When he did yell at me after I discovered his drug use, it was out of his own pain."

"Regardless. This afternoon's attack sent a strong signal that it's time for you to go home."

"I've thought about it," she admitted. She touched the bandage covering the slash on David's arm, and shivered. "But if it were my brother who was in this mess, I'd never run away from it. I won't do that with Tommy, either. Whether you can understand it or not, I have to know for sure what has happened to him before I can let go of the search. But you don't owe Tommy anything, David. You can leave. In fact I . . . I'd rather you did leave."

She couldn't look at him when she said that. Sending him away was the last thing she wanted to do. But before the attack, she'd never really believed that she was exposing him to serious danger by having him with her. Now she knew better. It was one thing to take chances with her own safety for her own reasons, but another to put David at risk when he had no connection whatever with Tommy.

"Take off and leave you here by yourself? Do you really think I'd do that?"

"I want you to."

The telephone beside the sofa shrilled into their debate. David reached over and snatched up the receiver. He listened for a second or two, then cold fury speared into his face. He leapt to his feet.

"You've got a hell of a nerve calling me, Pereira."

Their traitorous informant was calling them? Whatever for? You'd think his first rough dealings with David would already have sent the man running far and fast from his employer's predictable desire for vengeance.

She pushed herself up straighter on the pillows to get closer to the phone to try to hear the other end of the conversation.

"You're not going to get away with informing on us to your trafficker friends," David snarled into the mouthpiece. "The next time I see you, *cabrón,* I'm going to take it out of your hide. I promise you that."

The way he rasped out the Spanish word made her sure it was no compliment.

He angled the earpiece away from his ear to let her hear the high-pitched crackle coming over the line. She couldn't really make out Manuel's words, but the tone was clearly irate.

"Don't pretend you don't know that a couple of gangster types roughed us up today... What...?"

More loud crackle.

"Sure, you didn't. We talk to you last night and three guys come after us today, but you had nothing to do with it...."

Suddenly serious, David turned his back to her and jammed the receiver back to his ear. A frustrating silence took over his end of the conversation. He stood listening so intently that she surmised he had to be hearing something important.

She reached up and tugged impatiently at his arm. "What's he saying?" she mouthed. "What's he saying?"

David shushed her with an imperious wave of his hand. He pressed his fingers over his free ear to cut out any sound but the voice on the other end of the line.

Annoyed at being shut out, Cara swung her legs from the sofa.

"Ouch." A sharp pain needled through her ankle. She'd moved so quickly that she forgot to take care in putting her weight on her left foot.

She hopped closer to David and the phone. No matter how hard she stared at the receiver and David's face, she couldn't figure out what he was hearing.

"You're sure?" He'd lowered his voice a few decibels and his face had lost some of its anger. "Are they still there...? All right.... I'm not sure I'm buying all this, Pereira, but if I decide to come, where shall we meet?"

Meet? He was arranging to meet the man who'd set thugs on them only hours ago? Moving so that David could see her face, she launched a silent glare of disapproval at him.

He paid her no mind.

"That's in the *barrio,* right?...Yes, I know the place...." He nodded. "Midnight tonight.... I'm warning you, Manuel, this had better be on the level, or you'll need to find a damn good place to hide."

The second David hung up the phone Cara's indignation burst out.

"You're going to meet that—that—" she sputtered, breaking off with a furious shake of her head. "Begging your pardon, Commander, sir," she purred with heavy sarcasm. "Have you lost your ever-loving mind?" She ended close to a shout. "You're going to meet that two-timing pimp after what happened to us today?"

David met her fury with aggravating calm. He simply sat back down on the sofa and gazed up at her with provoking mildness.

"Pereira swears he had nothing to do with what happened at the procession."

"And you believe him?" She threw up her hands in exasperation and flopped down next to him.

"Maybe. But that wasn't the most interesting part of the conversation. He gave me some information which, if true, might provide us with our best lead yet."

"About Robert Kane?"

He nodded. "And Tommy." An eyebrow hooked upward in irony. "Still not interested?"

His news knocked some of the wind from her sails. "What about them?"

"A friend of Manuel's reportedly spotted the two at the gaming tables of a luxury resort only yesterday."

"A luxury resort? Where?"

"Well now, that's the tricky part. I don't know. Manuel wouldn't say. He wants to get paid before he tells us any more. Asked me to meet him in the *barrio,* where he lives. It's a straight business transaction. I give him five hundred bucks American. He gives me the name of the resort."

"For God's sake, David, you can't go there." Forgetting that it wasn't at all a good idea to keep touching him, Cara laid her hand imploringly on his arm. "Pereira might have those same men waiting for you. This time they could finish the job."

"You may be right," David allowed with frustrating coolness.

"Damn right I'm right."

She struggled to match some of David's unruffled manner. Only with him did she so easily lose her usual professional composure.

"But evidently you think he was telling the truth. You think it's safe for you to meet him."

"*Safe* is a pretty strong word. I'm not sure I'd use it. Let's just say that I'm almost convinced that Pereira had nothing to do with what happened this afternoon."

"*Almost* is a pretty weak word on which to bet your life, David."

"I agree. Regardless of what you think, partner, I'm still in possession of most of my marbles. I don't intend to go into the *barrio* without carrying a weapon wielding a little more firepower than a cane. I need to pick up a gun, and I know where to get one."

Evidently David was a more trusting soul than she. The idea of meeting the *mestizo* for any reason stood her hair on end.

On the other hand, Reid was an intelligent man. A man who'd proven only a few hours ago that he was well able to take

care of himself despite his injured leg. He wouldn't take un-
necessary chances. She frowned. Okay, so she wouldn't actually bet the farm on that. But he'd be armed. If those goons
showed up again, the odds against them would be a lot more
even than they'd been the last go-round.

"Okay," she said. "We'll go."

"What d'you mean *we?*"

She stared him down. "Don't waste your time arguing with
me."

It could have been wishful thinking, but she may have dis-
cerned a hint of admiration behind the displeasure in the wry
quirk of David's mouth.

"After what I saw you do to the hapless gentleman who
made the mistake of taking you on this afternoon, I wouldn't
dare. Hey. Why am I worrying?" He aimed a scowl at her
bandaged ankle. "Between the two of us, we can still count on
two perfectly good legs—just in case we have to run for it
again."

His glower didn't faze her. She chuckled. At times David
Reid could be too much the arrogant military commander. But
in his defense, he could also be an amusing, arrogant military
commander.

"I'll tell you one thing," she said, giving her head a decided
bob. "This time I intend to load up my handbag with rocks."

The rain that sluiced down on the city in late afternoon had
dripped to a halt by the time they grabbed a taxi from out front
of the hotel.

The driver didn't want to believe that David had gotten his
directions straight.

"No, *señor.* That is in the *barrio.* You don't want go there.
Is bad place. At night, very bad place."

David had come prepared for the man's reluctance to take
them where they wanted to go. More like where David wanted
to go, she grouched silently. She, like the driver, could do
without this risky midnight excursion. Her partner leaned over
the front seat and offered the driver a strong inducement to
follow his passenger's orders.

David's wallet was getting quite a workout lately. Darn good thing there was a bank ATM in the hotel lobby, and he didn't have to worry about finances. If she ever doubted that money made the world go round, she didn't anymore.

Regardless of what he'd said back in Baltimore, she was keeping track of his expenses. Whether he wanted it or not, when this was all over, she intended to send him a check.

The trip from shining wealth to wretched poverty was distressingly short. Their taxi followed the rough road snaking between mountains of moldering garbage to a tin-roofed huddle of huts jerry-rigged of plywood and tar paper. Beyond them, a dense jumble of squalid shacks ranged off up the mountainside into the gloom. In the distance, the twin spires of a church, silvered in thin moonlight, seemed to float from a pool of shadows.

A meager row of ancient streetlights was strung for no more than a few blocks down the road that passed for the shantytown's main street. The weak shafts of light they threw lost the battle of holding back the night.

David tapped the driver on the shoulder and brought the vehicle to a halt.

"We'll walk the rest of the way," he said, and ordered the driver to wait for them. Cara wasn't entirely sure the man would wait, even with the promised tip. This wasn't a place anyone would choose to be stranded in. As they scrambled out of the car, the driver threw them another strong warning to be careful.

The stench of human waste snaked from the dank waters of a nearby stream.

David switched on the flashlight he carried.

Back in the main part of the city, thousands of people still worked hard at having noisy fun amid the brilliant glow of hotels and amusement centers. Here, the two of them, with not another person in sight, were shrouded in darkness and brooding stillness. Not even the unhappy cry of a child broke the hovering silence. Maybe the unfortunate children living here learned early that crying wouldn't help.

It was a good thing David knew where he was going. She would have gotten lost within two minutes of wandering through a baffling, haphazard maze of narrow, filth-strewn streets and alleys.

Their harsh surroundings were softening her opinion of Manuel Pereira. If he'd been born into this pitiable level of poverty, she couldn't blame him for trying to squeeze them, or anyone else, for every penny he could get.

She sensed rather than saw the small shape that skittered across the alley only a few inches from her feet. Rats. An area like this must be overrun with rats. Her heart went out to the children, the babies, who lived here in these appalling conditions. Any doctor attempting to practice decent medicine amid this squalor would soon be overwhelmed by the lack of the most basic sanitation facilities.

David pointed to a small, cinder-block building whose few windows were heavily barred.

"There's the shop Pereira mentioned. According to the directions he gave me, his place should be right around here."

Somewhere close by, a dog erupted in a frenzy of barking.

The sudden commotion brought the two of them to a standstill.

From back in the direction of the stream, muffled shouts and a scurry of running footsteps rent the threatening silence. The unmistakable sound of a splash followed. Something large had just fallen—or was thrown—into the stream. Hundreds, maybe thousands of people either slept, or listened, their nerves on edge as her own, in the pulsing night. There was no reason to think the frightening sounds had anything to do with Manuel.

She had the sickening feeling that they did.

"Take this," David ordered, handing her the flashlight. He reached inside his jacket and drew out the black metal weapon he'd told her was a Glock semiautomatic. "This way," he said.

She took his arm and threw her light ahead of them as they hurriedly picked their way down the alley.

They almost tumbled into the ditch at the end of the lane. A sluggish, putrid stream snaked along the bottom of the gully. She played the light back and forth over the black water.

"There," she cried. "I think I saw something."

She walked a few yards upstream toward the faint glimmer of some small light-colored object caught at the dim edge of the flashlight's beam. A picture of Manuel's yellow hair flashed into her mind. At her side David uttered a soft curse. Apparently he'd made the same horrifying connection.

Her light fell on a long, rounded bundle of some sort lying in the water five or six yards away. A body, she recognized in horror. A body lying facedown and motionless in the stream.

"It's Manuel, David." She was sure of it, although she couldn't see his face.

David shoved the weapon back into his pocket. "You stay up here and hold my cane. Hold the light steady on the body."

The slope dropping down to the stream wasn't steep, but it was slick from the rain. David had to make his way down carefully to avoid sliding headfirst into the water. She followed, favoring her bandaged ankle, to give him what help she could. At the bottom of the ditch, he waded into water little more than a foot deep. Not deep enough to drown a conscious man.

Hoisting the inert body under the arms, he managed to drag it from the creek. She gave David his cane to make it easier for him to climb the hill and hooked a hand under one of the man's arms. Together they struggled to haul him, his clothing heavy with water, to the top of the embankment where they lowered him gently to the ground. The man's drenched clothing began to seep a black puddle into the earth around him. Carefully, so as not to worsen any of his injuries, she rolled the sodden victim onto his back.

She'd been prepared for the worst. Still, it was a shock to recognize someone she knew.

She knelt quickly beside Pereira's immobile body and shone her light on his wet face. The black eyes were wide and staring and glistened faintly in the cone of light. They did not blink. She pressed her fingers to the man's neck. No discernible pulse. She handed David the flashlight, hiked up her skirt and straddled the man to commence C.P.R.

It was difficult for David to kneel. Leaning on his cane, he bent and slipped a hand under the dripping blond head. Almost at once he drew his fingers away. Shaking his head slowly, he showed her his hand covered with dark stains of blood.

"You can't do anything more for him, Cara. His skull is crushed. He's gone."

She'd known that the moment she'd looked at the body after David had pulled it from the water, but she always viewed the death of a patient as a personal failure. When David laid him down before her, Manuel had become her patient. She refused to concede defeat until she'd done everything possible to avert it.

Today she'd accomplish no miracles. With a heavy sigh she gave up the useless attempt to save the man.

She sat back on her heels next to the lifeless body. In death poor Manuel looked pitifully young. No more than a teenager.

David fished a handkerchief from his back pocket and tried, without much success, to clean the blood from his hands.

"The kid was no role model." His quiet voice was filled with regret. "But he sure didn't deserve this."

"No one deserves this."

"Come on, Cara, we'd better get out of here."

"Aren't we going to call the police?"

"No. We'll let these people handle things in their own way. It's their neighborhood."

Others must have heard the scuffle. Not a single person had ventured out to help.

She had no right to condemn them. Perhaps mere survival in this awful place took all their energy. Maybe they had no pity to spare for one who came to grief in their midst.

Cara laid her hand on the dead man's chest and offered a silent prayer for him.

The possibility that Pereira might have been killed because of his connection with her lay like lead in her stomach.

"Come." David slid a hand under her arm to help her get to her feet.

To her relief the cab was still waiting for them. Its doors were locked, its engine was running and the driver was hunched over the wheel, peering anxiously through the windshield. He asked no questions when David squished back into the automobile, his shoes and the bottom of his trousers soaked. He'd barely pulled the door shut when the car sped off.

The compassion that she'd held onto for so long for Tommy as a friend in trouble gave way to disgust and rage.

If only she could see him right now and demand to know if he played any part in Manuel's death. If only she could face him and force him to explain why he'd thrown away his life. Why he'd brought so much pain into hers. Why he'd put not only her, but David, who meant him no harm, in danger.

But with the *mestizo*'s death, her last tenuous link to Tommy was gone.

Chapter 10

David heard the strain in Cara's disheartened whisper of good-night. Dirt smudged her chin and streaked her skirt. Mud daubed her white jogging shoes and the pink elastic bandage on her ankle. He'd knocked the largest globs of mud off his own black loafers, but they were still caked in the stuff.

She'd scarcely spoken a word on the way back to the hotel. Her lovely face was etched in lines of weariness. Dark circles of fatigue smudged her eyes.

This remarkable woman had slogged bravely through a day that had delivered a one-two punch that hit even a trained fighter such as himself in the gut. He wasn't about to let her walk all alone into a dark, empty room in a strange city.

"I'll come in with you for a moment."

She gave him no argument. He read relief in her eyes when she looked up at him and nodded. Inside, he reached in back of her to flip up the light switch just inside the door.

To him, any hotel room looked foreign and desolate in the middle of the night. Always a reminder that he was just passing through. Cara seemed to be suffering the same reaction. She wandered to the center of the room and stood there, looking around aimlessly, as if she didn't quite recognize the place and couldn't decide what to do next.

A little shiver rippled across the stiffness of her back. The shiver turned into a shake that threatened to take over her whole body.

Before her knees buckled, he hurried over and clasped an arm around her waist. Her hands jerked up defensively as if she meant to throw off his support. Instead her fingers fastened over the prop of his arm.

"I don't know what's come over me," she said in a reedy voice, as he led her to the sofa. "It's not as if I haven't seen death before. I've handled dozens of bloody emergency-room cases better than I'm handling this."

He understood her shaken reaction. She was trained to deal unemotionally with serious disease and critical injury. The professional detachment she'd developed, though, hadn't completely hardened her to the sight of violent death.

Neither had his. Finding the boy's bloody body had sickened him.

"Maybe this one came with a lot more personal emotional baggage than the others. It also came on the same day you had to fight off an attack. I can tell that your ankle hurts a lot more now than it did earlier. It didn't do your injury any good for you to be working it so hard tonight. Sit."

She sank onto the seat.

His contempt for Grant mushroomed. What kind of man could expose a woman, especially one he once professed to love, to sickening murder?

In the room's small refreshment bar he found a tiny bottle of brandy and poured it into a glass.

"Here. Drink this."

She used both hands to hold the glass steady as she sipped the liquor.

"I need to wash my hands," she said absently, holding up one hand, fingers spread, in front of her.

Her eyes widened and she darted him a stricken look.

"Oh, David!" she blurted. "*Your* hands."

She sprang to her feet, tipping the glass. A few drops of brandy spilled to the rug. She didn't seem to notice when he rescued the tumbler and set it on the table.

"You held Manuel's smashed head. Your hands were covered in his blood." She snatched up his left hand that still bore dark traces of red and inspected it.

"You've got to wash them. Right now. The bathroom's right through there. Give them a good hard scrubbing with soap and water—get every speck of blood off your fingers—don't forget your nails—it's important. I'm sure Manuel was promiscuous—he could have been involved with intravenous drugs—you never know—"

"Whoa!" He broke into her anxious, rapid-fire stream of instructions. "I'll take care of it. You sit down before you fall down. And finish that brandy." He stood over her, frowning, and made sure she obeyed his orders before he headed for the bathroom sink.

Several minutes later when she returned after cleansing her own hands, he was glad to see that the familiar medical practice of washing after treating a patient—albeit a dead man—had helped settle her some.

"It's almost two in the morning, Cara. Go to bed. If you like, I'll sit here until you fall asleep."

At a time like this, he asked himself, what kind of insensitive oaf would remain blazingly aware of the bed that dominated her room, and what happened in it the other night? After what Cara had been through today, he should be concentrating solely on looking after her. What the hell would it take to keep that damnable desire for her from roiling through him every waking hour?

"Thanks, David, but I wouldn't be able to sleep. I'd only lie there staring at the ceiling and thinking about Manuel."

Her face crumpled.

"Tell me the truth. Was that poor little man killed because of me? Because he was trying to get information about Tommy for me?"

He was convinced of it. Too much of a coincidence for it to be otherwise. But he wasn't about to heap any more grief on a woman who wasn't one to deny responsibility for her actions. An overzealous sense of obligation had driven her to Colombia in the first place.

He gave her shoulder a gentle squeeze.

"Take your sister's advice and stop blaming yourself for all the ills of the world. Manuel lived a precarious life. Who knows what kind of trouble he'd gotten himself into long before he ever met us." He hoped his shrug of dismissal was convincing. "He had dangerous connections. Most likely one of those connections chose tonight to settle an old score and we had the seriously bad luck to stumble into it."

A stretch of what he believed to be the truth, maybe. But not entirely impossible.

"I hope so." She kneaded tiredly at her forehead. He hated to see the mesmerizing blue of her eyes so dulled and troubled.

"I don't understand what's going on, David. I just wanted to help a friend. I had no idea it would lead to all this. I'd hate to think that I was responsible for—" She clapped her hand to her mouth, suppressing her cry of anguish.

He couldn't help it. The depth of her distress made him slide his arms around her shoulders and gather her to him. He recognized the tautness in her body, not much different from the tenseness that always gripped him just before embarking on another mission.

"Stop it, I said," he whispered against the fragile silk of her temple. "You've done enough thinking for one day."

He smoothed back her tousled hair and tightened his hold on her.

Alarm leapt into her eyes.

"No, David . . . I don't . . ."

Giving the lie to her weak protest, her hands crept to his chest and grasped his shirt as if it were a lifeline. With what could have been a faint sigh of defeat, she curved her softness against him and dropped her head onto his shoulder.

"Hush," he soothed, cuddling her close. "Hush. You've had one hell of a day. Let go of it." He rocked her gently in his arms until he felt some of the tension drain out of her.

He was holding her simply to comfort her, he told himself. Not because it filled him with pleasure. Not because of the comfort it brought him. He wasn't a boy. He could control himself. He wouldn't let their embrace get out of hand.

The justification he forced into his mind needed a lot more work to sound the least bit convincing.

His fingers encountered the pliant side of her right breast. By accident, he told himself. No way, what was left of his conscience countered. Her hand moved up to his shoulder, giving him the room to stroke gently back and forth over the yielding curve.

With a small sigh she shifted against him. The soft heat of her middle arched into him. He swallowed a groan. His manhood swelled to hot, throbbing life. He gritted his teeth.

This embrace isn't for your benefit, you jerk. It's for hers.

Cara clung to David's comforting solidity. She hadn't meant to thrust herself against him that way, but after the cold hard scene of death in the *barrio,* she so needed to be close to his wonderful warmth, his vibrant life.

She needed him to hold her. Needed to lean on the strength he never seemed to lose. Her own had fled when she'd had to walk away and leave that sad young man lying all alone in the dirt. Lying there perhaps because of her.

She squeezed her eyes shut against that dispiriting thought and snuggled her face into the strong steel wall of David's chest. The scent of him arrowed straight through her, leaving a nebulous, shivering need in its wake.

Her cheek picked up the vibrations of the low growl rumbling through his chest. A growl that sounded strangely like anger.

Before she could begin to wonder where the sudden anger came from, his fingers roughly clasped her chin and tilted her face upward. The miraculous heat of his mouth rid her of the chill that had clamped over her at the killing scene.

Large strong hands molded her breasts, blanketing her whole body in shuddering, wanting heat. The light fabric of her blouse and bra couldn't prevent her nipples from puckering and straining closer into the warmth of his palms.

Forever, it seemed, she'd craved to feel David's burning touch directly on her bare skin. Hard on her mental wish, he fumbled at the top button of her blouse.

Fearing that his large fingers wouldn't manage the tiny fasteners quickly enough, she slipped the remaining buttons out of their loops.

With the frustrating care of a person opening a longed-for Christmas gift, he slowly spread apart the sides of her blouse. The raptness of his expression as he gazed at her breasts barely concealed behind their small scallops of lace made her feel she possessed a sexual skill she never knew she had.

Slowly and reverently he drew the backs of his fingers down the valley of her breasts. A delicious quiver ran through her.

His trailing fingers reached the front fastening of her bra. He flicked open the hook and brushed aside the lace. The fullness of her breasts fell into his cradling hands.

"Your skin feels like warm, delicate satin."

She thrilled to the hoarse purr of his voice.

His thumbs brushed over her nipples, caressing both into tight, hard nubs.

A bright sting of pleasure shot through her. A soft cry of delight pulled from her throat.

His lips found the base of her throat. Her pulse hammered beneath the searing contact, and her head dropped back. With tormenting slowness his lips dragged a burning fuse down the rise of her chest.

In a flagrant plea for a more intimate contact she raised her hands to tangle in the thick waves of his hair, and arched her back to lift her breasts closer to his mouth.

He bent and brushed his lips teasingly over one piercingly sensitive tip. His tongue flicked out to taste.

A moan of purest pleasure escaped her. His muted groan echoed hers.

If he didn't give her more, she was afraid she might slip to the floor and beg him for it. Only his immediate, tantalizing response to that unspoken desire kept her from going that far. His hot, wet mouth engulfed the burning crest of her breast, bathing the whole of it in moist, aching fire.

Hovering want flared out and licked at her womanhood. Molten excitement rolled through her veins. She was sure she'd die if she didn't soon feel his searing mouth moving over every part of her.

She was ready to implore him for exactly that. He'd join her in that bliss in a heartbeat, she knew. His arousal pressed hot and hard against her. His breathing rasped as ragged as hers. One word from her and he'd stay the night.

Her whole body screamed at her to give him that word.

She moved a leg against his. Clammy cold brushed against her ankles. She glanced down. The bottoms of his trousers were still soaked from the stream.

The whole frightening day rushed back at her—the attack, Manuel's broken body lying forlornly by the ditch.

Her pleasure, her happiness at being held in David's arms flowed away like water from a smashed pitcher.

Not all of it, though. A different kind of happiness stayed with her. A feeling that went way beyond a desire for sex. Far beyond the simple affection and admiration she'd had for David Reid since they'd met. A feeling that lodged deep inside her, so overwhelming it almost felt like hurt. So powerfully emotional, she flailed about for logic to counter it.

What she thought she felt for David made no sense.

How could she be in love with him? Only a teenager fell in love this easily. This fast. Or this hard. Especially not this hard.

The strange feeling flooding her heart had to be the result of the guilty loneliness that had plagued her for so long. Or stress. Or the horror of the depressing scene they'd gone through an hour ago.

That was it. She grabbed for the rational excuse with both hands. She and David were making love in reaction to the psychological trauma of today's attack and Pereira's death. This growing ache in her heart for him was simply part of that perfectly normal reaction to severe mental stress.

Was this what she wanted? Making love with David Reid as a form of therapy? She didn't turn up her nose at treatment of any kind that helped make a hurt better. But the therapy of sex with David, no matter how wonderful, how consoling, would only complicate her life and lead to more pain.

Pointless to hope for anything more than the relief of sex from a man who'd made it quite clear that he was with her only because of a mission he never wanted any part of in the first place.

She already knew firsthand how destructive a one-sided relationship could be. No matter how much she wanted David, she wasn't about to foist herself on a man who was unwilling—perhaps unable—to make any real commitment to her other than the purely professional obligation he'd taken on.

"David."

She wasn't sure her body, still straining for the relief only he could give it, would let her do what she wanted to do.

She pushed against his chest.

His hold on her didn't budge.

"David, it's been a terrible night." She tried again to escape his grasp, with no more success than the last effort. "We need time to recover from it before we get ourselves into something we might both be sorry for."

From the naked desire flushing David's face, his struggle to control his rapid breathing, she half hoped he might contradict her. Half hoped he'd simply continue to lock her to him and kiss her senseless. Wished he might order her once again to quit thinking so much and get on with what they both so obviously needed.

"Yes," he growled. "Of course." He opened his arms, allowing her escape.

She wrapped her blouse over her still throbbing breasts and tucked it into her skirt. Crazy to feel so dejected at getting precisely the response she'd asked for from him. She turned away, pulling her professional persona around her.

"Get out of those wet things as soon as you can," she ordered, pleased that her voice contained such a slight wobble he might not have heard it. "Who knows what kinds of contaminants were in that water. Take a shower when you get back to your room. I'll do the same. We should see about getting tetanus boosters when we get back to the States."

Putting more distance between them should help her resist the impulse to rush back into his arms. She hoped he wouldn't read that embarrassing admission in the quickness with which she scurried back to the couch. Picking up the tumbler from the table, she drained the last half inch of brandy left in it.

"I suppose we'll be leaving tomorrow," she said. "There's no point in staying any longer."

"I agree."

His voice was cold. And unlike hers, completely steady. Distancing himself from her, his anger was written in the careful stiffness of his body, in the guarded blankness of his face.

With humiliating eagerness to get away from her, he limped quickly to the door and yanked it open.

How could she blame him? She'd wantonly led him on, only to cut him off without granting him the physical release her teasing actions had given him every right to expect.

"We leave tomorrow," he said with curt directness. Without bothering to look back at her, he pulled the door shut behind him.

Exhaustion swept over her. She might have fallen to the floor if the couch hadn't been there to catch her.

The people who called her search a crazy obsession were right, she decided, with a surge of anger at the foolish compulsion that had led her here. She should never have come on a mission that led only to the death of a man she barely knew, and a tangle of emotions over a man who didn't want her, except in bed.

David was a decent man. He hadn't pressed her on that when he could have.

He couldn't help his lack of any serious feeling for her. Any more than she could help the feelings that raged through her for him.

David lay in his lonely bed, his body still aching from the strain of being denied what it so strongly craved. Cara never knew how close he'd come to laying her down on the floor of her room and taking her with or without her consent. She'd wanted the same thing, he was certain, until thoughts of the damnable Grant turned her off.

Only fair if she was having as lousy a night as he.

If he needed further proof that he was now nowhere near the man he used to be, the incident at the religious procession this afternoon had provided it. In spades. Before he was shot up, he could have prevented those goons from getting anywhere near Cara. He could have left them in the dirt in a few capable moves.

No more.

He'd mentally castigated Tommy for involving her in a killing. But David Reid had been the one to lead her to that scene of murder in the *barrio*. Led her there against his better judgment.

He frowned in puzzlement. It was so hard to refuse her anything. No one else was able to make him do something he didn't want to do. Why should it be any different with her?

His mouth jerked into an ironic smile. For starters, she never allowed him to refuse her anything. Not even when he knew refusal would be for her own good.

That enraging thought made him hurl a sharp curse into the quiet dark of his room. For the third time since he'd hauled his tortured body into bed, he reached over and clicked on the bedside lamp. He shot a baleful glance at the crumpled bit of paper lying on top of a glossy brochure on the nightstand.

Damn. He should never have stopped to make that quick search of Manuel's pockets just before he led Cara back to the taxi. If he hadn't found that wet and almost illegible note he wouldn't be facing this problem now. And he should never have given in to the damnable inquisitiveness that sent him back down to the lobby to search the rack of advertising brochures aimed at tourists for the note's same two words.

He snatched up the colorful pamphlet and absently flicked it against his chest as he pondered the fix he'd placed himself in. He didn't have to read the brochure. He'd already done that several times.

Manuel could have scribbled those words for any number of reasons, David argued lamely with himself. They didn't necessarily refer to the information Pereira had planned to give them. Maybe the enterprising young man had been planning to branch out his business to the resort trade. Maybe he was thinking about taking a vacation. The five hundred dollars he'd demanded for his information would have helped him do that.

David threw himself back down on the pillow. He knew damn well what the note meant. The only real question was: What was he going to do about it?

Undoubtedly the smartest thing to do would be to let Cara go on believing that they'd come to the end of her search.

The attack at the village was bad enough. Pereira's death scared the hell out of him for her safety. He wanted nothing more than to get her out of this threatening place as fast as possible.

He gave a firm nod of decision. That's what he'd do. She'd done more than enough for Tommy. Tomorrow he'd take her back to Baltimore.

He tossed the brochure back toward the nightstand. It skidded across the tabletop and fell to the floor. He left it there.

Chapter 11

David watched Cara toss her travel bag onto the bed and pull open the zipper. His own packed case waited by the door.

"After last night," he said with a hopeful nod, "I'm sure you've had enough of this whole thing. You're more than ready to go home. I know I am."

She gave him a dispirited smile. "I can believe that, David, after what I've put you through. Yes. I'm finally giving up on trying to find Tommy."

He should be glad. He shouldn't let that tone of flat defeat in her voice bother him. He kept his mouth pressed tightly shut.

She strode to the dresser and scooped up a sweater and a couple of blouses from the top drawer. She folded a blouse neatly into the case and stacked another on top.

"What other choice do I have?"

Just a rhetorical question, he reminded himself. No need to give her an answer.

"I may be too darn tenacious for my own good, but I'm not stupid. After all our work—" she flicked him a glance "—all your hard work, David, Pereira was our only lead. With him gone, our chances of finding Tommy are nil."

She walked to the closet and slipped a dress from its hanger. "It's just that..." She halted halfway back to the bed and chewed on her lower lip. "Well, I've come so far, it's hard to leave without being able to confront Tommy about—"

"Damn it, woman," David broke in. "Stop talking about that man. Stop living your life around him."

Fury seethed through him. With her it was always Tommy. She claimed she was never really in love with the man, but the louse still had to mean something to her. In spite of everything he'd done, everything that had happened to her here in Colombia, it was still Tommy.

David gnashed his teeth. The thought of her once being Grant's lover—the thought of her as being anyone's lover but his—inflamed him. A totally irrational reaction. He wasn't in the market for commitment. And even if he were, he wanted so much better for her than himself.

He heaved a sigh of frustration. This wasn't about him. Nor was it about his feelings. It was about Cara and her single-minded efforts to help a longtime friend. How could he fault her for wanting to see a mission through to the end? Exactly what he'd always done himself.

Until now.

That repugnant idea surfaced in his mind. Not only was his silence forcing Cara to quit, but he was quitting, too. The admission made him squirm.

He was quitting. Why? Was he afraid of what might happen if she ever did meet up with that jerk again? Was he throwing in the towel on a job he didn't like out of sheer jealousy of a man for whom he felt nothing but contempt?

That question was one he didn't want to touch. He wasn't ready to deal with what jealousy that deep might imply.

One thing he did know: The loyalty to a man and the devotion to an idea that drove Cara had to be respected, whether he approved of it or not.

Concern for her safety wasn't the only worry biting him. If she went home believing she'd failed, would she ever really be through with the detestable Tommy? Everything he'd learned about her made him doubt that. How many more years might she go on struggling under that needless load of guilt she carried?

He wanted her to be completely through with Dr. Thomas Grant. He wanted her to be happy. She'd known so much heartache, she was overdue for enough happiness to balance the scales.

He yearned to get her away from this dangerous place. Nevertheless he had to concede that a woman who strived so hard to accomplish what she'd set out to do had a right to make her own decision on whether or not to take this final step.

Angry at himself for not having the guts to look her in the eyes and go on lying to her—or at least, not telling her the whole truth—he yanked the advertisement from his pocket and thrust it out to her.

"Here. I found a note mentioning this place on Manuel's body."

Cara looked up from her packing and gazed at him across the bed. "On Manuel's body? What is it?" Dropping the dress she was holding onto the case, she took the pamphlet from him.

She opened the brochure and glanced through it. "I can't read this, David. It's printed in Spanish."

"You're holding a brochure advertising a luxury casino-resort on Colombia's Caribbean coast."

"A resort? You mean the one Manuel mentioned?"

He aimed a mental curse at the hope he saw springing into her face. Another at himself for putting it there.

"I've no way of knowing for sure, but I'd guess that it is."

She turned back to the cover page and took a second look.

"Cartagena. I can make out that much. This place is in Cartagena."

"It's a few miles up the coast from Cartagena, almost four hundred miles north of here. From those photos of what look to be swinging singles lounging on the beach and in the bars, I don't think the place is a family resort. I'd guess it's aimed mainly at well-heeled South American businessmen looking for a place to unwind without the missus and kids."

"Didn't Pereira tell you that Tommy had been seen there only two days ago?"

David nodded reluctantly.

"So there's a chance he might still be there." She showed the first vitality he'd seen in her all morning. "A chance I might finally be able to confront him."

The frown that hardened David's mouth pushed up from deep inside him. Maybe his personal sense of honor gave him no choice about passing the information along to her. It didn't follow that he had to make acting on that intelligence easy for her.

"This isn't just any resort, Cara. Our going there involves serious risk. Indications are that drug money is tied up in the place. There isn't any doubt now that Tommy is protected by powerful friends who don't take kindly to our efforts to contact him. Manuel's death proves that."

"But last night you said that it—" She shook her head and waved away the objection. "Never mind. I guess I really knew that you were only trying to make me feel better."

"I figure the kid got it because he started asking pointed questions of someone a lot closer to the center of the drug trade than we did."

Cara laid a pleading hand on his chest.

"Try to understand, David. It has taken me so long to come this far, I hate to give up when I might be close to finding Tommy. There's so much I've got to know for sure. If he's still on heroin. If he actually was behind what happened to Manuel, what happened to us. I've got to know that there's no hope for Tommy Grant before I can walk away from him."

"Walk away?" David erupted, throwing up his hands. "No one could ever accuse you of walking away from anything. I've had no luck whatever in getting you to walk away from this."

"You're wrong, David. I'm ready to do that. I'll make this one last effort to reach Tommy. If he's at the resort and I'm able to speak to him, I'll urge him to come back with me and enter the special treatment facility I told you about. If he refuses, that's it. This has nothing to do with guilt, David. If anything, what I feel for Tommy now is sheer rage at what he's done, for throwing his life away."

She spoke with more conviction than he'd ever heard in her voice before. Maybe if she cleared this last dangerous hurdle, she might truly free herself of her obsession with her former fiancé.

"It's not just for his benefit that I want to go to the resort, David. Frankly I loathe the idea of letting those horrible people send me packing. Even if I don't find Tommy there, at least I'll have the satisfaction of putting an end to what you call my mission by myself. It infuriates me to think of having that decision forced upon me."

David marveled at the fire in her eyes, the boldness in her voice. How could a man help but admire a woman like that, even if she was making life difficult for both of them?

He wasn't about to let that admiration show. Further encouragement was the last thing she needed.

"That's a nice, neat script you've presented there, Cara. But nobody tangles with Colombian traffickers and comes out unscathed. The last time I tackled drug lords on their own turf I was fully armed and backed up by a team of well-trained men." He paused to let that frightening observation sink in, then slapped his damaged thigh. "As you can see, I came out of that confrontation in a lot worse shape than when I went in. I won't expose you to that danger."

"Come on, David. My going to the resort to see Tommy is not the same as what you did. I'm not trying to hinder anyone's drug operations in any way. I couldn't if I wanted to."

"An Avianca flight leaves for Cartagena this afternoon," he said brusquely. "I'll investigate the place without you and report back."

"That's not going to work. If Tommy is there, he won't speak to you. He doesn't know you. I'll have to talk to him personally. I'm the only one who has a chance of convincing him to come back to the States."

"If my own disastrous experience with these guys doesn't make any impression on you," David said grimly, "maybe this will. A couple of years ago an American reporter tried to reach Dan Kane for an interview. The reporter's body was found shot through the head and dumped on a *barrio* garbage heap. He'd been to that same resort only a few days earlier."

He was happy to see Cara pale.

"It was that incident that prompted our people to look into the ownership of the place and make the connection to a drug consortium. Although they haven't been able to prove it to the satisfaction of the legal types yet."

"All right, David, you've succeeded in scaring me. But it doesn't change my mind. You're quite willing to accept danger. You knew that great personal risk came with being a SEAL. Do you think I can't do something of the same because I'm a woman?"

"Of course not. I've known military women who've made it their business to deal with personal danger."

"Then why not me?"

"Because I—"

He chopped off the astonishing words about to spill out of him unbidden.

"Call me overly sentimental," he drawled with more than a hint of sarcasm. "But I wouldn't much like to have to haul you out of a filthy stream like we did Manuel."

The way her jaw firmed and her chin jutted upward told him even before she spoke that he'd lost the battle.

"I'll be on that flight, David. You can't stop me. But you didn't sign on to tackle drug lords on their own turf, as you put it. I don't want you to come with me. I have good reason to take the risk. You don't."

His eyebrows shot up. "I've no reason to take the risk? My dear Dr. Merrill, in case you haven't noticed, I hold a deeply personal interest in traffickers. They wrecked my body and my life. They attacked you. They killed a man who was working for me. How many more reasons would it take to make it my business?"

"But there's really no need for you to go. If Tommy's there, I'm sure our relationship is more likely to protect me than to harm me. To put it bluntly, David, there's no reason for him to protect you. Another thing. Aren't you overlooking the possibility that perhaps these people aren't after me at all? Maybe they found out who you are and they're after you for whatever you did to them."

"Not likely. The names of my team haven't exactly been plastered on billboards around the world. If you go, I go. And if you think I couldn't find some way to stop you then, lady, you don't know me."

He advanced to crowd her toe-to-toe and stared icily down into her eyes.

"Here's the deal. I'll only allow you to get on that plane with me if you promise two things." He stabbed up a finger in front of her face. "First, this is going to be no more than a quick overnight trip. Since they don't know about Manuel's note, they won't be expecting us, and if we don't meet Tommy, it should take a little time for whoever's in back of all this to find out we're there. If we do run into Tommy, I'm relying on your instincts that he wouldn't cause you any harm, and his presence might afford you some protection. So far, their aim doesn't seem to be to take us out for good. But we don't know what the hell's going on here."

A warning glare came with the reminder.

"I'm also hoping," David continued, "that the resort management would frown on anyone opening up on us on sight with automatic weapons fire that's liable to take out other paying guests and result in some very negative advertising. But I don't care if the guy meets you at the damn plane and falls into your arms, we're taking the first flight out tomorrow morning."

He threw up a second finger. "Second. I want your solemn word that if we don't find the jerk there, you'll put him and his problems behind you once and for all and go home."

She snapped her hand to her shoulder in a Girl Scout salute. "Fair enough, David. I promise."

"Make no mistake, Cara. I intend to hold you to that pledge."

Under the gruffness he took pains to project at her lay the maddening suspicion that if this woman asked it of him, he'd parachute naked into the vicious green maw of the deepest Colombian jungle.

* * *

Drug money had transformed a wide crescent of white sand fronting the turquoise waters of the Caribbean into a tropical garden of Eden steeped in sun.

The resort pampered its high-rolling guests in sybaritic splendor. One side of its massive lobby opened on a waterfall cascading amid artful plantings of coconut palms and masses of jungle foliage. Gilded reproductions of spectacular pre-Columbian masks and artifacts glinted from whitewashed walls reaching to the vaulted ceiling. A South American contingent of jet-setters reclined on plush oversize chairs and sofas covered in fabric as brightly colored as the live parrots perching among the branches of the aged ficus trees planted in the marble floor.

All this beauty and opulence was bought at the cost of death and tears and untold numbers of ruined lives. That she had to be part of it for any time at all turned Cara's stomach.

David wanted one of the separate villas that would afford them more privacy and a secondary means of escape, rather than the single entry of a hotel room that could be easily blocked. Hearing the cost of the only one available made Cara's eyes bug out. She could very well find herself in hock to David Reid for the rest of her life.

He'd made it clear she wasn't to have a room of her own. He intended to stay within shouting distance, he'd told her. And she could see for herself that the women accompanying the other male guests weren't likely to be sleeping apart from their escorts. True, too, that the svelte, perfectly made-up women hanging on their arms didn't look much like wives. Insisting on her own room would only draw unwanted attention to the two *norteamericanos*.

Hoping to run into Tommy and get their difficult meeting over with, she'd screened every man she saw in the lobby and on their way to the villa. David was right about the place catering mainly to Latino businessmen, along with a smattering of Japanese tourists. She heard no English being spoken.

From its higher elevation, the lavish bungalow afforded a breathtaking ocean view, which David barely glanced at. No

sooner had the bellboy left, than her careful partner sat down
to pore over the detailed layout of the resort he found on a
desk. He then made a circuit of the house and its surroundings.

"Could be worse," he pronounced when he returned to her.
"The place is heavily landscaped and not easily accessible. If
any unwanted visitors show up at the door, we'll have another
way to make it out of here. There's a narrow access road that
runs to the back of the resort. The dirt driveway passes by this
villa at the bottom of a fairly steep slope. To get to it, we'd have
to pick our way around trees and shrubbery, but so would
anyone following us. No way out through the back, but the
front end of the road leads to the marina. If the need arises and
we can't make it to the rental car, we can head for the marina.
If we're very lucky, we can pirate one of the motor launches
docked there."

To her, that seemed like a major *if*. "Hopefully we won't
need any of those options."

She and David dined by themselves on the patio of their villa.
Their fish fillets sautéed in coconut milk was served by their
personal waiter. The fish—only hours out of the ocean—was
delectable. The atmosphere was spoiled, though, by the surly
waiter who made little effort to contain his animosity, or perhaps his resentment, toward Americans. After he'd cleared
away the remains of the meal, she wasn't sorry to see the last of
him.

"You stay in the bungalow," David ordered, "while I re-
connoiter the place to try to find out if Grant and Robert are
still here. I'll have to be a lot more careful with my inquiries
than we were in the city, and I can do that better without you.
I know the language. You don't. If I don't spot Tommy in the
lounges or dining rooms, I'll wander the casino and see what I
can pick up."

David's choice of phraseology didn't cheer her. She didn't
think he'd have too much trouble gleaning information from
any woman who had some to give. Nor would he be too fussy,
she suspected, about using whatever romantic techniques were

necessary to elicit the information. Simply a means to an end, he'd assert, rightly. Just business.

She still didn't like it.

"Come back and let me know the moment you find out anything," she said. "If you do see Tommy, don't try to talk to him without me. You might scare him away."

"If he's here, you'll know it two minutes after I do. The sooner you see that bast— The sooner you see Grant," he said, backtracking, "the sooner I can get you away from here. After I leave, lock the door behind me. I have my key." He frowned down at her. "Believe me, Dr. Merrill, if you so much as stick your pretty nose out of this villa without me tonight, I'll pack you out of this place so quickly it'll make your head spin."

He could make her head spin with a lot less than that, Cara admitted dolefully. Just looking into his eyes could rob her of equilibrium, and that was nothing compared to what his lips could do to her.

Dutifully following instructions, she shot the dead bolt after him.

Which left her all alone in a villa definitely built for two. Judging from the bedroom's overripe decor, David had engaged the honeymoon suite. A triumph of pink satin, garlanded in red silk roses, was borne aloft by a dimpled flight of gold plaster cherubs. The circular bed beneath the canopy was enormous enough for the two of them to get lost in.

The living room boasted a large, comfortable-looking couch.

She couldn't help but wonder what sleeping arrangements David had in mind. If he insisted on the two of them sharing that colossal bed, she was afraid she'd make it very easy for him to find her.

Spending the rest of the evening watching Spanish-language TV on the giant screen in the air-conditioned bungalow didn't appeal to her. She left a light on at the front of the villa to guide David back and clicked off the other lights in the house before wandering out to the darkened patio.

After the frenetic clamor and chill of the city, she savored the calming stillness and languorous warmth of the Caribbean evening. She kicked off her shoes and stretched out on one of the thick-pillowed chaise longues.

With David deep in her thoughts, she smiled to herself. He'd proven that she hadn't been mistaken in placing her complete trust in him. If he hadn't told her of the advertising brochure, she'd never have known about it. He must have had to call on the self-control of a saint to overcome his natural instinct to take command, and instead, to allow her to make her own decision about coming here. The respect his action showed her only strengthened what she already felt for him.

Not that those feelings made a whit of difference. It was only a question of time until he walked out of her life and back to his mountain, or to his Richmond home.

There was no point in brooding about a situation she couldn't change. More intelligent to try to enjoy the moment in a location specifically designed to afford her every comfort and pleasure.

Crimson bougainvillaea climbed the trellised arbor roofing the patio, and baskets of purple and white fuchsia hung from the rafters. Lovely terraced plantings of exotic flowers, many of which she'd never seen before, tumbled down the gentle slope to an inviting private pool.

Small mushroom lamps illuminated the half-dozen stepping-stones leading down to the pool, and threw soft washes of light over lush mounds of white and pink blossoms bordering the way. Their saucer-size blooms emitted a heavenly fragrance into the humid air. On the far side of the pool, another lamp, hidden among foliage, played over the narrow jet of water spurting in a crystal arc from a clump of ferns. The fountain splashed a gentle rhythmic music into the night.

A huge, two-person whirlpool tub waited for her use in the villa's palace-size bathroom. But she found the pool, its waters shadowed purple in the darkness, much more tempting.

What could ten minutes in the pool hurt, anyway? She was really fed up with allowing nameless hoods to dictate her every moment, her every move. A quick dip and she could be dressed and back inside before David returned.

She hadn't packed a swimsuit. This trip was far from being any sort of vacation. But the pool was naturalized amid greenery thick enough to screen her from prying eyes. From the high ground of the patio, she could spot only a corner of the red-tiled roofline of the villa next door. The pool, at its lower elevation, was even more secluded.

Feeling adventurous, she pulled the combs from her hair and let the golden strands fall down her back. She unzipped her dress, stepped out of it and tossed it on the couch. Bra and panties followed. She needed no more than the small puddles of light displaying each step to make her way down to the pool.

Set amid a narrow swale of perfectly manicured grass at the bottom of the steps, a curved ledge of smooth granite formed a kind of bench giving easy access to the water. She folded herself down on the large rock that still held some of the sun's warmth and slipped naked into the darkened pool. The water was pleasantly warm and deep enough for her to swim lazily around its circumference.

In contrast to the frantic pace she and David had set in Bogota, the quiet, seemingly isolated surroundings, the whole indulgent ambience of the place began to soothe her frazzled nerves. She flipped herself over on her back and closed her eyes, moving her arms and legs only enough to keep her afloat.

She wasn't sure how long she'd luxuriated in the pool, but she wanted to spend just a few more relaxing minutes here. She made another lazy pass under the jetting fountain. And another.

Above the trickling sound of the fountain, she heard the muted scrape of the sliding glass door opening onto the patio.

She didn't need to see David standing in the deep shadows above her to become vividly aware of his presence. She felt his gaze fall on her like a touch in the starlight.

Her heart took one hard leap within her chest.

An alarm tried to make itself heard in the recesses of her mind.

The warning was drowned out in the rush of dark excitement, as primitive and powerful as the wild and pagan depths of the Colombian jungle, streaking through her.

She'd never wanted anything in this world more than she lusted right now to experience David Reid's miraculous touch on every part of her. The soul-deep wanting flared out from her heart to take over her whole being.

She'd never been a seductress, but she knew exactly what she was doing when she set her feet on the blue painted floor of the pool and slowly uncurled from the water. With her back to the patio, she crooked her arms above her shoulders and lifted her hair to let the long, wet strands drift through her fingers.

David's plan to bundle Cara into the car and drive her away from here blasted from his mind the moment he saw her.

The beauty of her slender form etched in moonlight and rising like some mythic water goddess from the shadowy pool held him transfixed. For a breathless moment, his lungs failed to expand. His heart to pump.

A man with an ounce of decency would turn and go back inside, he told himself. A man with a shred of honor left in him would call out and make his presence known.

He stood silent, rooted to the spot.

God help him! If he didn't take her in his arms and feel her soften against him in the next minute he was liable to go berserk.

The graceful, languid movement of her arms, gestures as old as Eve, told him that she knew he watched her.

That heady observation joined forces with the unstoppable feelings she called up in him and compelled him slowly and irresistibly toward the small lagoon. He'd set his foot on the second stone step when she turned her head and looked up at him over her shoulder.

He felt the ground shift beneath his feet. Whether from another of the region's continual earthquakes, or from the impact of her soft smile of silent invitation, he couldn't tell.

Desire stormed through him, swamping his native caution, his fear that she might turn away from the ugliness of his body, his apprehension about what making love to her might do to him. The conviction that he wasn't nearly good enough for her

threaded into his mind. And fell before the vanquishing power
of his need.

His entranced gaze fixed on the long, elegant curve of her
back, on the flare of her hips veiled in sapphire water, he
shucked off shoes and clothes.

Still holding her back to him, she hadn't moved from the
middle of the pool. Her fingers gently stirring the waters at her
side, she waited for him.

Grateful for the darkness that cloaked his disfigured body,
he lowered himself to the curved stone at the side of the pool
and launched himself noiselessly into the tepid water. Not entirely certain he wasn't simply indulging in another secret midnight fantasy, he swam the short distance toward her and rose
to his feet half an arm's length in back of her.

Slowly, half afraid the ravishing dream in front of him might
dissolve into a mist, he reached out to touch his fingertips to the
exquisite tracery of her spine.

She let out a low, shuddering sigh.

The satisfying sound of her pleasure made the whole miraculous scenario real. Her ardent responsiveness to his touch—*his*
touch, no one else's—brought him a rush of raw male power.
Power that must have been there all along, but that he hadn't
been able to unlock.

He walked his fingers to the delicate, vulnerable curve of her
neck, and started downward again, slowly counting off each of
her vertebrae. His worshiping lips followed that entrancing
track beneath the water to the last hard rounded nub of her
backbone. Never before had he sought out intelligence on territory any more fascinating than this.

He smoothed his hands slowly up the supple column of her
back. Over the beautiful turn of her shoulders. Down the
trembling length of her arms.

"David," she breathed. "David."

Never had the name seemed so uniquely his as when it fell
from her lips.

Realization erupted into his mind like a flare of white fire.
The woman who filled his dreams was his. His to fully ex-
plore, to lovingly caress, to miraculously possess. His for the

here and now. He'd deal with the pain of tomorrow when it came.

Not for a moment did he allow himself to believe that what he was doing was right for either of them. Especially not right for her. But he'd shot way beyond being able to factor right or wrong into his compulsive need.

He stepped closer, enclosing her in his arms and bringing his torso and thighs into direct contact with her back and hips. A film of cool water slicked the heat of her satiny nakedness.

The shiver that raced through her leapt from her body to his.

A blaze of sensation engulfed him. His whole body so long tight and cold turned molten. A slow hot surf of thickened blood rolled through his veins and flooded his manhood.

A moan scraped up from the bottom of his chest.

Her head dropped back against him. She reached up to grasp his shoulders.

His foraging hands greedily encircled the soft, warm mounds of her breasts, the outline and weight of their luscious contours already etched into the skin of his palms. He rubbed them over her nipples. Her fingers spasmed over his shoulders. Her nails clawed into his skin. He didn't mind the slight pain.

Only by reminding himself that he could return later and pay greater homage to the arousing loveliness of her breasts was he able to slowly move his hands down over the hard ridge of her rib cage to the dip of her narrow waist.

His fingers broke the surface of the water and found her navel. He lingered to investigate the tiny, perfectly sculpted hollow, then splayed his hands over the silken curve of her stomach.

Every inch of the flawless body that came under his searching touch notched his delight, his thirst for her, higher. And with every inch, his palms and fingers grew more sensitive, meticulously recording the smallest change in the texture of her skin, the slightest ripple of pleasure that moved through her.

What she was doing for him went way beyond allowing him to enjoy simple sexual pleasure again. In making love with him, she was opening areas of his soul locked tight for what felt to be ages.

Tingling heat gushed into his lips eager to map the same enrapturing sector as his fingertips.

He nuzzled his face into her wet hair. The intoxicating scent of her robbed his brain of any further ability to command his actions. Propelled solely by impulse of his dazzled senses, he bent his legs slightly to match his body to hers and drew her closer, fitting the enticing roundness of her bottom against his throbbing arousal.

His pulse thundered out a volley of short, hard beats. His hand skimmed downward to comb through the silky floss at the base of her torso.

His open mouth, pressed to the side of her neck, filled with the taste of sweet wild honey. The rapid flutter of her pulse registered on his tongue. The sweet intimacy of it almost brought him to his knees, and stoked a craving to taste all the secret places of her body. Before the night was through, he promised himself, he'd accomplish that mission.

His hand continued its entrancing journey over the tiny distance to the wet satin joining of her thighs. The merging that on her bed a few nights ago had been barriered from his direct touch.

A tremor raced through her. She made a sound like a small night bird's cry.

A soul-deep ache to bury himself within the soft, healing loveliness of her took hold of him. Hauling in great lungfuls of heavy humid air, he battled with all his strength against the powerful urge to take her immediately. It was too soon. He wanted this experience to be as wonderful for her as he could make it. He wanted to imprint this one night of love with him so deep in her soul, she'd never forget it.

As he never would. It was all he'd ever have of her.

His slight nudge turned her effortlessly in his arms. She pressed the fresh, pure sweetness of her naked body into him as easily as if she truly belonged to him.

A wild shudder of pleasure ripped intimately through him.

He vised her against him so tightly that not so much as a whisper of air could come between them and he claimed her mouth.

The searing contact of the womanly body branding his lit a fiery pleasure in his pulsing center. He tore his mouth from hers only to let his bursting lungs gasp in air. With feverish cries she frantically sought his mouth again and raked her nails over the newly sensitized skin of his back.

God, how he wanted. He burned with wanting. Every cell of his body was trembling crazy with want.

Her fingers scraped down his spine to his buttocks. Pure torture to feel their slow journey over the top of his thigh. Sweet agony to wait forever for the intimate touch he longed for.

Just as he was about to rasp out an order, her fingers stroked along his rigid length and closed his pulsing flesh within their velvet flame.

A strangled cry thrust up from his soul and burst out into the shivering night.

Her consent drawn indelibly upon his body in the language of love, he stretched them both out upon the water. Their gazes locked, their arms moving in sync, he swam with her to the side of the pool and swept her from the water. She felt light, buoyant in his arms. He set her down on the rounded edge of the long, smooth rock and gently lowered her into the slight hollow carved in the stone's slanted surface.

She lay before him in silver rays of moonlight, clothed only in a transparent shimmer of water and a delicate filigree of shadows. With an angel's smile, she held out her open arms for him.

He choked back a moan of awe, of wonder.

Chapter 12

He started an awkward scramble from the water to reach her. Instinct halted him.

Not on land. His first incredible union with the woman who'd grabbed onto his life with both gentle hands and wouldn't let go should happen within the pool. In the water that sometimes allowed him almost to forget his broken body.

He moved back into the water and stood in front of her. Setting his hands at her waist, he slowly drew her up to face him. Without him speaking a word she seemed to understand what he wanted, and edged herself closer to the stone's rim.

Fighting grimly to hold his raging need in check, he forced his hands to cup her beautiful face with the utmost gentleness. Shaking with the effort to keep himself from clamping his open mouth over hers and invading that sweet moist entrance to her body, he managed to do no more than reverently touch his lips to hers.

He hoped his tenderness was showing her that he viewed this lovemaking as something very far from the meaningless coupling he'd proposed at the village. He wanted her to know that he realized her loving generosity was bestowing something very special, very meaningful on him. She could have no idea how much this act of love meant to a man who hadn't been able to bring himself to risk any intimate relations with a woman for almost two years.

He nudged apart her knees with his hips and fit himself between them.

Cooling water lapped at his legs.

Flame engulfed his throbbing center.

She drew her legs up on either side of his and tilted herself back a little, seeking their perfect position. The piercingly sensitive tip of his flesh slid over the soft, yielding center of her femininity.

His rasping moan built a chord with her tremulous cry. She gasped and trembled and clutched him.

The last of his control snapped. He spread his mouth wide over hers. The soft lush ripeness of her lips opened under his passionate onslaught. He plunged his tongue inside her. And craved as ardently as once he'd fought for life itself to drive another part of himself within her.

His whole body shaking in the violent grip of desire, he slid his hands beneath the silky firmness of her thighs and grasped the smooth rounds of her bottom to lift her onto him.

As wild now with need as he, she wound her arms tensely around his neck, her legs tightly around his hips. He braced her on the rock behind her and thrust himself into the burning mystery of her.

Never had he felt so consumed with pleasure, with a sense of fulfillment entirely new to him. Greater than the pleasure of sexual intimacy, oceans of satisfaction poured through him because this one particular woman above all others was sharing herself with him.

Her breasts were pressed against his. The furious throbbing of her heart matched the frenetic beating of his. Her rapid gasps rasped from her throat as quickly as his.

She ground herself against him, taking him deeper into the smooth, searing luxury of her body. Deeper still. He battled to keep himself from hurtling over the crest before he was sure she'd reached it.

Suddenly she bucked and bowed back into a quivering arc.
And spasmed tightly around him.

What was left of his rationality shattered into a million tiny
pieces of blissful sensation.

Mindless, he rode a pulsing crimson cloud of pleasure.

Cara dragged in great gulps of air as the scattered shards of
her mind slowly wandered back from the ecstatic oblivion into
which David had catapulted her.

Draped limply over his hard body, she had no strength left
to cling to him. He, too, was gasping for breath as his heart and
lungs like hers wound back to normal. His arms shivered with
the exertion of holding them clenched around her to keep her
from slipping down into the water.

She could stay like this forever, utterly replete, skin to naked skin with David, reveling in the wonder of feeling him still
a part of her.

"Holding you like—like this feels—wonderful—" he panted.
"But you've completely demolished me—I can't—can't keep
it up—any longer."

His chest expanded on a deep inhalation and he backed her
up to set her on the stone ledge. She found only enough strength
to drag herself onto the more comfortable grass as David
scrambled slowly from the water. He fell on his back next to her
and turned his face to hers.

His mouth worked as he struggled to speak, but evidently he
had exhausted his strength. She was happy to have him settle
for staring deeply into her eyes. She couldn't have answered him
right now, anyway. In the dim light his eyes were hidden within
dark shadowy triangles, but she could make out that the cor-
ners of his mouth were upturned.

She smiled back at him. Her hand dropped between them to
the grass. He found it and tangled his fingers through hers.

The two of them lay together beneath a purple velvet sky shot
through with diamonds. A gentle tropical breeze whispered
over her cooling skin. The same breeze carried the soft strains
of slow dance music being played somewhere inside the resort.

A sense of the utter rightness, of the utter inevitability of their joining cocooned her in a lovely feeling of complete satisfaction. The simple connection of his hand covering hers contented her in a way nothing else had for a very long time.

Not long, though, before that slight touch wasn't nearly enough. Marvelous to be free to touch him as much as her heart desired. She smiled up at the stars and pondered how best to go about doing that.

David lay completely still. She heard his slow, shallow breathing, saw the slight rise and fall of his chest. She whispered his name. Nothing. He'd fallen asleep. That didn't seem fair when a greedy desire to once more experience the wonder of having him inside her was again creeping through her.

That he remained dead to the world, though, did give her the chance to gaze her fill of him. Or rather of what she could see of him in the darkness. She propped herself up on an elbow and gazed down at his beautiful face.

Everything about him, the intriguing color of his eyes, the sexy shape of his mouth, the sound of his voice that played entrancing riffs down her spine had hooked on to her deepest being. And tonight she'd made the remarkable discovery that she fit to him as if her body had been custom-made for his.

There could be no more hiding from the truth. She'd come to Colombia to find the man she'd promised to marry and found the only man in the world she wanted to spend the rest of her life with.

She didn't have to be told that it was stupid to love a man who didn't want to be loved, but she was deeply in love with David Reid. It was clear to her now that love had begun to creep into her heart those first few conflicted minutes with him in the mountains. She couldn't think how it happened. She certainly hadn't planned it. But there it was: For all the complications it posed, her love for him was planted as immovable as Mount Everest in the middle of her life.

He'd staggered her with his dazzling sensitivity to her needs.

She'd expected that a man so blunt about his sexual desires, so full of anger, of hurt, would be rough, would take her quickly. But he'd spent long, delicious minutes offering her what felt like true tenderness, genuine caring.

David wasn't in love with her. She wasn't naive enough to believe that. But after what they'd just shared, she had to believe she did mean something to him. Her few intimacies with Tommy were quick exercises to satisfy his undemanding needs. David had transported her to a whole vibrantly different world. Her experience wasn't great, but it sure felt to her that the two of them had done a lot more than just have sex. They'd truly made love.

Her heart swelled with affection for him. She wasn't sure he realized how much he'd given her, how grateful she was that he'd gone out of his way to make her feel that he cherished her—at least for tonight. She wanted to give back to him that same kind of caring.

She stroked lightly across his breast to awaken him. He trembled slightly but his eyes remained closed.

His skin was still damp. In the darkness she skimmed her fingers down the long, hard line of his body from shoulder to foot. To her, nothing could mar his masculine beauty. Not the series of scars she could feel zigzagging from his hip to his left breast. Not the gouge in the muscle of his thigh that her fingers encountered, nor the ridge of the healed half-circle tear at his knee.

The ugly evidence of his long-ago suffering twisted her heart. She wanted nothing to ever hurt him again. How better to express that wish than to give him the pleasure of making love once more.

To awaken him, she bent and pressed her lips to the center of his chest.

His heart took a quick bounce beneath her lips. The hand lying limply at his side twitched a little. That was all. After the way he'd responded to the slightest of her caresses in the pool, how the heck could he simply go on sleeping now, with her touching him, kissing him this way?

She smiled to herself.

Sleepy time is over, Commander.

She flicked her tongue back and forth over the nipple dotting the top of a scar. His eyelids stayed irritatingly closed. She noticed, though, that his fingers curled tightly into his palms.

Pretend to go on sleeping peacefully, would he, while the warm ache between her legs grew uncomfortable? Forget it.

Okay, mister. You ready for a full-fledged assault on your so-called nap?

She licked her lips to wet them. With deliberate slowness she drew them down over the taut leanness of his stomach. And lower.

She heard his choked grunt and was pleased to watch his fingers dig deep into the grass.

Let's see how much more of this you can take, partner.

Hovering over the most delicate part of him, she held her mouth a tiny fraction of an inch above it, taunting him with what she hoped would provide a thoroughly agonizing moment. The faint whimper that came from him told her she'd succeeded. She pursed her lips against the thin, silky skin. His flesh swelled against her mouth. His breathing jogged into a pace that was far from shallow.

He still refused to declare surrender by opening his eyes, or reaching for her.

She now faced a needling problem of her own. Without lifting a finger, David was laying on friendly fire that was turning her battle tactic back on herself. With devastating results. Parts of her were pulsing into painful heat, and she was encountering serious breathing problems of her own.

But the lazy devil deserved to undergo a lot more teasing. She couldn't really say, though, that it was only to torment him that she stroked the tip of her tongue along his satin-sheathed hardness.

His hips convulsed quickly. He let out a full-fledged groan.

Torture for herself as well as he when she forced herself to pull away from the delicious taste of him.

She moved up and bent over his face to nudge his nose with hers.

"You faker," she breathed against his lips. "You aren't asleep at all. You just want to lie there like a lump and have me do pleasant things to you. Admit it.'' Not that it posed any hardship whatever for her to do those pleasant things to him.

"I admit it," he rasped. "I'll say anything you want. Only please, please don't stop what you were doing."

He lifted his hands between them and closed them around her breasts. The softness between her legs grew hotter.

She was ready to surrender, but he didn't need to know that just yet.

Looking down at him, she pushed out her lips in school-marmy disapproval. "You don't deserve it."

"I know. Do it."

She rather enjoyed seeing the pleading look on the face of a man who so often felt free to tell her what to do. "So the commander still thinks he can give me orders?"

His head moved into a shaft of moonlight. The dangerous glint she caught in his eyes suggested that this teasing maneuver might be about to backfire on her.

"The commander can give as well as he gets." His voice rumbled low with warning.

His thumbs wiped firmly over her nipples.

"Do it."

Tough not to let him see how much the touch affected her, when he'd managed to take a lot more without flinching.

"I'll think about it."

He grasped her shoulders and dragged her up with the power of his arms until the crest of one breast fell into his open mouth. His teeth pulled gently on the nipple. Her breath caught in her throat.

"Please," he growled. "Kiss me the way you did before."

Impossible to hold out any longer against a desire that was as compelling in her as it was in him. She scattered kisses down the heated skin of chest and stomach until her lips found the glorious fullness between his thighs.

His hands tangled in her hair, holding her to him.

Her kisses outlined his beautiful hard length.

He writhed and groaned beneath her gentle, merciless assault on his senses. The taste of him intoxicated her, but it was the sweet, vulnerable intimacy between them that truly filled her heart with joy.

"Enough," he rasped out. "Or this will be over real quick."

In an instant he'd grasped her arms, pulled her up and rolled her beneath him.

His lips drew a delicate web of pleasure sensors over her breasts, her stomach, her hips, fine-tuning every nerve to the slightest nuance of sensation.

Making love with David was a revelation, not only about him, but about herself. He brought her feelings as new as spring. Feelings she'd known forever. In an incendiary mix of passion and tenderness, he was teaching her the glory of equal partners giving and receiving pleasure. Bringing her a fresh and excitingly full understanding of herself as a woman.

She abandoned herself to all the magnificent roiling power of it.

"Open your eyes," he gasped. "I want you to know it's me. I want you to see *me* join myself to you." His voice rasped low and dark and rich with emotion.

She captured his head in her hands and looked into eyes whose pupils had turned into deep wells of ebony fog.

"I do know it's you, David," she breathed. "I'll always know it's you."

Holding her gaze, he slowly slid inside her and began to move in a delicious rhythm whose sensual beat her body instinctively strove to match.

She tried to keep her eyes open, but her will to control any part of her was swept away in engulfing ecstasy. The last thing she saw as her eyelids drifted down was his doing the same.

She felt the steaming shudder of his release and fell headlong into hers.

An eternity later, she lay sleepily wrapped in his arms, her head pillowed on his chest.

"I can't believe how selfish I've been tonight," he murmured.

"Huh?" Her fuzzy brain struggled to parse the ridiculous sentence he'd just uttered.

"I never should have made love to you without seeing to your protection. My only excuse is that I honestly didn't expect it to happen." No more than did she. "I thought I could keep myself from—" He broke off sharply. "I know that's no excuse at all."

"If you're talking about the possibility of a child resulting from our union, you can stop worrying. I took care of that myself back in med school."

For some dumb reason hearing David more or less say he was worried about making her pregnant disturbed her. His reaction was a lot more mature and logical than hers. To her, the idea of bearing David's child felt wondrous.

"Not just that," he said. "I also want to keep you from worrying about any medical problems that are out there. Even before my marriage, promiscuity never appealed to me. I took my marriage vows seriously. Which was the reason why my wife's unfaithfulness came as such a shock. Since then I, uh, I haven't . . ." His words trailed off.

She lifted her head and nodded encouragement at him to keep talking.

His sigh spoke plainly that he would just as soon not continue. Not wanting to press for what he wasn't ready to share, she settled back down on his chest.

"You don't have to worry about disease," he went on, "because I haven't been with a woman for the past two years."

Her head jerked up. "You haven't?" she blurted out, astonished. "But you're so good at—at what we've been doing tonight. You're so expert at making love, I was sure you—"

A chuckle rasped through his chest and burst out in a soft whoop.

Laughter wasn't the reaction she expected.

"How about letting me in on the joke." She didn't see anything all that amusing about the situation.

"Umm—" The string of irritating chuckles trailed off. "I don't think you really want to know."

"I do, too."

Ought she to feel insulted here, she wondered, or what?

"Did that laugh mean that you think I'm not nearly the expert in the art of lovemaking that you are?" An observation she could hardly deny.

"Far from it, Cara. You're a wonderful lover. Believe it. What you gave me tonight, I've never, ever experienced before." He drew his fingers slowly through her hair. "And you're one hell of a doctor."

It was hard to stay disgruntled with him beaming up at her that way. He seemed as happy as a kid who'd just found a pile of presents under a Christmas tree.

She shook her head in bewilderment. "You're not making a whole lot of sense, David."

"Yes, I am. You just don't know it." His face finally sobered. "Okay. I guess you've a right to hear exactly what you've done for me."

He hauled in a deep breath. "This isn't something a man wants to admit to a woman—" He paused again. "Especially not one he's holding naked in his arms, not one who's just given him the most satisfying, intimate experience of his life. But up until I kissed you in the courtyard of the church the other day, I thought I might be, uh, immune to female blandishments."

"'Immune to female blandishments,'" she repeated dryly. "What the heck does that mean?"

"To be blunt, it means that since the night Anita ran away from me, I was afraid I might be impotent."

"You?" Her voice came out in a squeak. "You, impotent?" Didn't seem possible. David Reid was the sexiest male she'd ever met. The only male who ever kicked her female reactions into overdrive with only a look.

"Well, Commander—" She struggled to keep a straight face. "My extensive medical training allows me to assure you that impotence is no longer a problem—if it ever really was. I hereby pronounce you completely cured."

"Yeah." He grinned. "I sure am." His hand slid possessively over the curve of her hip. "But it wouldn't hurt to make absolutely sure of that one more time, would it? Purely in the interest of scientific investigation, of course."

And purely in the interest of scientific investigation, she agreed.

She fell asleep in his arms, the sweet memory of holding him within her still singing through her veins like music.

She woke alone on the grass.

Chapter 13

David had covered her with one of the hotel's white terry bathrobes. She pushed herself unsteadily to her feet and hunched into the robe. Still lethargic after an exhaustive night of lovemaking, she slowly took the steps to the house.

David was fully dressed and waiting for her at the glass-topped dining table inside the bungalow.

"Breakfast is here," he said without preamble. "Eat quickly and get dressed. We're leaving in a matter of minutes."

He poured her coffee and waved her to a seat at the table.

"Uh...what?"

She raked her hair out of her eyes. Her mind was still cottoned in the aftermath of deep sleep. The effects of the magical night with David still resonated through her body. It took her a moment or two to kick her brain into gear and walk to a chair.

"Come on, Cara. Get moving."

She obediently picked up the cup and sipped the coffee.

What happened to last night's sweet sighs and whispers about how wonderful she was? What happened to his focused concentration on pleasing her?

His brisk efficiency in the bright light of morning slammed her down to earth with a thud. Already he was distancing himself from her.

She'd expected something different? She was a doctor, for heaven's sake. She understood the male sexual response. She knew that a man's raging hormones would make him say anything, do anything in the middle of sex that he'd conveniently forget in the morning.

A woman heading toward thirty ought not to have mistaken a man's demonstration—extremely vivid demonstration—of his sexual expertise for true tenderness. She never should have read nonexistent evidence of genuine caring into the simple influence of pleasure and moonlight.

The realization slashed her heart. David had used her to restore his virility. She didn't begrudge him that. She only wished he wanted more from her. Wished he wanted as much from her as she did from him.

He gulped down his coffee while standing.

"I meant to get you out of here last night, but I—" He stopped to clear his throat. "I never should have let myself get sidetracked like that."

Sidetracked? That's how he thought of the soul-stirring wonder of what they'd shared? As a mere sidetrack on the way to more important plans?

"Tommy and Robert Kane were here yesterday morning. They left at noon."

Tommy? She'd completely forgotten Tommy until David mentioned him just now.

"It took some doing, not to mention parting with another healthy stack of dollars, but I managed to find out that Robert—and lately, Tommy—are frequent guests here because Dan Kane's headquarters are located somewhere in the vicinity. That's too damn close for comfort. We're taking the first plane out, regardless of its destination." He shot her a dark look. "Don't give me any grief on this, Cara. I'm holding you to the promise you made."

"You don't have to call me on that promise," she said quietly. "I didn't intend to break it."

Her concern for Tommy was over. The debt her vow to marry him had lain on her was paid in full. Lying in David's arms last night had washed away the last traces of guilt over her former fiancé. Thomas Grant was a grown man entitled to make his own decisions about his life. If those decisions were hopelessly wrong—as they were—that was his responsibility, not hers.

No. Her wanting to get out of here as quickly as possible had nothing to do with Tommy. She simply couldn't bear to spend any more time with David. Not with him acting as if last night were nothing more than an insignificant sexual interlude. How could she stand the torture of feeling his soul twinned to hers while he obviously felt no such bond?

The past year, and more, had stretched her coping skills to their limits. She was afraid there wasn't enough left to deal competently with the aching hollow David's departure was sure to leave in her life.

She picked up her cup and headed into the bedroom, drawing the louvered wooden doors shut behind her. She'd lain naked and wanton in his arms last night. This morning she didn't care even to have him watch her get dressed.

She showered quickly and pulled on a pair of jeans and her last clean shirt for the trip home. She was tying the laces on the second sneaker when she heard the sound of a scuffle from the outer room. The grating of a strange man's voice.

Cold fright scuttled through her. Someone was in there with David. From the harsh growl of the man's voice she didn't think it was a waiter.

She shot from the edge of the bed.

A foot-high, heavy bronze cherub stood on the dresser. She grabbed it. Holding the statue at the ready, she rushed to the bedroom door and reached for the knob.

The door was flung open from the other side. She leapt back an instant before it would have smacked into her.

A mean-looking Colombian blocked her way. Her heart sank. Cupid wasn't going to do much good against the weapon the gangster trained on her. She lowered her arm and let the useless statue drop to the carpet.

David! She didn't hear his voice. What had they done to him? Her gaze darted frantically around what she could see of the living room beyond the goon's bulk.

David stood flattened against a side wall, a cheek pressed against the flowery pink wallpaper, his arms and hands splayed above his head. The same thug who'd come at him with a machete back at the village now jammed the ugly black snout of an assault weapon into the small of his back.

The terrifying sight turned her blood to ice water.

The butt of David's pistol poked from the back of the man's pants.

Her own assailant grabbed her arm and pushed her ahead of him into the living room.

David couldn't move his head much, but his gaze found hers when she moved into his line of vision. How could the eyes of a man with a gun on his spine reflect such deadly calm, when she had to fight to keep from trembling in fear?

"Are you all right?" His voice was hard but steady. She tried—unsuccessfully—for the same effect.

"I'm okay. You?"

"Yeah."

A ridiculous exchange when they were both in a situation that could never be listed under the heading of okay. But that David was still in a condition to talk to her, when she'd feared the worst, brought a bit of comfort.

"Passport. Give!" David's attacker demanded.

"There. In that black bag on the table."

Not taking his eyes off David for a moment, the man backed up to the carryon and rummaged through it. He came up with the blue passport and shoved it into a pocket."

"You?" he growled at Cara.

"In my handbag on the couch."

Her man did the honors, appropriating her passport.

David's attacker had to reach high to grab a fistful of David's hair. "Move, Americano." He pulled him from the wall and aimed him toward the open patio door. *"Muy vite."*

"I need my cane," David protested loudly. "I can't walk without it."

The cane was the only weapon he had left. And that was lying on the floor near the breakfast table.

His attacker only laughed. Clearly the brute hadn't forgotten the mayhem David had wrought on him using that same cane.

Her own personal goon wasn't holding on to her at the moment, although he still had her covered with his weapon. Maybe she could pick up the cane on the way out. She started toward it. Her captor caught her wrist and forced her after the other two.

Without the assistance of the cane, David's limp was worse than she'd ever seen it. He was dragging his left leg slowly and painfully.

It wasn't David's fault that the goons had been able to make their way to the house through the plantings. She was sure he hadn't overlooked the fact that a possible escape route could work two ways, but there wasn't a whole lot he could have done about that.

The two prisoners were ordered down the slope. David's foot caught in a tangle of vines and threw him to the ground.

She tried to rush forward to help him. The thug in charge of her yanked her back.

The machete man kicked David's injured thigh and ordered him to get up. David moaned loudly. Bile rose in her throat. She shot a look of pure loathing at his tormentor.

David made it to his feet and soldiered on, limping badly, down the narrow dirt driveway.

She had no choice but to follow.

No help was in sight. Apparently seven o'clock in the morning was too early for vacationers to be up and about. Even if a resort worker did happen to spot what was going on, what with traffickers owning the place, she had a strong suspicion the staff might not be too quick to help.

The weapons prodded her and David along the pier to the end where a narrow wooden ladder led down to a small runabout waiting in the water. A third man had been left at the controls.

She managed to scramble down the ladder to the deck without falling. No thanks to her guard who made no effort to help her with the awkward jump.

David stood hesitantly looking down at the boat, apparently trying to figure out how to get himself into it. He'd have trouble maneuvering down the ladder. His guard gave him a vicious shove. He fell from the planking and landed hard on the floor of the boat. His face contorted and he yelped loudly.

The fall must have hurt him terribly. Usually he tried to squelch any sign of pain.

She'd never hated anyone in her life, but black hate for these gangsters burst into her mind.

"You scum," she shouted. "You contemptible dirtbags."

The men ignored her. Maybe they didn't understand what she was saying. Maybe they couldn't care less about a woman's ineffectual anger.

David sat crumpled on the floor of the boat. She was pushed down beside him. Their two guards settled onto vinyl-cushioned benches on either side of the boat and held their weapons on the Americans. The helmsman touched a switch. The powerful motor growled to life and the vessel leapt out to sea.

In a matter of minutes they'd left the resort far behind. It looked as if they were heading for the middle of the Caribbean.

Heaven help them! Were they about to be dumped into the ocean to feed the sharks? After what had happened to poor Manuel, the idea didn't seem as crazy as it should. She wouldn't put anything past these horrible people.

David sat as still as stone, holding his slitted gaze in the direction of the coastline. Perhaps he could still make out land. All she could see was the blue haze of the Caribbean.

She laid her hand on his back. Not only to offer him what little encouragement she could, but because she needed the comfort that touching him provided. His stillness was deceiving, she discovered. She could feel the coiled tension in the muscle beneath her hand.

The boat turned east, bringing the shoreline into her view again. They passed a village clinging to the edge of the land in the distance, and several small fishing boats bobbing in the surf. The sight brought her a smidgen of relief. Surely she and David wouldn't be tossed into the ocean in plain sight of witnesses.

A naive hope, she discovered. None of the fishermen so much as looked out at their boat as it sped past. Probably they knew all too well to whom it belonged.

She glanced at her watch. They'd been traveling for almost an hour. They had to be miles and miles up the coast from the resort. Up ahead, the indistinguishable green blur of an isolated island gradually solidified into a thick ridge of palm trees and the dark roofs of several buildings. Apparently their destination.

The helmsman slowed the motor and expertly eased them alongside a concrete wharf jutting into the ocean. A small fleet of boats were wharfed at the long pier boasting its own fuel pump. The pier seemed considerably out of scale with the modest size of the island. But then it needed to be to accommodate the grand white luxury yacht moored to the other side.

David needed her help to climb out of the boat and up the ladder to the pier. That he'd asked for help at all showed her that his fall had left him in bad shape. Their captors allowed her to support him as they were herded past a large warehouse near the wharf. Inside, workmen were stacking bales at the open door. Piles of long wooden boxes lined the back wall.

They climbed a beautifully landscaped path to the palatial residence set on the crest of the island. A silent servant held open one side of imposing double doors that looked as though they'd been salvaged from an ancient church.

The marble foyer opened onto an enormous room in which touches of gold gleamed ostentatiously from every ornately carved surface. The owner of the place obviously possessed a lot more money than he did good taste.

A gray-haired man elegantly dressed in beige linen slacks and red silk shirt stood in front of one of the tall arched windows open to the rose garden behind it. He was a slight man, thin and hollow-cheeked, but his authoritarian stance indicated his position as master of the house. He pulled a long cigar out of his mouth and watched their approach over a priceless antique rug the size of a football field.

A few feet to the right of Dan Kane—who else could it be?—a dark-haired man scarcely out of his teens huddled deep within a large brocaded wing chair. His head drooped over hands clasped tightly between his knees. On the far side of the sofa between them, another man sat in the same type of chair set with its back to her. She could see only the top of a man's blond head.

"Tommy!"

Her fiancé stuck his head around the side of the chair.

Heavy drug use had ruined Tommy's work and his life. It hadn't yet damaged his attractive, boyish grin. Its meaningless charm no longer tugged at her heart, or her sense of guilt.

"Well, Cara. I never expected to see you here."

Dr. Thomas Grant uncoiled himself from the chair and ambled toward her. She walked hesitantly toward him. She'd invested so much emotion, so much time in reaching this moment, but the reality of it left her feeling curiously unaffected.

"Tommy? Are you all right?"

"Sure, hon. I'm fine."

He certainly looked a lot better than the last time she'd seen him. He was clean and well-dressed and seemed to be completely lucid. She thanked God for that.

After what Tommy had done, the last thing she wanted was an affectionate greeting from him. She didn't even want to touch him. He, on the other hand, found nothing incongruous in winding his arms around her in an indolent hug and dropping a light kiss on her cheek.

Instinctively she glanced over at David. The look on his face as he stood watching them was one of pure revulsion.

She gave Tommy a few maternal pats on the back and extricated herself from his loose embrace.

"What are you doing here, Tommy? How did you get here? I've spent months looking all over for you."

Predictably her questions—remarkably mild compared to her desire to scream a demand for immediate answers from him—

roused his ire. "You didn't have to, you know. I didn't ask you to come looking for me."

"Didn't you realize I would worry when you disappeared? The last time I saw you, you were—"

"I said, I'm fine," he cut in.

"I can see that, and I'm relieved."

"Dr. Grant, please introduce our guests."

A superfluous command—not a request—from the man in charge. Kane had already been given their passports and studied them. He didn't move from his place at the apex of the group. Quite obviously they were to come to him, not vice versa.

"Of course, Mr. Kane." Tommy practically bowed before he led them forward. "I'd like you to meet Dr. Cara Merrill, my former fiancée." *Former fiancée,* Cara noted. Well, it might have taken her a while to understand that he wanted nothing more to do with her. Evidently it had taken him no time at all. "I've never met the man with her."

With a courtly gesture, Dan Kane reached for her hand and lifted her fingertips to his lips. "My dear boy, how could you bear to leave such a lovely woman behind?"

Kane's voice and words were pleasant. The look in his coldly assessing eyes was not. A gaze of black glass snapped to her partner.

"David Chandler Reid." Kane did not offer his hand. Nor did David. "Your passport claims that you're a retired naval officer. Exactly how retired are you?"

"I've been a civilian for almost two years."

"Really." Kane looked as if he wasn't going to buy much of what David might say. "Tommy has given me his version of what Dr. Merrill may be doing in Colombia. Why are you here?"

"I'm a friend of Dr. Merrill's. She wanted an interpreter on the trip. I speak Spanish. She doesn't."

"An interpreter who asks many troublesome questions and frequents places not usually visited by tourists."

"They're no worse than some of the other places Tommy has led me to back in the States," Cara offered. Just looking at this

steely man sent shudders down her back, but she wasn't about
to let him see it.

"An interpreter who does very well for himself in street
fights, and who involves himself in the death of an insignificant *barrio* dweller."

"Not by our choice, Mr. Kane," Cara countered.

David seemed content to let her do most of the talking. If
he'd thought it best, he wouldn't have hesitated to take control
of the interrogation. And she'd learned that his stillness didn't
mean that he wasn't paying extremely close attention to everything that was going on.

"Robert." The sharpness in Dan Kane's tone made the
young man in the chair jump. He wasn't the only one. "Since
our guests are here largely because of your imprudent actions,
shouldn't you bid them welcome?"

Hard to feel welcome, she thought, when half a dozen armed
men ringed the room.

Robert rose partway from his chair and aimed a sickly smile
in their direction.

"Please sit," Kane said, gesturing to the sofa in front of him.

They sat. She and David on the sofa. Tommy in his chair next
to it. Kane remained standing, his eyes fixed on his so-called
guests. She felt more like his prey.

"Tommy, what are you doing with these people? What is all
this?"

"It's not my fault, Cara. Nobody can blame this on me. I
didn't even know you were in Colombia until a few hours ago."

Evidently aware that Tommy wasn't one to give brief and
direct answers, Kane took over the explanations.

"My son met Dr. Grant on a trip to Miami. Robert suffers
from juvenile onset diabetes. You understand, Dr. Merrill?"

Cara nodded.

"My boy isn't good about taking care of himself. He col-
lapsed in the street in the throes of a diabetic reaction. Fortunately Dr. Grant was nearby. He took care of Robert, saved him
from lapsing into a diabetic coma. Perhaps even saved his life."

"A stroke of luck for both of us," Tommy added. "I was
working at a free clinic just up the street from where Robert

passed out. After he felt better, we spent several days together checking out Miami's club scene.'' He tried another smile. ''Robert's a lot of fun, Cara. You'll like him. When he suggested I come back to Colombia with him, I thought, why not? Robert needs me to oversee his condition. There are good Latino doctors available, but he feels more comfortable with a fellow American. Don't you, Robert?''

Comfortable wasn't the way she'd describe the cherubic-faced young man who nodded weakly. Robert looked the least comfortable of anyone in the room. Which, considering how she felt herself, was saying something. Having Dan Kane for a father, she decided, couldn't be easy.

''This place suits my needs perfectly,'' Kane said. ''But for a young man...'' He shrugged. ''I thought it would be good for my son to have a companion, an American near his own age. I was not aware that Robert's friend came with such... encumbrances.''

Encumbrances such as a jilted fiancée stupid enough to want to help? Or like drug addiction? Would a trafficker consider that an encumbrance? Either way, she wasn't interested in hearing about this man's family problems.

''Tommy, the commander and I were viciously attacked a few days ago.'' She turned and pointed to the machete man. ''That man there was one of them.'' She didn't see the other two in the room. ''An acquaintance of ours was brutally murdered. Tell me the truth. Did you have anything to do with either of those events?''

''Of course not. How could you think that? I didn't even know about the incidents until word came early this morning that someone at the resort was asking about Robert and me. Mr. Kane questioned us and found out that Robert had...well...'' Tommy's words trailed off after a nervous look at his host.

''My son has acted rashly. And I'm afraid his rashness has caused serious problems for all of us. Very serious problems.''

She didn't like the way Kane emphasized the seriousness of the problems his son had caused.

"Robert found out that you were in Bogota looking for me," Tommy went on. "I guess he was afraid that if you succeeded in finding me, you might take me back to the States with you. I had no idea that he'd sent his personal bodyguard to attack you. Without his father's knowledge, I'm afraid. I could have told Robert it would probably take more than that to scare you off. I was horrified when I learned that he'd actually had someone killed to prevent him from leading you to me."

"You were horrified that someone was killed, Tommy?" she burst out. "These people are drug traffickers. They kill people one way or another all the time."

Perhaps not the wisest comment in the world considering their position, but she'd had it with phony politeness.

Tommy simply ignored her comment. He'd always been good at dodging facts he didn't like. Maybe she'd been doing a little of that herself. Maybe, at the time, she'd gotten something out of having him be so dependent on her.

Tommy leaned forward to speak across the low coffee table to his friend. "I wish you'd talked to me first, Robert. You didn't need to try to scare Cara away. Why should I want to go back? You and I are good friends. I'm happy here. You and your father have been more than generous to me."

No surprise that David had been right, as usual, Cara thought. Her partner's cold-eyed view of Tommy's probable reluctance to return home had been a lot more realistic than hers. Looking at the situation from Tommy's point of view instead of her own, she could almost understand his choice. Why give up a life of luxury to return with her to an uncertain future back in the United States?

If only he weren't with such hateful people.

"You don't have to stay here, Tommy," she said. "I've found an excellent rehab program—"

He slapped the arm of the chair. "I don't need a rehab program. And I'm tired of you telling me what I should or shouldn't do. You pushed me to keep on with the residency when I told you it was too much for me. I thought I might be able to cope better if we were married, but our engagement just added one more pressure on me. You're too much for me,

Cara. I started in on the drugs because of you. You kept at me and at me until I needed to find some kind of relief."

David's hands clenched into fists.

Tommy's nasty words hit her like a blow. How could someone she'd been friends with for so long—a man who once claimed to be in love with her—charge her with something so patently untrue?

"Oh, Tommy, I just tried to help. That's the only reason I came here. To try to help. And you started in on the drugs long before I tried to get you off them."

"I don't need your help. I'm fine now. Drugs aren't a problem for me anymore."

"He's right." David bit out the words. "Drugs aren't a problem because he can easily maintain his habit here. Ask him why he's the only man in this very warm room wearing a long-sleeved shirt."

David reached over to grab Tommy's arm. The nearest gunman took a menacing step forward. At the small motion of Dan Kane's head the guard halted.

David shoved up Tommy's sleeve so hard the button popped off.

A glimpse was enough to show her the fresh tracks of a continuing heroin user. She squeezed her eyes shut and turned her head away. Tommy was no longer her responsibility, but the evidence of his continuing addiction was hard to take.

"I intended to give you back your ring, but your new friends here—" she angled her head toward the group of kidnappers "—prevented that. The ring is in my purse at the resort. I'll leave it in the guest safe. You can pick it up there."

"It appears," Kane said, "that the tender reunion is over. Now, suppose you tell me the real reason you two have been tracking my son."

"We haven't been tracking your son, Mr. Kane. We've been trying to find Tommy."

"Do you expect me to believe, Doctor, that you came all this way simply to see a man you were once engaged to? I didn't notice any excess of affection in your greeting to Dr. Grant.

Even less in his reaction to you. That story, though, could provide good cover for American agents."

His hard gaze landed on David. "Which are you and the doctor, Commander Reid, DEA or CIA? Both agencies have caused me considerable nuisance over the years."

"Neither of us are government agents of any kind," David said, as calmly as if he'd been asked the time of day. "Our reasons for being here are exactly as Dr. Merrill has explained."

"Ridiculous. You've been trying to reach me through my son. Your government has been trying to nail me for years. One of the reasons I'm now a citizen of this country."

"For heaven's sake, Tommy," Cara said, "you know darn well I don't have any connection to the DEA or the CIA. Neither does David. He's not on active duty. This has gone far enough. I'll appreciate it if you'll tell your friends to take us back."

Dan Kane stepped forward.

"Unfortunately, Doctor, I can't allow that. Even if you are no more than who you claim to be, my son's foolishness has exposed us both to retribution from my superiors. They will not take kindly to reports that Robert's misguided actions have brought possible government agents into our midst. I'm not happy that you were able to trace my son from Miami to Bogota to this area. Until now I had managed to keep Robert's involvement in our family business fairly quiet."

Poor Robert sank lower in his chair.

"It's now up to me to correct his mistakes. If your devotion to Dr. Grant is genuine, Dr. Merrill, it's admirable. As a man who sets great store by the loyalty of those around me, I can appreciate the apparent loyalty you've demonstrated."

Kane sighed. "However, I'm afraid that you and Commander Reid know too much, have seen too much. And long experience leads me to believe that despite your protests, you probably are undercover DEA. Believe me, dear lady, it pains me to have to do this, but surely you can understand a father's duty to protect his son from the consequences of his indiscretions.''

He nodded toward the nearest gunman. ''Take them outside and get rid of them.''

Chapter 14

His hands fisted into tight knobs, David watched Tommy leap from his chair.

"Oh, Mr. Kane, no. Please."

"You . . . you can't just go around murdering American citizens," Cara said. "You won't get away with it. Our government will track you down. You mentioned retribution from your drug trafficking colleagues. You ought to be more worried about retribution from American authorities."

Damn, he was proud of her, David thought. She certainly didn't wilt under pressure. Only afterward. Her hand sought his. Her fingers were as cold as ice and he could feel the brittle tightness in her body. But she'd spoken up firmly. She held her chin tilted upward and she didn't tremble. Much.

"The American government may track me down, Doctor?" Kane's thin smile was not designed to reassure anyone. "Colombia has no extradition treaty with the U.S. Only one of the benefits of living here. Let me tell you what the reaction of the U.S. government will likely amount to. There'll be questions asked at the embassy in Bogota, of course. They will trace your movements to Cartagena, where you simply disappeared. You must take my word for it that there will be no record at the resort that you were ever there. After many months of investigations a strongly worded letter of the 'We will not tolerate...' variety will go out to the Colombian government.''

Kane took a long, slow drag on his cigar. "No, Doctor. Retribution from the American government is not something that greatly concerns me.''

The slime was probably right, David conceded. U.S. authorities had been trying to get their hands on him for years. One way or another Kane always managed to elude any reckoning.

Eventually Elliott's special contacts might be able to provide some information about their disappearance. By then, of course, he and Cara would be long past caring.

"But, Mr. Kane," Grant continued, "now that Cara and her companion understand that I'm not interested in going back, they'll leave Colombia. Won't you, Cara?''

"Of course. Believe me, Mr. Kane. We want to leave here as much as you want us to. I have no more interest in Dr. Grant. Take us back to the mainland and Commander Reid and I will leave the country immediately. I give you my word on that.''

The drug lieutenant's cruel face registered not a flicker of softness. David hadn't expected it to. Kane couldn't afford mercy. He lived under the same harsh rules with which he controlled others.

The gunman followed his orders and marched forward to stand behind the sofa. David felt the cold, hard stab of the weapon at his neck.

"Talk to your father, Robert," Tommy pleaded. "I've known Cara for years. We were engaged, for God's sake. How can I stay here if she's...if anything happens to her here? If she's harmed, I'll have to leave. I *will* leave, Robert. I couldn't possibly stay.''

The spineless little jerk had finally summoned up some backbone, David observed. Not that it would do Cara any good whatever. He understood people like Dan Kane. Their own comfortable survival came before any other consideration.

And if he were in Grant's shoes, he'd be more than a little concerned about his own safety. Evidently it hadn't yet occurred to Tommy that his presence here was the underlying cause of the events that provoked Dan Kane's displeasure. He'd be willing to bet that sometime soon Grant would meet with an unfortunate accident that Robert couldn't possibly blame on his father.

Robert finally found his voice. "Dad, please."

He stood up to face his father. The younger Kane was the taller and heavier of the two, but that gave him no edge in this confrontation. His shoulders slumped. His hands were clasped tightly in front of him.

"Please, don't do this. Tommy will leave me. I have no other real friends. You know that. I don't want to lose this one. Please, Dad. Let me have this. They'll go away. After all, what can they do to you? What can anyone do to you?" Kane gave no sign that he'd heard the bitterness in his son's voice. "Let them go. Please, Dad," Robert begged on the verge of tears.

His entreaty brought forth only silence.

The guard behind David prodded him to his feet. Cara rose with him. He staggered a little and steadied himself on her arm.

A thin stream of smoke snaked from Kane's lips as he studied his son. Kane held his arm out to the side and flicked the ash off his cigar, confident that the gold ashtray would be in its proper place beneath his hand.

"All right, Robert. For your sake, I'll do as you ask. Take them back to the resort," he told the gunman.

Robert's double take at his father made it obvious that he hadn't really expected his request to be granted. He ventured a hesitant smile. "Thanks, Dad."

Cara let out a sigh of relief—a relief David didn't share.

"But remember, Dr. Merrill, Commander Reid, should you decide to inform on us, no city in the United States lies beyond the reach of my Colombian colleagues."

"Thanks, Mr. Kane." Looking pale, Tommy slumped down in his chair.

The bastard had caused Cara a lot of grief. If the guards hadn't been around, he'd have punched out Grant's lights for accusing her of being the cause of his addiction. The man had to be granted a grudging bit of respect, though, for finding the nerve to speak up for her when it counted.

"Goodbye, hon." Apparently Grant didn't have the strength left to rise. A good thing. If he'd had to watch that jerk kiss Cara goodbye, he probably would have puked. "You don't have to worry about me anymore. If anyone back home asks, tell them I'm doing great."

"I really hope that's true, Tommy."

Kane waved dismissively. "Very well, José. Take them back now."

Even if Cara had noticed the sharp look Kane sent his man as the guard walked them from the room, David doubted she understood the meaning of it.

He did.

As he'd suspected, they'd received no reprieve at all. Kane had simply taken steps to quiet his son's fears, and Grant's. The guard didn't carry that Uzi as a fashion accessory. Kane's original order to kill them was to be carried out at sea and their bodies dumped into the water to disappear.

Still, the first scrap of hope he'd been able to work up since Kane's men invaded the villa surfaced in him. He was going to be put into a boat again. On the island, surrounded by armed mercenaries, he didn't stand a snowball's chance in hell of saving Cara or himself. In a boat with this single guard the odds would be a little better. He might find some frighteningly slim opening for action. Their first trip had presented him with no opportunity to act. Not with that second weapon constantly pointed at Cara.

As they were escorted along the pier he looked back for a moment to fix the whole scene in his mind: The yacht being loaded, the warehouse filled with drugs and weapons, the position of the house and what he judged to be the bedroom wing. Six men inside, another four out here. Maybe more out of sight. Only the supervisor of the workmen carried a weapon.

His prayers were answered. The same unarmed man waited in the boat for his passengers. As they were ordered in, David put his arm around Cara as if to comfort her and pressed his cheek to hers. "It'll be okay," he said loudly. "We're on our way home."

He dropped his voice to a hurried whisper. "Watch me. Jump when I move."

She was smart enough not to show any reaction, ask any questions.

He boarded the boat carefully this time. No point in leaving himself open to further injury. As it was, he'd need every ounce of strength, every bit of training—plus a whole lot of luck—to handle a situation Cara's presence made the most dangerous he'd ever faced.

They were allowed to sit together on one side bench. Their guard took a seat opposite them. Fortunately the man wasn't the machete-wielding attacker, who'd learned better than to let his eyes wander from the male prisoner. Machete was a lot smarter now than he'd been at the village. At that time he probably hadn't expected what seemed to be an ordinary American couple to put up any resistance whatever. Very likely he'd been following orders from Robert not to let any of his father's mercenaries in on his plan, and had hired two stupid punks on the spot for the bungled attack.

David smiled grimly to himself. Right now that son of a bitch very likely was undergoing a painful reminder of exactly who he was working for. And that wasn't Robert.

David permitted himself no more than a moment's satisfaction that so far his dramatics had paid off. Ever since the men had broken into their villa and disarmed him, he'd been emphasizing his weakness, making a great show of his inability to walk properly. Not entirely an act. It wasn't hard to cry out in pain and develop a heavy-duty limp when a kick and a fall sent spasms of agony shooting through him.

His plan was painfully simple and extremely hazardous. Without it he and Cara would be dead within the hour. And it depended entirely on her ability to act quickly when the time came.

The guard settled back on the seat, his legs thrust out in front of him. The boat wasn't speeding, as it had been on the way to the island. Anyone would think them a group of friends out for a pleasant morning excursion on the water.

The guard stretched an arm lazily along the top of the bench. His weapon rested loosely in his lap.

Good, David thought. He wanted this man to assume he must be in complete control of the situation. What well-armed man would feel that a cripple and a supposedly helpless woman posed any real threat?

He'd never been so glad in his life for the SEAL training that let him feel as much at home in water as on land. Maybe more so. He didn't fear the ocean as much as he feared that Uzi, especially with Cara sitting right beside him. He'd sell his soul for a knife, though, let alone his usual combat equipment.

He couldn't make his move until they were far enough away not to be spotted from the island. Unfortunately that made for one hell of a swim back to the mainland if anything went wrong with his planned maneuver.

The island melted into the crystal blue of the Caribbean.

He smiled at Cara and hoped his hasty warning had been enough to allow her to read the mental message in his eyes to get ready to jump overboard the second he lunged for the weapon. A woman in such good physical shape had to be a swimmer. He'd pick her up after he'd dealt with the guard and the helmsman. It was important to get her out of the way while he did that. If either of the two got their hands on her to use as a shield, commandeering the Uzi wouldn't do him much good.

His jaw hardened. He simply refused to consider the possibility of failure. The consequences to Cara would be too horrendous.

David's smile didn't do anything to calm the roiling questions in Cara's mind, but she managed to curve up her own lips in return.

What the heck did he mean, *jump when he moved?* Evidently he intended to take some kind of action. But why did they have to act at all? They were on their way back to the resort, weren't they? She clung to Kane's last order mainly because she so much wanted to believe it. There was that damnable weapon lying in the guard's lap, of course. But maybe a mercenary like that automatically carried a gun with him everywhere.

How was she to act? What was she to do? She wished she had some clue as to what David expected of her. Knowing him, he'd tackle the armed guard. That left the guy driving the boat for her to take care of. She gave the man a quick assessment. He was no taller than she, and from the thinness of his arms probably was no fitness buff. But still . . .

If only she had David's cane. The boat offered nothing in the way of a weapon. There was a life ring fitted against the stern, but there wouldn't be time to free that and hit the helmsman with it. Besides, she doubted if a round, bouncy ring would put much of a dent in the guy's head.

He was standing at the wheel, looking out over the windshield and hemmed in somewhat by the seat behind him. That might give her some advantage for a few seconds.

David gave a low groan and shifted his position. The slight movement garnered the guard's quick attention. For a moment, the Colombian watched David rubbing his thigh, then went back to his idle scan of the ocean ahead.

The gunman never noticed, as she did, that David had braced himself firmly on his good leg.

Oh, Lord. She wished he'd given her a little more time to figure out an effective course of action.

Not the briefest instant elapsed between the flick of his eyes toward her and his leap toward the guard.

Instinct took over. She hurled herself toward her target, barely aware that she'd planted a foot on the bench and vaulted over the boatman's chair. She hit him squarely between the shoulders with her locked arms. The force of her blow doubled him over the low windshield.

Without a guiding hand at the wheel the boat lurched to the right and slowed. She caught a quick glimpse of David plummeting over the side with the guard as the Uzi arced through the air above them.

She could spare David no more attention. She was too busy focusing all her energies on the single goal of dumping her man off the boat, so she could take control of it. She clamped her arms around his legs and heaved with all her strength, trying to roll him over the windshield and onto the bow.

Her action worked too well. Before she could grab the wheel and throw it into another sharp turn to pitch him off the boat, he scrambled to his knees and turned to deal with her. He grabbed her under the arms and yanked. Instead of pulling back, she threw herself forward to use his own momentum against him.

The metal edge of the windshield scraped across her chest as her thrust and his pull hauled her across it. She found herself lying on top of him on the slightly curved deck of the bow.

He swung at her. She couldn't do anything but take his punch in her ribs. Gasping for breath she rolled off and kicked at him furiously.

The boat tilted. He slid toward the prow. The line coiled above it had come loose during their struggle. The steersman grabbed for the rope whipping out across the deck. He missed and tumbled over the prow.

She heard a sickening thud, but she had no time to worry about what had happened to Kane's skipper. The commotion on the vessel had set it rocking and the deck was slipping out from under her, too. She flailed desperately for the line strung out across the bow.

And grabbed a handful of nothing.

She tumbled backward into the ocean. Water filled her nose and mouth and closed over her head. She felt herself plunging downward and fought the fear threatening to engulf her.

Stay calm, she told herself. *You're a good swimmer. You're not going to drown.*

She kicked off her heavy, waterlogged sneakers and struggled toward the surface. She came up coughing and sputtering. Sucking in mouthfuls of delicious air, she tried to spot anything at all other than endless ocean.

She saw the stern of the empty boat heading off into the distance. No sign of anyone else in the water around her. No sign of David.

Cold terror speared through her. She countered with the thought that a swimmer as strong as he couldn't possibly drown in only a few minutes.

But if the guard had the chance to use that weapon . . .

She couldn't remember hearing gunfire or shouts. The whole incident had unfolded in eerie silence. She dived back beneath the waves to look for David.

In a cloud of whirling bubbles a fair distance away, she could barely make out the two submerged dark shapes locked in silent, slow-motion combat. She could recognize David only by the blue of his shirt. The guard wore white.

Neither held the gun. With bare hands they struggled with each other. She couldn't tell which man was winning the life-or-death battle. She swam underwater toward the pair to give David what help she could.

One of the men began to drift downward, his arms and legs spread out uselessly in the water.

Utter panic seized her. Oh, God. Was it David? She couldn't see clearly. Her head was ringing. Her lungs were screaming their need for air. Survival instinct forced her to the surface.

She gulped in air, preparing to jackknife down again. A head broke through the waves too far away for her to identify. The survivor, whoever he was, began to swim toward her.

David. It wasn't so much his face that she recognized, as the strong, even motion of his arms. She went so limp with relief that she slid underwater.

Within seconds she was being dragged upward.

"Are you all right?" David shouted as she bobbed to the surface.

He was constantly asking that stupid question, she grumbled to herself as she coughed out what felt like half the Caribbean.

"No, I'm not all right," she gasped. "I'm stuck without a life vest—in the middle of the . . . the damn ocean. There's not a rescue ship in sight—and there could be sharks zooming in on us right this very minute. Neither one of us is all right, you turkey."

The dark look on his dripping face brightened. "Yeah. You're all right. Do you see the boat?"

"There, behind you." She pointed.

David turned to look. "Looks like torque has set it running in a circle. A fairly slow circle."

"It's too far away. We'll never be able to reach it."

"Where's the shore?" He kept his eyes on the boat.

She squinted into the distance all around her. "I can't see it."

David glanced at the sun and jerked his chin toward his left shoulder. "Neither can I, but it's that way, a very long swim. The boat's a lot closer. It's that or the sharks."

"Jeez, David. I didn't mean there really were sharks around." She jerked her head from side to side searching fearfully for the ominous fins.

"I did. They just haven't hit this neighborhood yet."

"You can't board a moving boat. It could hit you in the head. One slip and that propeller would be slicing into you."

"We've no other choice. I have to try."

He took her hands and set them lightly at his shoulders, making himself a flotation device of sorts. She appreciated the rest holding on to him gave her. On beach vacations she'd stayed in the ocean a lot longer than this without tiring. But that hadn't been after she'd had to fight for her life. And not when she'd been so terribly scared.

"I have to get to that boat quickly, Cara, and I'll have a better chance of boarding her if I don't have to worry that you're beside me in danger of getting run over by the keel. Can you tread water here until I come back for you?"

She understood exactly what he was saying. They had to get out of the water before a passing shark found himself an easy meal. David couldn't waste time swimming at her slower pace, along with trying to look after her in the boat's vicinity. Which he'd do, she knew, whether she wanted him to or not.

"You go ahead, David. I'll be fine. I'll follow you slowly so I won't get tired and I'll be closer to the boat when you come back for me. The bowline is dragging in the water, maybe you can grab that and haul yourself in."

"Right. I'll look for it."

"Good luck." She let go of David's shoulders and waved him on.

"That's my girl." He lifted a hand out of the water and stroked her cheek.

Then he was gone, swimming away from her with the powerful strokes she'd seen him use back in the wonderful safety of his lake.

If this was to be the end, she wanted him to know that she loved him. She opened her mouth to call those words after him, then choked them back. David had his hands full trying to keep them alive. He needed no distractions.

All too soon she could no longer make out his form in the water.

She tried to convince herself that he actually would be able to heave himself into a moving powerboat. If he didn't, they were both going to end up as shark meat. She forced the horrible thought to a corner of her mind and concentrated on trying to keep her eyes on the boat that looked much too far away.

Moving slowly through the water with minimal motions of arms and legs, she felt terribly alone in the vastness of the ocean.

Time lost meaning in the tiring rhythm of keeping herself afloat. It felt as if David had been gone for hours. Her arms were growing as heavy as lead. Her eyes were burning from the bright sun bouncing off mirrorlike waves.

Horrible images of what might be happening to David kept assaulting her mind. He was knocked unconscious by the boat. He slipped under the keel and his back was chopped up by propeller blades.

He was gone. The ocean had taken him. And she was so tired. Maybe it would be better simply to let herself slide beneath the surface and end it that way. Certainly better than being devoured by sharks.

But David would never forgive her if she gave up. Even if he wasn't around to know it.

For sure she'd started to lose it. Now she was hearing his voice calling her name. Something landed in the water near her. The splash woke her from her daze. A life ring.

"Grab it, Cara."

The boat was stopped in the water a few yards away. It took the last of her strength to hook her arm through the ring and hold on while David reeled her in. He leaned over and vised a hand around her wrist to pull her into the boat.

She flopped onto the deck like a landed fish, gasping and unable to move.

David went down on one knee beside her and gathered her to him, holding her tight to his chest.

"It's all right. You're safe. It's all over."

She *was* safe. Safely enveloped within the strong circle of his arms that felt so much like her only true home. Utter heaven to be pressed against the warm solidity of his chest. The unique scent of him, underlying the salty smell of his ocean-drenched clothes, assuring her more than his words that everything really was all right.

He ran his lips over her forehead, her cheeks, pressed his mouth against hers. She had no energy to do anything but lie back and revel in the wonderful feel of his kisses calming her fears, easing the pain of her exhausted muscles. She couldn't make out the words he murmured against her skin, but she loved their tone.

His gaze darted fearfully over her, his hand ranged over her legs, her arms, as if he expected to find some horrible evidence that she'd suffered some hurt.

"Are you okay?" His voice rasped with concern.

The words made her drag up a bit of a smile. "Yes." She didn't have the breath to speak in more than a whisper. "I'm okay."

"Thank God for that" came out on a shaky breath.

"Did you see anything of the other two on your way back to the boat, David?"

"No. They're gone."

The deaths of the two men didn't leave her as unaffected as they had David. No matter that they'd meant them the worst kind of harm, she was sorry they hadn't made it.

He held her until she was able to move a little under her own steam.

"I have to take the wheel, Cara. We've got to get going before somebody comes out here looking for José and his pal."

He used the support of the bench to push himself to his feet. She thought about feigning deeper exhaustion than she felt, simply for the pleasure of remaining in his arms. But she couldn't argue with the frightening logic of what he'd said.

"Right, David. Do you need me to help you with anything?"

"No. You just go ahead and lie here for as long as you need to. I'm going to head for Cartagena. There's an American consulate there, where I can contact Roger Elliott. We'll need his help to get out of Colombia. I'm afraid you'll need to write off your things back at the resort."

"A few clothes and my credit cards in exchange for our lives? Not a bad deal, I'd say."

He chuckled and dropped down again to touch his lips to hers.

She was sure he intended only to give her a light kiss. But his lips lingered, nibbled hers. Then his mouth was pressing harder, hotter against hers. She gave him entry, and his tongue slid inside to meet hers. The pain of her exhausted body suddenly didn't seem important as the energy of liquid heat began to rise in her.

Before he managed to take all her wits from her, she laid a restraining hand on his chest.

"You've got to get this boat away from here, David. We're still too close to the island for comfort."

"Right. The wheel."

She was glad to see his obvious reluctance to leave her as he stood up once more and headed for the helmsman's chair. That he liked their embraces and their kisses as much as she did brought her a little happiness. Maybe he didn't want her for anything more, but that at least was something.

In a few minutes she felt recovered enough to go stand beside him.

His initial grin on seeing her slipped into a frown.

"What the hell did you think you were doing when you tackled that boatman? You were supposed to jump overboard when I moved."

"Well, how was I supposed to know that? There were two bad guys, two of us. Seemed the right thing to do. Hey, it worked, didn't it? You're still here. I'm still here."

He made a grumbling noise in his throat. "Well, I don't want you tackling any more bad guys. Understood?"

She was too relieved that the two of them had made it through those last few terrifying hours to let David's bossy tone bother her.

She laid her hand on the large hard knob of his shoulder. His shirt, like hers, had already dried in the sun.

"Don't worry, David. I don't intend to make fighting bad guys my life's work." She slid him a sideways grin. "And I never had to do it at all before you showed up."

Chapter 15

They spent the night on cots in the safety of the consulate, while the powers-that-be busied themselves with the logistics of getting two nondocumented aliens out of the country. They left Cartagena early in the morning on a small private jet.

The distance David had begun to put between them before their scary run-in with Dan Kane was nothing compared to the taciturn coolness he'd shown her since their arrival in Panama. After depositing her at a hotel, he went off to stay at the military base.

He'd been gone for hours, doing who knew what, while she sat in the hot sticky room where the air conditioner didn't work and made reassuring phone calls to her family.

He couldn't be bothered joining her for their last meal together? Fine. She turned on the nightstand lamp, the only functioning light in the room, ordered room service and picked at her food alone.

David, now merely her ex-partner, probably wouldn't show up before meeting her for their noon flight back to Miami and then on to Washington.

She was a grown woman, a respected professional. She wasn't about to go off and mope over a man. Love affairs ended for someone somewhere every day of the week. No one died of it. You cried a little, maybe. Then you got on with your life. Soon it wouldn't hurt at all to think of David Reid, she told herself.

Twice.

Three times.

This empty feeling in her heart couldn't possibly last forever. She'd simply wait it out.

A soft rap came at her door. She forced herself to walk toward it at a reasonable pace. The last few steps moved a lot faster.

David stood in front of her dressed in navy whites, his officer's hat tucked under one arm. He'd picked up a plain black cane from somewhere.

He looked as if he'd just stepped down from a movie screen. But then, he always did look like some fantasy hero.

She opened the door wider to invite him in. Lightness, she decided, was the way to go.

"Does this mean you've reenlisted?"

"Huh? Oh, you mean the uniform?" The hat arced to the bed. "No, just borrowed."

Apparently the strained humor of her flippant remark had gone right by him. Not surprising. He looked as if his mind were miles away. Not the most flattering reaction in the world from a man who'd made incredibly passionate love to her only two nights ago. Incredible, at least, from her point of view.

He plowed a hand absently through his hair. "Have you had dinner?"

Her eyebrows shot up. She pointed to the dishes on the tiny table right in front of him. David Reid, not notice things? Had he already written her off so completely he hardly saw her or her surroundings?

He glanced down at the remnants of her meal. "Oh. Good. I wanted to come back here to have dinner with you, but I couldn't get away."

How hard did he try? she wondered.

"That's all right." She shrugged. "No problem."

"I just got word that a Congressional fact-finding commit-
tee is heading for the States in a couple of hours. There's room
on the flight. Can you make it?"

So soon? She wouldn't even have the night to decompress
from spending every waking hour—and lately, every sleeping
hour—with David to saying goodbye to him for good.

Her nonchalant toss of her head wouldn't betray any of that.

"Sure. It's not like I have a lot of packing to do. I'm wearing the only part of my wardrobe I have left." Someone had
shown up with a pair of sneakers two sizes too large, a tooth-
brush, a tiny tube of toothpaste and a comb.

David commandeered a couple of olives and a slice of to-
mato from her plate and downed them.

"I hope you've been able to settle down a little after what
happened yesterday," he said.

"I'm getting there."

Settled down? Her stomach was churning with wanting to
throw herself into his arms, but no way would she be the one to
make the first move. It looked, though, as if David was so pre-
occupied with matters other than herself, any move from him
would be a long time coming.

"You feel okay about Tommy?"

"Okay? I'm not sure that's the right word. I still wish I'd
been able to get him out of that awful place. I did my best. It
didn't work, but that isn't my fault."

"No, it isn't. I'm glad you understand that."

"I do, David. But that doesn't keep me from feeling sorry
about what's happened to him."

David gave a sigh of amused resignation. "You win the prize,
hands down, for being the most maddeningly single-minded
person I know."

The sudden gentling in his voice shot her mind back to the
very best of their time together.

Her hair combs and pins hadn't made it out of the Caribbean. Her blond locks hung loose around her shoulders, and
humidity had glued one thin strand to her cheek. David care-

fully fingered it back behind her ear. His light touch was enough to set her heart pounding.

"You've been gone so long—" She bit her tongue, wishing she'd been able to resist saying that. "What have you been doing all day?"

His hand hovered over the roll she hadn't bothered to eat. "May I have this?"

"Help yourself."

The roll disappeared in a couple of bites. The evidence that perhaps he hadn't taken any time at all for dinner made her sorry she'd doubted his excuse that it truly had been business of some kind that had kept him away.

"I've been debriefing to various higher-ups on what we found out about Dan Kane."

"Oh, David. Should you have done that? We promised not to make any trouble for him."

His face hardened. "A promise extorted by a drug criminal bent on murder is no real promise at all."

"Maybe not, but he threatened to come after us if we talked about him."

David hooked his cane over the back of a chair and stepped closer. At last he seemed to be totally focused on her. He reached out and lifted her hands, folding them within his at his waist. The stimulating warmth and strength of his hands flowed into her, considerably brightening her gray mood.

"I don't want you to worry about him or anyone else coming after you. I promise you'll be safe in Baltimore. Forget Dan Kane."

"That'll take some doing. You were the assigned hero in our partnership, David, not me. Every time I turn around, I'll be looking to see if someone is following me."

"I don't want you to live like that. I want you to remember only the pleasant parts about our stay in Colombia, the nice people we met, the spectacular mountain scenery."

She agreed that the scenery had been spectacular. But, for her, the pleasant parts about Colombia were the times she'd spent in David Reid's arms. She sure wasn't likely to forget that.

"To remind you of those good times and help you forget the bad," he said, "I have something for you."

He fished in a pocket, brought out a small red box with elegant gold lettering and handed it to her.

"A present, David? For me?"

"A present. For you."

She opened the lid and caught her breath at the beauty of the jeweled brooch sparkling up at her from its tiny bed of black satin. Emeralds shaped the petals of a five-pointed blossom centered on a brilliant diamond.

"Colombian emeralds," he said, "to replace the flowers you had to throw away that day back in the village."

"Oh, David, it's beautiful." The pin was the most exquisite piece of jewelry she'd ever seen. And surely the most expensive.

She ran her finger over the delicate golden curve of the flower stem, then replaced the cover and held the box out to him. "This is remarkably generous of you. Believe me, I do appreciate the thought, but I can't accept the gift. It's too—"

"I'll be very disappointed if you don't. Think of it as a thank-you gift."

"A thank-you gift? What for?"

"For bringing me along on a mission that gave me back a measure of self-respect. For making me feel I might actually be useful for something again. There was some truth in what you told me that first day. Maybe I had pulled up the drawbridge for good. But you got me down off that mountain. Others had tried. You were the one who did it. I owe you for that."

"I can't take credit for it. If you hadn't been ready to rejoin the world, you'd never have come. But after all the help you gave me, I'm glad I might have been able to return something to you."

"I don't think you understand that what you did for me was nothing less than give me back my interest in life. It's probably no news to you that I'd just about lost it. Please." He gently pushed the box back to her. "Take the gift. It would make me very happy for you to have it."

It was beyond her to disappoint him. The pin's cost didn't matter. The fact that the gift came from him made her love it as much as she'd loved the armload of flowers he'd placed in her lap in the boat.

"All right, then. I'll keep the brooch as a memento of the pleasant parts of our trip to Colombia." It would only painfully remind her of David Reid and of their one magical night of lovemaking.

"Do you remember that darling little girl who sold the flowers to us?" she asked. A sharp pain knifed through her heart. She and David would never create a child together. For some absurd reason, what didn't even exist felt like a terrible loss.

"I remember." His voice resonated with a depth of emotion that surprised her. "I'll remember everything that happened between us there."

She hoped so. She didn't like to think that he might easily consign to oblivion all memory of the wonderful hours they'd spent by the pool.

He took the pin from its box and set the little container on the table. "Here. I'd like to see how this looks on you."

She laughed softly. "Diamonds and emeralds. Just the thing to dress up wrinkled, slept-in, ocean-washed shirt and jeans."

"You don't need any dressing up. On you, a potato sack would look good."

He fastened the brooch on her blouse below her left shoulder. His knuckles whisked down over the rise of her breast. A prickle of heat spread through her.

"Thank you, David."

She lifted herself on her toes to drop a quick kiss of appreciation on his cheek.

As if she'd sprung some delicately set trap, his arms closed around her. His mouth captured hers. Before her mind ever issued the command, her lips had parted to take him in.

In a matter of seconds she was drunk on the taste of him, dizzy with the scent of him, excited with the feel of her softness molding the hard planes of the body she so loved.

With no awareness of how they'd got there, she found herself lying across the bed, the arousing weight of David's body pressing down between her thighs.

His hips flexed, thrusting his rigid center against her.

The barriers of their clothing held him frustratingly separate from her.

Unbearable.

Frantic to hold him naked in her arms, she began to tear off her clothes. He started to shuck off his uniform. His shirt went flying after hers. He stretched an arm to the lamp beyond her head and plunged the room into darkness.

She couldn't see where shoes, pants and underwear landed.

She didn't care.

The only thing that mattered in the whole world was that she was lying within the sweet sensual cage of David Reid's body, his arms, his legs, holding her imprisoned, his arousal burning a demanding ache into the joining of her thighs.

Neither could spare the time for gentleness or tenderness in this embrace. Desperate need flared like a tongue of flame between them.

His drugging kisses swamped her in a powerful undertow of pleasure. Hurled her into a whirlpool of sensation that drowned her senses. Wrenched away her mind. Her hands, her mouth, her whole body strained to experience more and more of him, to soak up everything he could possibly give her.

His wondrous lovemaking in the pool had taught her how to turn back on him every lightning flash of delight he speared through her. She'd learned how to draw from him that throaty groan she so loved hearing. How to make him thrash as wildly as she in frenzied craving for more and more intimate touches of fingers, lips, tongue.

Their hearts pounded to the same riotous beat as together they raced toward the crest, their breath mingling in their gasps of completion.

Only when both were too wrung out to so much as lift a hand to the other's body did they fall away from each other.

"Heaven help me, woman—you take everything a man has to give. And then some."

Not everything a man had to give, she thought. Not yet. And she so yearned to possess the most important part of David Reid. His heart.

He gave her little time to piece her mind back together.

"We have to get going, Cara. The plane won't wait."

The passion she'd just shared with him filled her heart and soul to overflowing with feelings that went an eternity beyond mere sexual desire.

A square of half-light dribbling in from the outside world showed in the open window. She could just make out the chiseled profile of David's face as he lay next to her. An aching longing to bring her love to life for both of them pushed through her.

The blanket of semidarkness wrapping around them, the awesome power of his response to her gave her the courage to take what felt like the greatest risk of her life.

"David," she murmured into the shadows. "I'm in love with you."

"No, you aren't." His answer, quick and devastating, punched into her ears. "You can't be. Not really. You only think you are because of all we've gone through together. Facing death can muddle up the emotions. I've seen it happen."

An avalanche of icy unbelief swallowed her up. She lay there stunned, her breath hooked in her throat, and stared blindly into the gloom. She felt David roll from the bed, heard him fumble for the pants he'd dropped on the floor.

No pill, no medical treatment could take away the pain lancing through her. Worse by far than what she remembered of her childhood's fractured leg. Worse than the attack of acute appendicitis that almost killed her ten years ago.

Under cover of the darkness she darted to the safety of the bathroom and locked the door behind her before snapping on the light. The sudden sharp glare hurt her eyes. She had to squeeze them shut for a few seconds. She twisted on the shower faucet. Fighting against tears, she stood shivering under weak spurts of cold water.

She still couldn't believe it. Complete denial. She hadn't known what David's reaction would be when she offered him her love. But the possibility that he would coolly and calmly deny the validity of her feelings hadn't crossed her mind.

She stepped out of the grungy shower stall and toweled dry, planning to shut herself in here until she was sure he'd left. After the unwelcome surprise she'd just handed him, he probably couldn't wait to get out of the room.

The knock on the bathroom door made her jump. "Here are your things, Cara."

Shielding herself behind the door, she pulled it open only a few inches. He pushed the wadded-up ball of her clothes in to her.

When she came out he was waiting for her near the bathroom door. He was fully dressed and the bedroom light was on.

The realization that he hadn't the courage to so much as reveal his injured body to her, when she'd laid bare the depths of her soul deepened her hurt.

"Ready?" he said. "Then let's go."

That he could maintain that damnable remote calmness that was so much a part of him, when her own nerves were scraped raw, unleashed her anger. She shoved him away. Hard.

"Damn you, David Reid," she yelled, lashing out in a murk of pain and panic at losing him. "What happened to that promise to protect me that you made? You didn't protect me at all. You went ahead and let me fall in love with you." Whether or not the muddled accusation made any sense to him, it did to her. "I can't forgive you for that."

"I—I'm sorry. I didn't mean to—"

"Don't give me *didn't mean to*. You don't do anything you don't mean to do. How dare you brush aside my feelings the way you did?"

She wanted to hit him. She wanted to hold him. More than anything, against all logic, she still wanted him to tell her he loved her.

None of her heartbroken tirade made the slightest impression on him.

He picked his hat up off the floor beside the bed and set it firmly on his head. "We don't have time for this. Your driver is waiting to take you to the airport."

What did he say?

"Take *me* to the airport? Aren't you coming, too?"

"No. I'll be staying for a couple of days. I have things to do here, people to talk to."

Anger gave way to sheer fatigue. She dropped to the edge of the bed.

"What is it, David? Are you so damn deep into control that you can't bear the thought of spending a few hours shut up in a plane with a woman who loves you?"

She raked her wet stringy hair out of her eyes, but didn't look up to meet his gaze. She couldn't bear to see any more of his aloof composure.

"You're supposed to be so damn brave, but I know the truth about you. When it comes to leaving yourself open to your feelings, you're not brave at all. I think you're terrified of letting go and allowing yourself to fall in love—not necessarily with me, with any woman. I believe that to you, love equates with the idea of losing control of your emotions. Assuming, of course, that you have any."

Her final dart had no more effect on him than had anything else she said. He glanced at his watch that, unlike her, had come through their adventures unscathed.

"Time to go home."

David was her home. Unfortunately he couldn't see it that way. Though he was standing only a couple of feet away, there was no way she could bridge the kind of distance he put between them.

On your feet, woman, she told herself. *Don't let the man leave, with you looking like a whipped puppy.* She squared her shoulders and briskly shoved herself upright. "I'm ready."

David handed her into the military automobile waiting in front of the hotel. She turned to the open window, needing to say goodbye, needing to tell him—she didn't know what.

David's rap on the car roof signaled the driver to take off.

His empty gray gaze betrayed no emotion whatever before he turned and walked back into the hotel.

* * *

Inside the hotel entrance, David had to stop and dig out a handkerchief to wipe away the heavy beads of sweat trickling down his forehead. He'd come within seconds of losing his fight to hold his face impassive as Cara left him for good.

He'd never forget the look on her face as he turned his back to her. But he'd had no choice. If he hadn't cut her loose right then, he was afraid he never would. Everything in him was driving him to hold on to Cara Merrill and never let her go.

Her miraculous disclosure of love had nearly broken him.

She'd never know how close he came to confessing that despite all his efforts against it he'd fallen desperately in love with her.

She'd been so right about its effect on him. His love did terrify him. *Love* was too insignificant a word for what he felt for her. He was consumed with desire, with need for the woman who'd invaded his walled-in life and taken him prisoner, heart, mind and soul. Only it didn't feel like an invasion. It felt like a melding of her life with his. As if they'd joined forces against the world.

Her charge that he had no trouble in holding himself in complete control twisted an ironic smile to his lips. Self-control didn't exist where she was concerned. He'd come tonight only to tell her that he'd booked her on the flight, give her the brooch to remember him by and return to the base.

That plan failed the moment she opened the door.

Cara Merrill had done so much for him that he couldn't tell her about. In her arms he'd found a sense of contentment he hadn't known for a long time—maybe never. She'd kindled a fire in him that would never burn itself out. A fire that laid bare the depths of his loneliness. A void she alone could fill.

A silent wail reverberated through him. How could he keep on going without her?

It was for her sake that he'd never act on his love. Bad enough that if he gave in to his feelings for her, he'd burden a woman who deserved the finest man in the world with only half a man.

There was something he feared even more.

After seeing the lengths she'd gone to out of loyalty for a man she pitied, for whom she felt responsible, he was deathly afraid that once she got a good look at the ugly reality of his body, she'd slip back into the Florence Nightingale role she'd played with Tommy.

He couldn't stand that.

Taking care of people was a vital part of her nature. She'd want to take care of him. The thought of having her act as his nurse, or offer him the mother-burden duty she'd shown Tommy, turned his stomach. As the old song said, he had to have all of Cara Merrill, all her passion and loyalty and commitment, or he wanted nothing at all.

That was precisely what he was going to get. Nothing at all.

Bone-deep ache settled inside him.

He'd made love to her for the last time. Okay, so he'd made that promise to himself before, and broken it. But tonight that vow was carved in stone into his brain.

If he managed to live through what he planned to do in the next forty-eight hours, he'd make sure that he'd never lay eyes on her again.

"Mrs. Delaney was the last patient, Doctor."

"Thanks, Patricia," Cara said to the nurse. "You can go now."

"I don't mind staying to help you with those Medicare forms."

"No need. I can manage." She saw the stack of paperwork as her salvation. At least for a while. It would keep her busy for another couple of hours. "Go on home to that good-looking husband of yours and your darling little boy."

"All right, if you're sure."

"I'm sure. Now scat." She waved the nurse out the door.

Thank heaven for the rigors of her job. If she didn't have her work to fill twelve- and fourteen-hour days, she'd be a candidate for psychiatric treatment by now.

* * *

Over a month, and not a word from David. She'd given up listening for the receptionist's response after every ring of the office telephone. Never had it been David calling for her. And none of the calls that came to her apartment were from him.

She'd left a single message on his machine at the mountain house, another at Chandler Hall. Sometimes the urge to call him again was so strong she had to leave the condo to counter it. One really dismal day the longing to see him was so powerful she'd driven across the Potomac before gathering enough good sense to turn back.

She refused to run to him. She had her pride. Too disgustingly pitiful for a woman to chase after a man who didn't want her.

Weekdays were almost manageable. Sundays, like today, were the worst. All she could do was veg out in T-shirt and shorts in front of the TV and hope for an emergency call. One of these days she'd have to accept one of her family's continuous invitations to come visit. Even though she loved them all, she wasn't ready yet to watch the joyful success of other people's relationships, when hers had foundered on the immovable rock called David Chandler Reid.

David had brought to life within her a passion even stronger than her emotional commitment to medicine. Then he'd left that passion with nowhere to go.

The condo's front door buzzer sounded. She clicked off the movie she wasn't really watching and went to collect the mushroom and green pepper pizza she'd ordered.

The man filling the doorway wasn't holding a pizza box.

It took her a second to believe what she was seeing. When she did, her hand flew to her mouth. She went weak in the knees.

"D-David. I—I—come in."

"No. I can't stay. I just came by to make a delivery. I signed on to help you find Grant and bring him back. I've done that."

He stepped aside and pulled another person into view.

"Tommy," she gasped. "How—?"

His handsome face looked drawn and gaunt, and he'd dropped at least ten pounds.

"He's clean," David said. "At least for now. I detoxed him the hard way at my mountain house." His jaw tightened. "I put the guy through hell, and frankly I enjoyed every minute of it. But it'll take more than a month off the stuff to get him to kick the habit completely."

"Your commander is a hard man, Cara. It took me a while to appreciate all he did for me." Tommy closed her in a loose hug. "Thanks for sending him back. I'm sure he's right that sooner or later Kane would have gotten rid of me."

"B-but I didn't—" She was having difficulty taking all this in.

She was only faintly aware of the brotherly kiss Tommy laid on her cheek. She was more concerned with trying to gauge David's thoughts from his flat, blank expression.

"Hey, hon," Tommy said. "What I said back there on the island, I didn't mean it. My head wasn't on straight at the time. I'm sorry I caused you so much trouble."

Right now, she didn't really care about hearing Tommy's story. David was beating a quick retreat down the hall toward the elevator.

"Wait, David," she called, pushing out of Tommy's embrace.

After one quick look in her direction, David stepped into the elevator. By the time she reached him the doors were almost closed. Through the last few open inches of the closing door, she saw that he made no effort to hold it open.

Chapter 16

Cara steered her car down the long, winding country road that led to David's place.

Pride didn't cut it. It hadn't taken her long to find that out. What did holding on to useless pride get her, anyway? Not a blasted thing.

Besides, technically David had come to her first, hadn't he?

Still, she kept telling herself, it wasn't because she simply couldn't stay away from him that she was on her way to his darn mountain. She'd come only to thank him for what he'd done for Tommy.

The dryness of high summer had converted the driveway's mud to easily negotiable hard-packed dirt. She was able to drive up to the house and park next to David's pickup. The truck, she saw, held a couple of large suitcases and several boxes.

The unlikely and nameless cat was curled up in the sun at the bottom of the steps. It found the energy to open one eye when she stooped to pet it, and flicked the tip of its tail in lazy acknowledgment.

She found David doing his thing in the lake. Where else? She smiled to herself at the predictability of it and walked out to the end of the jetty. He was already looking in her direction, but she cupped her hands around her mouth and called to him.

"Hey, David. Come on out."

She could imagine his irritation at the intrusion as he turned and swam toward her. Tough. She'd had to put up with a lot more than mere irritation over him.

"One of these days," she shouted, "you're going to get so waterlogged you won't be able to squoosh yourself back onto dry land."

She was knocking herself out trying to keep things light and not let any of the desperation she felt into her voice. From what she could see of his face half-hidden in the water, he didn't crack a grin. She wasn't surprised when he halted at the end of the wharf and made no effort to climb up on it.

"Don't bother giving me any orders to vacate the premises," she said. "I won't go."

"I wasn't going to waste my breath. You didn't go the last time, either."

Her skirt billowing out around her, she sat down on the planking and circled her arms around her drawn-up knees.

"You went back to Kane's island," she said, with an accusing frown. "You shouldn't have. You could have been killed."

"I wasn't."

"Thank God for that. And thank you, David, for what you did for Tommy. That was incredibly courageous of you."

"Not so courageous when you consider the backup team I took with me. I simply served as the intelligence officer. The team did all the grunt work. They took out the guards and nabbed Dan Kane and Tommy."

"Robert?"

"Last I saw of him, he was high-tailing it out to sea in a speedboat. We let him go."

"I'm glad you blew up the drug warehouse."

"By the time we got there the yacht was fully loaded and ready to put to sea. We blew that, too. Those drugs were only a drop in the bucket compared to what floods into the country every day. But if what we did saves a few lives, or prevents only one kid from getting hooked, it will have been worth it. And there were several dozen assault weapons that won't be used against the cops, Colombian or American.''

Both of David's hands were spread wide on the planking, holding himself in place. Looking at the long, lean fingers brought her a painful recollection of how exciting those hands could be when they were stroking over her.

She bit her lip and looked away.

"But why did you go back for Tommy? You loathe the man."

"I figured I owed him something for stopping Kane from having us taken out and shot right then and there. Besides, you'd tried so hard to get Tommy back, you deserved to succeed at that. But don't get the idea I went back out of sheer altruism."

His face hardened into a scowl. "I don't like to fail at a mission, and I don't like to be pushed around by scum like Dan Kane. I wanted to put the slimy bastard out of commission for good so we wouldn't have to worry about him coming after us."

"Out of commission?"

"He'll be in jail for some time. Our people were eager to get their hands on him for what he did in 'Nam and what he's done since then. The Colombian authorities were quite willing to help us get rid of him. Elliott had no trouble mounting the mission."

It was difficult to keep on chatting about everything but what she really wanted to talk about: their relationship. Which, of course, was over, even though she was having a lot of trouble getting that hurtful fact through her heart.

"I came to see you because I thought you might like to know that Tommy checked himself into the treatment facility I mentioned. Whether or not that will complete the job of getting him clean that you started, who can say. But from here on he's on his own."

"I wouldn't make book that the jerk will have the sense to use the chance you gave him."

From the rigid set of David's jaw, she could well imagine that Tommy's month in the country had been no vacation.

"Either way, he's not my problem anymore."

"Yeah. Well . . ."

David's interest in Tommy's future seemed to have reached its limit. An uncomfortable silence fell between them, broken only by the soft slap of the waves ruffling the surface of the lake. She'd said her piece. What she ought to do now was bid David as cheery a farewell as she could manage and leave. But the thought of making the long walk back to her car all by herself and then leaving David for good made her feel ill.

"So," she said, glancing up over her shoulder to the house. "I saw the stuff in the truck. Looks like you're getting ready to leave."

He nodded. "Yes. Tomorrow morning I'll be heading back to Chandler Hall and my grandmother. I've really missed Anne. She's a great old lady. She never gave me any hassle about my holing up out here, although I knew she was worried about me."

"Have you made any plans...?" She felt so full of sighs, she was running out of voice. "You know... for what you'll be doing from now on?"

"For starters, I have a round of apologies to make to my friends for turning them away all this time. Then I'll be going to work. The navy has asked me to help set up a new SEAL training program. I thought I'd give it a shot."

"You're going back on active duty?"

"No. The doctors would never sign me off on that. I'll be working as a consultant, mostly from home. Computer work. Research. Evaluating different training techniques. That sort of thing."

Sounded as if he was on his way to rejoining the human race. She was glad for him.

"That's great, David. I know you'll be good at it."

There didn't seem to be much left to say. At least not much that he would want to hear. She clambered to her feet. "Well, goodbye, Commander. Good luck with your new job."

"Yeah. Thanks. You, too... uh, with your old one."

So that was that.

"You ever need a doctor, you know where to find me."

The flicker of a humorless smile came with his quick farewell salute. "Right. I'll keep that in mind."

She'd bet the M.D. shingle hanging on her office door that he'd never make it back to Baltimore again. At least not to her street.

"Well . . . See you later, Commander."

This would be a whole lot easier if he'd just end their meeting by swimming away instead of floating there holding his gaze on her.

"Mmm . . . See ya."

Impossible to leave without touching him. She went down on one knee and reached out to lay her fingers over his. The tremor that moved through him kept on going through her.

He let out a sharp breath.

The gray gaze that continued to do quivery things to her insides wasn't coolly blank. It hadn't been since he'd glided up to speak to her. What she thought she saw in their depths now was pain. And indecision.

Pretty much what she felt herself.

She felt as if an impenetrable wall of glass lay between her and David. On the other side of the wall she could see everything in the world she wanted, but she couldn't reach it.

She didn't believe in fate or magic, but there'd been something of both in her relationship with David. How could she turn her back on that without one last effort to make him understand what she could see so clearly? That they were meant to spend their lives together. If they didn't, she had the horrible feeling that some vast celestial plan would surely go awry.

He'd labeled her loyalty to Tommy as sheer stubbornness. Maybe it had been. But didn't she owe even more of that same kind of stubborn loyalty to the man she truly loved?

She might be about to make a fool of herself again, but she'd already done that over David Reid. What did one more time matter?

"Whether you want to hear this again or not, David, I'm going to say it. I love you. And that love is now as much a part of me as my breathing. It will never change."

The curtain of his eyelids dropped over his eyes. His face jerked to the side, as if he'd just received a blow.

"I refuse to believe that you don't have any feelings for me," she continued relentlessly. "How could that be true when you made love to me in a way I'll never be able to forget for as long as I live? That I'll never want to forget for as long as I live?''

His face contorted. He shoved himself off from the wharf and swam in a small agitated circle back to her.

''Cara—please. I—I can't—I—''

Any sensitive person would back off in the face of the man's obvious distress. But this was too important. This was about the rest of her life. And his.

No matter how much it hurt either one of them, she intended to press him until she heard him say flat out that he didn't love her. David Reid could be as evasive as the best of them. He'd given her no inkling of his plans that last evening in Panama. But he was no liar.

''I love you, David. That gives me the right to demand to know how you feel about me. Maybe I'm just dense, but the response I sense when I'm in your arms doesn't square with what you say. Or rather what you don't say. So you'll have to spell out for me exactly what those feelings are. Or aren't.''

A breeze swept off the lake and chilled her to the bone. If only she could take back that last stupid throw of the dice. She didn't possess enough bravery to stand here and listen to him say she meant nothing to him. But it would take nothing less to rub her nose in that devastating truth and finally make her believe it.

Weak with apprehension, she thumped her bottom back down on the dock and folded her arms in front of her in a show of determination that was just that—a show.

''And I'm going to sit right here until you do.'' To her ears, her voice sounded much too loud and strained.

David muttered a curse and threw her a dark, snared look.

''You'd do just that, wouldn't you?''

He hauled in a huge breath and blew out the mouthful of water that came along with it.

''Okay. Here it is. Frankly I wish I had the nerve to go ahead and lie to you.'' He sighed. ''But with you sitting there looking at me like that, I can't. I'm in love with you.''

A shower of happiness sparkled over her. ''Oh, David.'' She melted toward him. ''I knew it. I knew it.'' She reached out to lay her fingertips across his wet, warm lips.

He propelled himself backwards a couple of feet out of her reach.

"Can't you understand, Cara? It's because I love you that I refuse to inflict a cripple like myself on you. How can a woman like you really love a man who can't even walk properly, whose body is a mass of ugly scars?"

Her face must have displayed the blank incomprehension in her mind.

"Believe me, David, no woman with an ounce of sense would turn away from you. I speak from experience. Your limp never seemed the least bit important to me. I was too involved admiring—and doing my best to fend off—that incredibly attractive and damnably forceful virility of yours."

Her compliments seemed to confuse him. His gaze jerked down one side of the lake and then the other as though he though he might come across the real meaning of her words lying around someplace on the shore.

"You've never seen all of me, Cara. I'm such an awful mess that it made my wife sick to her stomach."

She rocked back on her heels. This was all about his damaged body? She knew a ten-year-old boy who'd lost a leg who was handling that physical challenge a lot better than David was handling his. She opened her mouth to pitilessly order him to get over it.

The words never made it past her lips. The bleakness she caught in his eyes gave her a sudden flash of complete understanding.

David's reaction to his feelings for her wasn't really about how he looked. It wasn't solely about his injuries at all. It was about his spirit. His reluctance to show himself to her was a symptom, not a cause.

All along he'd been trying to tell her what he might not consciously comprehend himself. She'd listened, but she hadn't really *heard*.

This was a man who'd been honed to the toughest standards of stoic, macho military expertise. A man who not only took pride in, but who defined himself by that powerful self-image. A man accustomed not simply to competence, but to excellence in performing any task he undertook.

As she did with her profession, he saw his work with the navy as much more than just a job. He viewed it as a special vocation, almost a sacred calling.

The burst of weapons fire that tore into flesh and bone had also shattered his basic sense of *self*. In the blink of an eye he found himself in a world where—in terms of what he'd been— he no longer counted. Undoubtedly, his wife's desertion had administered the coup de grace to the last of his already precarious self-esteem.

When he spoke of being afraid he might be impotent, he wasn't merely talking about sexual impotency. He was confessing his fear that sustaining massive trauma to nerves and muscles somehow made him less of a man.

Not only did he have to recover from his physical wounds, he'd had to completely reinvent himself mentally, rebuild a definition of himself from the ground up.

No wonder he'd retreated to his mountain.

"I don't want to talk about this anymore," he said, once more turning out toward the center of the lake. "Goodbye, Cara."

"Is a decorated naval officer afraid of a little serious conversation about this?"

"There's no point," he continued. "I don't even know what your *this* is supposed to be."

Evidently he hadn't considered that when he jackknifed beneath the surface, he'd give her a pleasant glimpse of a bare and very attractive male behind. She waited until he came up several yards distant.

"I'm not entirely sure, either. Let's find out together."

He didn't turn, but he didn't continue swimming either. He tread water with his back to her.

"Please, David, come and talk. Maybe you don't need to, but I do. Remember what we shared at the pool? Remember how wonderful that was? Come back and talk out of respect for what happened between us then."

If that plea didn't work, nothing would.

She allowed herself a bit of hope when he turned and swam slowly toward the dock.

"Thank you," she said, when he'd reached her.

"That last tactic of yours comes pretty close to blackmail."

"I'm sorry. But it's not easy to get you to do something you don't want to do."

A strange snort of laughter burst from him.

The deep vulnerability she'd just discovered in him called up her strongest nurturing instincts. She wanted to cuddle him in her arms and murmur comforting words.

Exactly what he wouldn't want.

Instinctively she knew that too much gentleness on her part, any hint of pity or sympathy, would send him racing for the farthest end of the lake. She had to tread carefully, but not softly, on a battered ego.

"I don't suppose I can get you up on dry land."

"I'm fine right here."

"How about if I jump in there with you?"

"No. You said you wanted to talk. So talk."

"Okay." With no time to think through how to bring up the subject in a way he wouldn't find threatening, she had to go with the direct approach. "I'd like to hear what your concept of manhood is."

"Oh, for— We're about to get into psychobabble here, aren't we?"

Best to ignore that one, she decided. "Then I'll give it a shot. You just listen and tell me if I'm right."

His wary sideways squint warned he wasn't going to stick around for long. She had to talk fast.

"I think your idea of real manhood involves a male who possesses the kind of perfectly trained body you once enjoyed. A man who's capable of the kind of action they make movies about. Like invading a drug baron's stronghold, rescuing someone and blowing the place to kingdom come."

His eyes rolled heavenward. "Yeah. We're into psychobabble, all right."

At least he seemed to have understood that she was saying he still possessed a good deal of that particular kind of manliness.

"I agree, David, that men like those in special forces such as your Navy SEALs are due considerable admiration and respect. But their work demands that they focus strongly on the physical aspects of masculinity. I think there's a lot more to manliness than that.''

''And you're going to tell me what that is, whether I want to hear it or not.''

''Right.'' She hoped her smile was broadcasting something to the effect that *See? This isn't so bad after all.*

''In my concept of manhood, a real man—whatever shape he's in—is one who has strength of character. Trust me, David Reid,'' she said dryly. ''You've got strength of character coming out your ears. A real man is one who looks out for the people in his life, even those who have no rightful claim on him. You went out of your way to help a stranger—namely me—who came to you with an outrageous request that you accompany her to South America.''

''Not that big a deal.''

''Yes, a big deal. Your first instinct, telling me to get lost, was the sensible one. You came anyway. On top of that you risked your life, not only for me, but for a man you had no use for.''

''Still don't,'' he added.

She sighed. He was going to fight her every step of the way. Well, she could be every bit as stubborn as he. She had Tommy to thank for developing that trait in her.

''Let's just go on. My version of a real man is one who's tough, yes, but one who can be gentle and tender, too.'' She tried to fill her voice with all the richness of her feelings for him. ''You were certainly all of those with me.'' Especially when she was in his arms. ''What I'm trying to say, David, is that my idea of a perfect man is exactly who you've been since the day I met you.''

His eyes flared wide. His mouth dropped open. What he was thinking she didn't know, but she sure as heck had his attention. To hold that interest she quickly plowed on.

''Think about it. Doesn't it count for something that a man of the calibre of Roger Bryce Elliott thought enough of you to put in effect a plan to nudge you out of your seclusion, along with helping his grandson's doctor? I'm sure he had that in mind when he sent me to you. He probably didn't think for a moment that I'd lead you into the kind of trouble that we faced. Together,'' she added, to remind him of how well they'd worked as partners. "I wouldn't be at all surprised if, when he put me in touch with you, he was also engaging in a little matchmaking between us."

"That's ridiculous. Elliott isn't the type to—"

"Play Cupid? Maybe not. It doesn't matter. The point is, I think it's high time you quit focusing on your physical weakness and recognized your real masculine strengths. So you're not Rambo anymore. So what? Personally I've never been that fond of the emotionless Rambo-type."

"But I . . . uh . . . you don't . . ."

David continued to shake his head uncertainly and begin several sentences he never completed.

She felt him slipping away from her and fought back creeping panic.

"What is it, David? Are you still carrying around some weird picture of yourself that your wife's stupid reaction branded into your mind? Are you afraid I might have the same reaction?"

His mouth thinned to a straight, hard slash. He rocked himself back and forth with his hands on the edge of the dock.

"That's it, isn't it, David? That's why you never let me get a real good look at you in the light."

She reached out to lay her hand on his cheek and gave a slow shake of her head.

"A waste of time, love. I know perfectly well what your body looks like. I've known that right from the day I worked the cramps out of your leg and felt the outline of the scars beneath your slacks. When we made love in the dark, my fingers, my lips painted a very clear picture of every lovable inch of you in my mind. Your wounds might once have looked pretty scary. Perhaps in your mind, they still do. Even if they did, it wouldn't matter to me. But believe me, David. They don't anymore."

To prove it, she proceeded to describe the location and appearance of each of his fading scars. His gaze never wavered from hers as she spoke, but his hand moved down to double-check the fading evidence of his injuries.

"You've got to forgive yourself for not being physically perfect. I love you as you are. I've only known you as you are. And I could never ask for anything better in a man. Listen to me, David, your body excites me. I want it. I don't think I can ever get enough of it. Come on, my darling," she challenged. "Sweep away all those old ghosts. Climb out of the water and show yourself to me in the bright sunlight."

She was so sure he'd do it. So sure she'd won.

Seconds went by.

A minute? An hour? She couldn't tell. The longest wait of her life.

"I see."

The black desperation that had hovered behind her shoulders since she'd begun speaking to David finally rushed over her. Hot moisture stung her eyes.

"You can't bring yourself to trust me, can you? I've long been ready to trust myself to you, David. I'm not sure that's true anymore. I don't want a man who can't see what's truly important about himself."

She struggled to her feet and turned from him so he wouldn't see the tears threatening to overflow.

"Get this through that rock-hard head of yours, my love. It's not your disability that keeps you from me. It's your ridiculous belief that your physical weakness—which isn't all that great now—somehow makes you less of a man."

She wasn't sure he was still listening behind her. Maybe he'd swum away. Maybe she was talking to the wind.

She forced herself to speak louder through a constricted throat. "Holding on to that stupid idea is wrecking our chance for happiness. Can't you see that, David? Can't you let yourself see that?"

No sound from the water in back of her. She knew it wasn't medically possible, but it felt as if her heart were shrinking away to nothing inside her.

"All right, Commander. Just remember that you called our breakup. I didn't. This time I won't come back."

David watched Cara's retreating form. His heart seized up.

What she'd said was true. Suddenly it was all blindingly true.

He'd gone to Colombia with her, not just for the chance to get back into action and prove he might still be good for something. Right from the start his heart had recognized the woman who could make him whole in the most important sense of the word.

He'd trusted his SEAL buddies with his life. Cara Merrill had taught him to trust her with more than his life, with his heart and soul.

With every step she took away from him, the walls she'd knocked down began to close in on him again. He couldn't make it without her. He knew that better than he'd ever known anything.

Damn the idiotic pride that had driven away the woman he loved. How could he have been so stupid, and so cowardly, not to recognize before now that he'd let the absurd notion that he could be nothing if not a SEAL rule his life for so long?

Terrified that it might be too late, he heaved himself up on the dock and clambered to his feet.

She'd already made it almost to the top of the steps.

"Cara, wait."

His shout echoed from the mountains, growing fainter and fainter until the sound of it died.

If she didn't stop, he'd live the rest of days in flat, black loneliness. And he'd have no one to blame for it but himself.

She halted and turned slowly, as if afraid of what she might see when she looked back his way. As she took each downward step, he steeled himself for her first good look at him up close.

She set her foot on the dock. His pulse set up an anxious pounding in his ears. Rationally he knew that the reaction no longer made sense, still, he couldn't help but hold his breath. He needed her desperately, but the slightest sign of repugnance on her face would instantly kill off all emotion for good.

Her hesitant smile grew into a grin as her watery gaze raked his naked body from head to foot and back again. He expected that very personal inspection to linger on his mangled leg. Instead, the intimate scrutiny came to a halt at his middle. And brought about his perfectly obvious reaction to her.

She halted a whisper away from him. He could plainly see that her misty blue eyes shone with nothing but love and desire. All for him. Only for him.

Reeling from the toe-turning impact of that astounding discovery, he reached out and pulled her to him. His mouth met hers, his tongue delving in to meet hers in an ecstatic sensuous dance. Between bursts of soft laughter and gasps of pleasure, a chorus of *I love yous* tumbled from their lips.

She glanced down at his manhood standing stiffly at attention between them.

"Since you're evidently so pleased that I came back, I guess I'll have to demonstrate exactly how I react to the sight of you naked." The soft huskiness of her voice told him her thoughts were traveling down the same engrossing road as his. "Doesn't seem fair that you should be standing there as bare as a newborn babe, while I'm burdened with all these clothes on a hot summer day."

That got hotter by the second as she rectified the unequal clothing situation.

Stepping back to him, she laid her hands flat on his torso just above his navel and snaked her hands sinuously up his chest to circle them around his neck.

Quickly and happily he ran up the white flag to that loving and overwhelming assault.

Together they fell to the smooth warm wood of the dock and loved each other as if they'd spent a lifetime apart and couldn't bear to wait another second to reunite their bodies.

Their intimate sharing ended in a ruffle of chuckles and soft laughter at the frantic hurry of their lovemaking.

David looked at the most beautiful woman in the world, who lay beneath him, and shook his head.

"I've been such a damn fool."

"Yes, you have been," she readily agreed.

He laughed again. He'd done more laughing in the relatively short time he'd spent with her than in the past couple of years.

He cut off the laughter. Time for that later. He had work to do. The most important work of his life.

"When I thought I'd never see you again, Cara, I felt so...so..." He shook his head helplessly, unable to come up with the word. "You can't imagine."

"Yes, I can, David. It was the same for me."

"I need you, love. Not for anything to do with taking care of me medically. I need you in my life. I need you to fill my days.

To fill my nights." His voice cracked. "I need you so much it should terrify me. It doesn't. It feels exactly right."

"The way I need you doesn't scare me a bit, either, David. It comes with loving you."

His hands tenderly cradled the face that would continue to haunt his dreams for as long as he lived.

"Marry me, Cara. You've got to marry me." If she didn't, nothing else he ever did would mean a damn thing.

Before she even spoke, he could read her answer in the flash of elation sparking into her eyes. It felt to him as if her whole trembling body smiled up at him, setting him alight with joy right down to the soles of his bare feet.

"Of course I'll marry you, my dearest love. But you'd better be real sure that's what you want. You know how I am with promises. I can't seem to let go of them. I warn you here and now that I'll hold tight to our wedding vows forever."

"I'm banking on that, my darling. And I vow here and now that I'll never let you go. And I'll never stop loving you. Never."

Cara smiled. "Never sounds just about right."

She tightened her arms around him and gave him her lips. In the brilliant sunlight, their loving bodies sealed the vows of their hearts and souls.

* * * * *

COMING NEXT MONTH FROM

 **SILHOUETTE**®

Intrigue
Danger, deception and desire

THE SOUL MATE Carly Bishop
THE BABY EXCHANGE Kelsey Roberts
EDEN'S BABY Adrianne Lee
PASSION IN THE FIRST DEGREE Carla Cassidy

Special Edition
Satisfying romances packed with emotion

OF TEXAS LADIES, COWBOYS...AND BABIES
Jodi O'Donnell
KEEPING KATE Pat Warren
NOT BEFORE MARRIAGE! Sandra Steffen
THE CASE OF THE MAYBE BABIES Victoria Pade
THANK HEAVEN FOR LITTLE GIRLS Tracy Sinclair
IN A FAMILY WAY Julia Mozingo

Desire
*Provocative, sensual love stories for the
woman of today*

THE TEXAS BLUE NORTHER Lass Small
THAT BURKE MAN Diana Palmer
THE COWBOY AND THE CRADLE Cait London
A WILFUL MARRIAGE Peggy Moreland
THE LONER AND THE LADY Eileen Wilks
SEDUCING HUNTER Cathie Linz

COMING NEXT MONTH

BORROWED BRIDE
Patricia Coughlin

Connor DeWolfe had sworn to protect Gaby—even if
that meant kidnapping her when she was on the way to
her wedding! He had to convince her that she was
marrying the wrong man—and that she was in danger.
Gaby trusted Connor with her life, but not with her
body—or her suddenly reckless heart.

CODE NAME: DADDY
Marilyn Tracy

The world believed Alec MacLaine was dead. *He*
thought the woman he'd loved had been killed. But *if*
she was alive, she was in mortal danger. He had to get
her and *fast*! He had even more to protect than he
knew, for Cait had a daughter...

SILHOUETTE™ ®

Sensation

COMING NEXT MONTH

MADDY LAWRENCE'S BIG ADVENTURE
Linda Turner

Maddy Lawrence never thought she'd meet a bold swashbuckler in real life. Yet it was a very real, flesh-and-blood man who took her on an incredible adventure that became the wild romance she'd always dreamed of...

LEADER OF THE PACK
Justine Davis

Trinity Street West

Wounded, Ryan Buckhart sought an escape from months of undercover police work. He could only go to one place, to only one woman. He'd never stopped loving her, but she was no longer his wife...

SILHOUETTE®

Spring is in the air with our sparkling collection
from Silhouette...

SPRING
fever

Three sexy, single men are about to find the love
of a lifetime!

Grace And The Law by Dixie Browning
Lighfoot And Loving by Cait London
Out Of The Dark by Pepper Adams

Three delightful stories...one romantic season!

Available: March 1997

Price: £4.99

There's nothing quite like a family

REUNION

The new miniseries by
Pat Warren

Three siblings are about to be reunited.
And each finds love along the way...

HANNAH
Her life is about to change now that she's met
the irresistible Joel Merrick in HOME FOR HANNAH
(Special Edition February 1997)

MICHAEL
He's been on his own all his life. Now he's going
to take a risk on love in MICHAEL'S HOUSE
(Sensation March 1997)

KATE
A job as a nanny leads her to Aaron Carver, his
adorable baby daughter and the
fulfillment of her dreams in KEEPING KATE
(Special Edition April 1997)

RACHEL LEE

◇

A FATEFUL
CHOICE

**She arranged her own death—
then changed her mind**

*"Ms Lee's talents as a writer are
dazzling. Put this author's name on
your list of favourites right now!"*
—Romantic Times

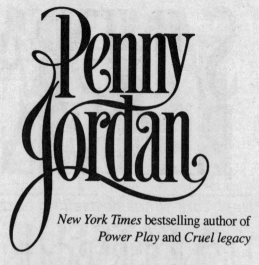

Penny Jordan

New York Times bestselling author of
Power Play and *Cruel legacy*

POWER GAMES

The arrival of a mysterious woman threatens
a son's manipulative hold over his
millionaire father in PENNY JORDAN'S
latest blockbuster—a supercharged tale of
family rivalries

**AVAILABLE IN PAPERBACK
FROM MARCH 1997**

New York Times bestselling author

LINDA HOWARD

ALL THAT GLITTERS

Married for love...or money?

Jessica had once been a wife in a marriage rocked by scandal. But in Nikolas Constantino's arms she found a peace she had never thought possible.

"You just can't read one Linda Howard!"
— bestselling author Catherine Coulter

"Howard's writing is compelling"
— Publishers Weekly

KEEPING COUNT

How would you like to win a year's supply of Silhouette® books? Well you can and they're FREE! Simply complete the competition below and send it to us by 30th September 1997. The first five correct entries picked after the closing date will each win a year's subscription to the Silhouette series of their choice. What could be easier?

$$6 + 3 + \square = 14$$

$$\square + 2 + \square = 15$$

$$\square + 1 + \square = 16$$

$$\square + 6 + \square = 17$$

$$\square + 3 + \square = 18$$

$$\square + 1 + \square = 19$$

$$\square + 5 + \square = 20$$

PLEASE TURN OVER FOR DETAILS OF HOW TO ENTER ☞

How to enter...

There are six sets of numbers overleaf. When the first empty box has the correct number filled into it then that set of three numbers will add up to 14. All you have to do is figure out what the missing number of each of the other five sets are so that the answer to each will be as shown. The first number of each set of three will be the last number of the set before. Good Luck!

When you have filled in all the missing numbers don't forget to fill in your name and address in the space provided and tick the Silhouette® series you would like to receive if you are a winner. Then simply pop this page into an envelope (you don't even need a stamp) and post it today. Hurry competition ends 30th September 1997.

Silhouette 'Keeping Count' Competition
FREEPOST, Croydon, Surrey, CR9 3WZ

Eire readers send competition to PO Box 4546, Dublin 24

Please tick the series you would like to receive if you are a winner
Desire™ ❑   Sensation™ ❑   Intrigue™ ❑   Special Edition™ ❑

Are you a Reader Service Subscriber?   Yes ❑   No ❑

Ms/Mrs/Miss/Mr_____
                                              (BLOCK CAPS PLEASE)
Address _____

_____

_____ Postcode_____

(I am over 18 years of age)   mps
                                                        MAILING
                                                        PREFERENCE
                                                        SERVICE
One application per household. Competition open to residents of the UK
and Ireland only.
You may be mailed with other offers from other reputable companies   DMA
as a result of this application. If you would prefer not to receive such
offers, please tick box. ❑

                                                                      C7C